Ebook ISBN 978-1-83751-643-8

Kindle ISBN 978-1-83751-644-5

Audio CD ISBN 978-1-83751-635-3

MP3 CD ISBN 978-1-83751-636-0

Digital audio download ISBN 978-1-83751-639-1

Boldwood Books Ltd
23 Bowerdean Street
London SW6 3TN
www.boldwoodbooks.com

For Sofia Lyons-O'Sullivan... An angel at work

PROLOGUE
THE GARDEN SHED

My outward appearance resembles that of a carefully mown and manicured Wimbledon lawn; pristine, clipped and ready for action. Not a weed in sight. Bring on the players. I perfect the look with an air of crisp efficiency. People imagine the foundations, the layers underneath my manufactured guise to be solid and hard-earned. A person of substance. How do I know? Because I'm treated with respect due from such summations. I read people well, but they have no idea who I really am or what lies beneath.

Below this surface mantle there are no soft silts and sands; no gentle porous foundations. My life has no rich varied layers of experience. Below the smell of freshly cut grass, a giant batholith lies embedded in my core. I was only ten when this black mass of spewing magma ex-

ploded through my being, killing off everything in its wake, and it slumbers dangerously close to the surface, threatening to expose itself at any time as life erodes its delicate casing.

Meanwhile, I pretend. I pretend all is right with the world. I keep the façade firmly in place to fool those around me. I know I mustn't tell, but I can't forget.

I remember. Every detail. It never goes away.

It's the pendulous jowls and wet salivating lips. That's what I see. The thin veneer of sweat coating the fat alabaster face is what I smell. The sweet cloying stench still hangs heavy in the air. It clung to my pores long after the scalding showers scorched my body and I'm still not clean, my nostrils thick with memories.

The garden shed was coloured a faded apple green. Flakes of paint rained to the ground when the door was yanked open.

'Green snowflakes.' He laughed. 'Look.' His eyes, shrivelled black raisins in a wobbly jelly, glanced briefly down at the ragged chips but he was too eager to get inside. There was no time to linger.

The inside was kitted out like a 1960s sitting room. A drop-leaf table was pushed tight against the damp rotting slats. It would be opened out once he'd caught his breath; crisps and custard creams blackmailing my silence. A two-seater sofa was wedged between the walls and bolstered up the flimsy structure. There was nowhere else to sit. I willed the walls to crumble, bury the shame.

Net curtains, stapled in place, sealed us off from the outside world. Thick dirt was so engrained it had solidified and ensured the flimsy material wouldn't budge. The floral chipped teacups and sugar tongs teased with homeliness and I often wonder where he got his props. The room smelt of urine, sweat and old age; and death.

Cobwebs decorated the corners with neatly spun gossamer threads. That's how they looked when I walked in the first time, having been enticed with sweets and treats. But the black hairy arachnids lay in wait; teasing with their silken perfection. That's the way clever predators operate. They lure the unsuspecting with illusory delights. But the spiders didn't hang about. They scuttled off, disseminating their pristine homes, when his blubbery white hide appeared and wobbled in excitement.

It wasn't long until I began to change my route home from school. Left down Burton Avenue, right into Salisbury Road and third left into Park Lane. At the main road I would scamper across when the lights turned green. I tried not to look panicked in case anyone intervened. I measured my pace. He might be there, sitting on a bench, watching me. 'Remember. It's our little secret. You mustn't tell.' A waggling admonishing finger kept me quiet.

Then I would hurry on through the park, not daring

to look back. *My heart hammered in my chest, beating like a kettle drum. But there was no escape, no matter how fast I ran, or how hard.*

Five more minutes and I'd be home. I counted the numbers backwards from three hundred. That was on a Monday. On Tuesday I took the direct route and avoided the park. Wednesday I spun a coin. Thursday was games afternoon so I got dropped off. On Fridays there was nowhere to run. He only worked a four-day week and would be waiting for me. 'Fun Friday' he called it and he was never late.

He became my stalker. I learnt the word later when it needed no explanation. My anxious alertness turned quickly to fear and then to terror. I became a prisoner in my own skin, the invisible walls impenetrable. He was everywhere, all day and all night; watching and waiting.

'Boo. There you are. I wondered where you'd gone.'

The tree trunk wasn't wide enough; I'd seen him but I wasn't fast enough. Again it was too late when I walked in and he was chatting to the shopkeeper, soft candy grasped in fat sausage fingers.

'Here, do you fancy some? My treat.'

But worst of all was the nightmarish anticipation of Fridays. There was one at the end of every week.

'Hi, Snippet. Let me walk you home. I could do with the company.' He called me Snippet. It was his pet name.

It rhymed with whippet, his scrawny breed of dog. We were both thin and wiry and got patted on the head.

He'd come to school and chat merrily to a teacher, blocking the exit gates. His sweaty palm would grip mine tightly all the way back and he would only let go when he loosened his belt and unzipped his trousers. By then we'd be inside; the door locked behind us.

It was the stalking that left the scars, the deepest gullies. His death brought a joyous finality to the physical torture, a fleeting release. Outside, through the newly barred windows of the shed, his rheumy watery eyes glistened through a small rip in the curtains. They made a silent unblinking plea; easy to ignore. Instead I smiled back, waved my skinny fingers and skipped away. I was barely thirteen after all, not quite done with skipping.

But I still look over my shoulder. Sleep eludes me. When I try to eat, my food tastes of vomit mingled with a sticky sweetness. My senses are full; full of sounds, sights and tastes but without the pleasure. The joy of touch eludes me. The flaccid monster that grew and grew in my hand, 'the big friendly giant' saw to that.

I should have told. It was my own fault. Not his death, but the 'not telling'. But I was only ten when it all began. Who would have listened? My age and innocence flew quickly by, but after his death I learnt to keep the illusion in place, skilfully, and for long enough so that no one would think me capable of murder. It never crossed their minds.

My stalker was Uncle Chuck Curry; 'Chuckles' to his friends; the big, fat, happy clown. He only lived two roads away and was my mother's stepbrother; the perfect babysitter.

A wolf in sheep's clothing. That was Uncle Chuck; the harmless cheerful buffoon. His appearance was his disguise. He nurtured the look with jam and cream doughnuts. What wasn't to like? And then, of course, he warned me not to tell. If I did, he'd lock me in the shed and throw away the key.

1

6 MONTHS PREVIOUSLY

I feel as if I'm in an isolation bunker, the chill in the air quite deathly. The flesh along both arms is stippled with pimples. It's as if the world has come to an end but with foresight, I've been clever enough to brick myself in.

The concrete stairwell is positively empty. I'm not surprised as I pinch my nose against the rank stench of urine. Yellow stains clog up the corners and remnants of rancid hamburger baps exude stale fumes. I shiver, fearful of breathing in the toxic mix. No one else is risking the fallout.

Tucked neatly behind the swing doors at the top, three flights up, my ears are primed against the slightest noise. Through the thick swing doors I pick up the faintest of buzzing. It's the office workers mo-seying around the lifts, talking in hushed voices, waiting for the tin cubicles to ferry them back down to the car park and ground zero. Their laziness plays into my hands because no one bothers to descend on foot. They never do. If I'm right, she'll be the only one to turn up.

It's been roughly three months since I heard about her impending baby. Thinking about it still makes me mad, leaving me unable to unlock my jaw-line which is clenched, day and night. My fury is sealed within for the whole twenty-four hours of each day.

Suddenly the swing doors open slightly and my hand shoots out flat against the wall to steady myself, but they close again and no one appears. Retreating voices fade as the clatter of metal heralds the arrival of the lift. Fate has played into my hands as they must have decided against the exercise. My heart threatens to crack its confines and a few seconds pass before I manage a deep breath to slow its rhythm.

My watch shows it's still only ten past five. I have six minutes left to wait. She's that regular. At the end of the working day there are lots of random people who head purposefully towards the underground car park where their vehicles are squeezed into obscenely tight spaces. Random is a good word, it smacks of chance. The coincidental angle needs to be water-tight. Today I am just another random person, out and about. Coincidence alone can't put me in prison.

Poor Danielle has had her wing mirrors clipped more than once. I'm surprised she doesn't rein them in. She still refuses to leave her car near the CCTV cameras to find out who is causing the damage and insists on being as close as possible to the stairwell entrance. This suits me fine. Using the lift for her is never an option. She suffers from claustrophobia, avoiding confined spaces, always on the lookout for an escape route.

Suddenly, at 5.16pm, the steel doors push open again but this time more widely. Quiet as a mouse, prepared to scuttle away once the coast is clear, my ears prick up. Wide eyes devour the spectacle.

Swollen feet make her waddle like a duck. Her ankles are retaining water; it's most unattractive, and the baby bump bulges through the tight outline of her sheer blue dress which hangs below her calves. The fact that she's displaying the bump so blatantly, a boastful statement, hardens my resolve. Her swollen breasts strain provocatively. My anger and loathing make me want to break cover and spit in her face. But I don't. I watch and wait.

Like a teetering toddler, she takes a tentative step towards the banister, and extends her right hand to grip the metal. Her left hand is holding firmly on to a soft leather laptop case, but she doesn't reach the banister. I watch agog as her foot gives way and her tumbling body begins a heavy descent over the cold slabs. Piercing screams follow and my hands automatically reach up to cover my ears.

Wow. I wasn't expecting such a display. She looks like a tumbling cheese in one of those country fair competitions, turning over and over until coming to a rest at the bottom of a steep hill. It's very startling.

For a moment I'm tempted to run down the stairs and offer help as the squeals are deafening and she seems in so much pain, but I can't alert anyone that I'm close by. That might make the stalking issue a criminal offence and I have no intention of being punished for being an innocent bystander, so I slink away.

I slide gently through the thick doors and walk quietly towards the lifts, head down. My soft leather pumps don't make a noise and I melt easily into the waiting queue. All eyes are steeled forward and no one looks in my direction. Strange though that no one seems to hear the screams, but perhaps I'm imagining that they're still audible as there's a definite ringing in my ears.

The lift doors creak open and, swallowed up by office workers, I'm shoved to the back of the tin cubical. We are like sardines in a can. Two young girls step back when someone indicates that the occupancy limit is eight people. Perhaps in their statements, when they come forward as being present on the day of the incident, they will recall how they were asked to wait for the next lift. An obese man, his body sweat engulfing us all with its putrid excretions, insists they wait. I can't help thinking that if he got out an extra four people could get in. On another day I might have dared to point this out.

As the doors finally close I find myself crushed between two suited men rapt in serious low-toned conversation, humming with importance, and I close my eyes tight as the lift chugs slowly downwards. I try to think of what I might cook for supper, what I might watch on television. You see, like the tumbling cheese I'm not a fan of enclosed spaces.

At ground level we all spill out of the lift and head off in different directions, casually walking past paramedics who are already on the scene. They must have been close by. A blue light flashes silently, steadily on top of an ambulance whose back doors are flung wide. A flustered medic is talking into a handset, relaying details of the incident and is ordering a stretcher to be lifted out.

No one stops and asks what's happened, which is strange. If I didn't already know, I'm sure I would have stopped. However, this works in my favour as no one takes any notice of me either, everyone keeping their eyes down, glad not to be part of an unfolding drama. It's too late in the working day.

I weave in and out of the line of all the CCTV cameras like a speeding motorist jumping lanes with aplomb until I'm back out on the street. It is part of a ritual to note where the snooping monitors are placed and I'm adept at avoiding their big brother recordings and today, I'm confident that my image won't be flagged up.

Yet, if my face does get captured and I've missed one, or someone vaguely remembers me, my testimony will claim coincidence. I happened to be shopping in the vicinity at the time; that's all. I have several receipts from the adjoining mall stowed away safely in my handbag.

As I reach the Tube and begin my descent into the bowels of the earth, at last breathing more easily, I remind myself that I didn't go near or speak to the woman who fell. She wouldn't have recognised me even if I had. Long gone is my dejected air and sunken cheekbones. The leggings and baggy shirts have been replaced by designer chic and my straggling locks have been shorn.

If she did glimpse me, she would have seen a stranger. It has all been a matter of coincidence.

2

PRESENT DAY

I'm lying prostrate on the therapist's couch like a patient waiting for a massage to begin. I'm fully dressed but the aim will be to strip my soul bare. This woman though isn't into gentle manipulation but rather into kneading deep-tissue knots embedded savagely along the spine accompanied by hands-on aggressive probing.

'Names,' she begins. Pause. 'Do these men have names?' She peers at me over the top of her half-moon glasses tempting me to respond using the severity of her stare as a challenge. With eyes closed, I hope she'll be fooled into believing that I'm considering a carefully constructed and thoughtful answer.

It's the way the questions are phrased that rankles. Sarcasm oozes from the single opening word, 'names'. My knee-jerk reaction is to say, 'No. They don't have names. One went by the letter "x", one by "y" and then there was "z".' But I don't. I hide my irritation and decide to play fair. The sooner we get it over with, the sooner I can escape.

'Jeremy is a name I think you mentioned before.' This is followed by a meaningful silence. My left eyelid peels gently back and through the narrow slit I see my interrogator twirl the end of a pen round in her mouth. She has checked her notes to find the name and is sitting patiently. I've heard somewhere that's what therapists do. Ask a question, wait quietly, and bore their clients into responding. It's an easy way to earn money.

'Yes,' I say. Jeremy. How could I forget? He was my first love; the deepest cut is what they call it. At the time he could do no wrong. Or let me rephrase that. I believed he could do no wrong. I conjure up his face, the beautiful perfect features. Only a woman in love would call them perfect. His nose was slightly hooked, his lips well formed but rather thin and the third tooth on the right overlapped its neighbour, giving rise to an endearing lisp. Endearing at first, irritating in retrospect.

'What happened?' She's going to pick at the sores,

try to find out what makes me tick and why a re-straining order has been slapped on such an inno-cent-looking young woman. Silence. I have all the time in the world.

Outside the birds are tweeting, cheerful back-ground music. The large sash window is ajar, letting in the first warm wafting breeze of summer; early June, my favourite month. A thick red book, a tome by Freud or Pavlov no doubt, holds it open, jammed in at one end. Perhaps the cord has snapped.

'Nothing much really. He went off with someone else.' It sounds so simple, so normal but I'm not going to own up to the shock I felt on discovering that he'd been sleeping with three women at the same time.

'We were young,' I continue, reluctantly, as I scan the room through lazy eyes. Bookshelves line the walls and stretch heavenward towards corniced ceil-ings. Psychotherapists must be well paid.

'Did you feel betrayed?' she asks, her voice soft and marshmallowy. A strange question really. At the time I kept going back for more, disbelieving and listening to the excuses, desperate for a few crumbs of encouragement. I used to ask him questions, willing the truth to set me free but he wasn't that no-ble. He was the first guy, since my father, that I couldn't let go. The worse Jeremy treated me, the more determined I got to hold on. The more elusive, the more driven I was to see him. Stalking isn't a word I would use. I was keen to catch him out, so I followed him around, day and night, until he disappeared.

'A complete bastard.' Thinking out loud, I'm shocked by the venom in the three words and wonder if the excavation of my soul might be starting to bear fruit, finally revealing its hidden depths. I know that's what Ms Evans is digging for.

'In what way?' A neatly shaped eyebrow raises. Miss, or perhaps to be more accurate, Ms Justine Evans as depicted on the gold embossed nameplate, asks questions for a living. I have a few questions I'm tempted to throw her way. For example, portraying single status for professional purposes gives me a clue as to her character. She doesn't want to be defined by marriage. She likes to play-act that she's single and it's tempting to ask why.

'He wouldn't phone for several days and this would force me to turn up at his flat, very late at night banging loudly to be let in.'

It was his fault entirely that I was forced to hang around outside and lose what dignity I had left. Following him every day to work might have been a bit over the top but I was in love and when he told me to back off, it only made things worse.

'He forced you? To turn up like that, I mean.' Ms Evans, 'call me Justine', is trying to pass the blame my way, make me own up to being desperate and neurotic, perhaps slightly unhinged. Ms Evans has a plan but then so have I.

'Perhaps that's a bit harsh but we were virtually living together so I would expect to see him at the end of the day.' My smile is like a politician's, a fixed grin set firm to sell my pitch. As his girlfriend, Jeremy had sworn undying love within the first three weeks of hooking up and I took it for granted that we would end up together. Together forever. We kept moving through difficult phases in our relationship, that was all, or so I told myself.

Ms Evans will guess I'm lying. We lived in two separate flats a couple of miles apart and even after a year, Jeremy showed determined reluctance to move in together; in fact to do anything together any more.

'What about the sex?' Ms Evans' lips have a gentle upturn at the corners.

The clock is ticking onwards and my one-hour slot is nearly up. Although I'm being treated like a sick criminal, I think it's quite amazing that the cost of my treatment is being funded by some governmental body; probably a specially set-up unit for the criminally insane.

'That was the hardest thing to give up.' This is what she's expecting to hear. I don't disappoint.

Ms Evans' legs are neatly crossed, silken nude-coloured stockings giving a hint of an inner sexuality. I wonder when she might uncross them and for what sort of clients. I suspect sex is a major topic on most of her questionnaires and maybe the answers get her excited.

'Was it special?'

What does she mean 'special'? We had been lock and key, first-time lovers who couldn't get enough of each other. Several times a day, inside and out, up-stairs and down, covertly and brazenly. Isn't that how it is with all first-time lovers? La-di-da-di-da.

'I thought so.'

'Before we round off our session, perhaps you can tell me how you finally accepted the end of the relationship.' This will be central to her enquiries. Once a stalker, always a stalker.

'I didn't. He disappeared off to America and I've never been able to track him down. I did try but eventually "out of sight, out of mind".' This is something else she needs to believe, my ability to move on.

I don't tell her about the fury, hurt and devastation that clung to me after he left. Clothed in a cloak of self-loathing and failure, I spent day and night trying to track him down. Not to mention the three futile trips to the States. A blackness suffocated my soul. Until I met Scott.

'Next time we can perhaps talk a little bit about Scott. He was "your saviour" I think you called him.' She smiles, but again I sense sarcasm lurking below the measured statement. Scott is the reason I'm here so I knew she wouldn't want to waste too much time on his predecessor.

'I met him on the rebound. He treated me even worse than Jeremy.' A tinny laugh pops out, accompanied by a distinct puff of disbelief. *Puff the Magic Dragon.*

'Okay. Next week you can tell me all about Scott.' As her notebook closes, an acknowledgement that the session is over, a crinkly smile replaces the professional mask.

Standing up straight, I flick back my hair in an act of defiance, and pass the buck firmly towards my interrogator. 'I've no idea why Scott has had a restraining order slapped on me as I wouldn't go within a hundred miles of him.' No need to tell her about my plans.

Without reply, the prim consultant opens her

desk diary and pencils me in for the same time next week. I thank her, but unsure for what. When I leave, Ms Evans dictates her conclusions into the little Dictaphone on her desk and her secretary types up a report which gets sent off to all interested parties. That is, all parties interested in my psychotic and unbalanced state of mind. Not to mention those footing the bill.

I close the door quietly behind me and wander out through the ornate portico entrance, pleasantly calm and weirdly refreshed from the lie down, and head back out into the sunshine. I glance heavenward, pause, and let the heat seep through my pores.

* * *

I trace the winding path back towards the road, through the carefully manicured grounds with the mature stately trees lining the route. The Abbott Hospital grounds have the distinct feel of an upmarket stately home. Luxury and insanity nestle side by side; an unlikely union.

Up ahead a thin wiry man pushing a bicycle approaches. He's not dressed in striped pyjamas, and isn't wandering haphazardly in a delusional psychotic state. That's the thing with mental issues, they're hard to spot. But this guy, Bob Pratchett, is a regular.

'Hi. All okay?' He pulls up alongside, his smile beaming like a toothpaste advert. It's a bright, overly forced, 'see how at ease I am with the world' kind of smile, yet his rounded shoulders and fidgeting fingers suggest that he's anything but.

'Hi. I survived,' I say. Bob is wearing a weird baseball hat, askew at an angle, with *Boston Red Sox* emblazoned in red across the brim. His mouth displays small perfectly-formed pebbles for teeth but his lips are wet, small spots of saliva congealed in the corners. He's like a salivating mongrel, rabid and malnourished.

'Perhaps you fancy a coffee sometime? We could swap stories and perhaps tell each other the truth, the whole truth and nothing but the truth.' His hearty laugh convulses his body as he makes the courtroom pronouncement.

'Sounds good,' I lie.

'Don't talk to anyone from the Abbot Hospital. They're all mad. Walk straight on past.' My mother's warning is still with me even after all these years. She wasn't quite so vehement though after the beatings sent her scrambling through the wrought-iron gates in search of drugs and a sympathetic ear to ease her

torment. Mental illness is something horrendous that happens to other people, she told me. Her assurances and smile convinced me that this was indeed the case.

'Great. Let me know when suits.' With that, Bob pushes his bike on past, whistling a distinct triumphant ditty. 'See you later,' he calls over his shoulder.

When I reach the end of the driveway I stop and look across the road at my childhood home. A chill shiver runs down my spine. The sun has dipped behind a cloud, hiding under a large fluffy map of Australia, and has taken the heat with it.

It's hard not to remember what happened. Even my determination to gut, cleanse and rebuild the interior of my household legacy can't wipe away the memories. As I wait for a break in the traffic, I wonder if I should invite Ms Evans across to my home one day. She could witness first-hand the source of my discontent; where it all began and perhaps where it's all likely to end. It might help with the answers.

My therapist will soon start probing, digging deeper into my family past. Her concentration will be on my violent alcoholic father and my neurotic drug-addled mother. She will try to make me accept that my parents are to blame for my sick unhinged behaviour. Opening up and talking about them should help me address the issues and lead to a 'cleansing of the soul'. I know the terminology. She believes my parents are at the root of all my problems and who am I to disagree?

As I step out into the road a car horn blasts through the air. Shit. I automatically reel backwards, catapulted out of my reverie. A large black Range Rover misses me by inches as it swerves across the white line.

I am a black cat. I have nine lives. My mother told me she had nine lives. I scuttle across to the other side, and pray I'm that lucky.

3

Covent Garden is packed, but then it's a Friday. End of the week, time to let the hair down. The milling throngs have been my camouflage. I've wafted in and out unnoticed for the past few weeks, floating by like a soft breeze, but today I will emerge, a phoenix rising from the ashes.

The café where I've settled is a small French bistro. Tables and chairs are slotted neatly into the confined outside space. I'm sitting at a table for two, having swivelled my chair round, strategically pointing it to face the length of pavement he walks every Friday for his lunchtime session. He won't be able to go past without spotting me.

The sun is directly overhead, but under the

striped awning there is welcome shade. I remove my hat, Audrey Hepburn chic, and lay it carefully on top of the red and white chequered tablecloth. Today has been a long time coming but it has finally arrived, my patience rewarded.

Then I see him as he turns the corner and heads in my direction. His hands are casually tucked into his pockets and sunglasses perch on top of his blond wavy hair. Oakleys. Only the best for Scott. Suddenly his pace falters as if everything has gone into slow motion. For one awful moment I think he might turn round and go back the way he's come, but he doesn't. His hands hang by his side, the casual air replaced by unease and a furrowed brow.

I hold my breath, still as a canny predator, and watch. I feign sudden recognition and spring up in my seat. After months of planning, Scott is in front of me, staring as if at a ghost. Face to face at last. Pistols at dawn.

'Oh my God! Scott!' My face reddens. The heat is helping my meticulously rehearsed embarrassment as a creeping swathe of crimson sweeps across my cheeks.

'Beverley?'

Perhaps he isn't sure if it is really me, the wanton curls and weight loss might be bolstering his surprise but there's an unmistakable element of shock in his intonation. I suspect he's praying that he might be wrong.

'What are you doing here?' My eyes are wide and my mouth agape. I've been practising in the mirror, perfecting the look of surprise. 'Oh my God,' I repeat. 'Is it really you?'

I push back my chair, standing up to proffer the customary kiss on both cheeks as would be expected between old friends and ex-lovers. I've toyed with the gesture, wondering whether it might not be better to let him take the lead but decided that a co-incidental meeting requires knee-jerk reactions, nothing stilted. The staged coincidence needs to be convincing.

'I work round the corner,' he says. 'But then you know that.'

'Are you still at the bank? It's great to see you. It seems ages. How long has it been?'

'A while.' Deadpan; not a smile nor flicker of emotion.

'Here. Sit down. Have a drink. Old times' sake?' I lift my handbag off the spare chair and pat the seat. 'One can't hurt. Surely.'

He hesitates. My surmise was that he would be curious, anxious and perhaps afraid that the meeting was orchestrated, but he'll need to find out. My next comment helps him make the decision.

'It's weird but I thought I spotted you earlier, round the corner by the market.' I straighten my skirt and sit back down under the awning. 'You were with a young girl.' My stomach knots and I bite the inside of my cheek but still manage a lightness of tone.

He sinks down into the seat, cramming his long legs uncomfortably under the table. His muscular thighs bring back memories.

I toss my hair from side to side, teasing the fringe. 'I've grown my hair. What do you think?'

He gives it a cursory glance. 'Yes, suits you.' He doesn't mention the weight loss, suntan and flawless complexion or my expensive outfit. It's taken time and effort but I'm looking good. His mind is else-where. Either that or he wants me to think it is as he won't throw me any crumbs by engaging.

'Where?'

'Where what?'

'You said you spotted me earlier. Whereabouts?'

'The French cheese stall.' I point to the carrier bag by my feet. 'Camembert, Brie and Roquefort. Old favourites, eh?' I tease. He'll remember the al fresco picnics on Hampstead Heath with the baguettes of French bread, the runny cheeses and chilled white wine. He might have tried to forget but I'll not let him.

'Oh,' is all he says.

'Are you okay? Perhaps a cool beer? It's so hot.' My smile is wide, a bright, innocent beam. I run the back of my hand across my forehead, wiping away theatrical sweat. 'My treat.'

I can hear the cogs in his brain working, ratcheting up. *Click, click, click.* The perspiration on his forehead might be from the heat but there's definitely a frisson of fear about his demeanour. I snap my fingers at a hovering waiter.

'A bottle of Peroni?' Scott doesn't humour me when I raise a questioning eyebrow, a knowing glint that this is his favourite tipple, especially in the heat.

'No thanks. Water's fine. Still, please,' he says, making his request directly to the waiter.

'Another glass of white wine for me, please. Sauvignon Blanc.' I drain an almost-empty glass and hand it across. 'I should have ordered a bottle. It's cheaper if you have more than two glasses.'

'Beverley.' The single word speaks volumes. I can hear Ms Evans using the same modus operandi when she threw out the single word 'names'. Perhaps they're in cahoots.

'Yes, Scott.' But I'm ready for him, my answers are

carefully prepared. My sessions with Ms Evans are helping with the manufacture of pertinent replies.

'What the hell are you doing here? You moved to Cornwall. Why are you back?' An angry skiff of spittle spurts from his tight lips and lands on the table. I swish it away with the end of a serviette.

'I've moved back to London. Dad died, by the way, and left me the family home. I'm back in Southgate.' I lower my eyes, teasing out a teardrop by squeezing my lids tightly together. It's better that Scott thinks I'm grieving, rather than know the truth.

I want him to remember my soft side. He probably guesses that I feel no sadness, only relief, as I told him often enough about my childhood when we first got together. Never the really bad stuff, but enough to warrant sympathy to keep him close.

'Sorry. I didn't know.'

'How could you?' Our drinks arrive and I reach for the wine, sipping at the cool nectar. 'Anyway, Cornwall was a perfect haven after all the drama but you didn't seriously expect me to stay there forever? It's miles from anywhere. God, this wine is good. Cheers.' I raise my glass then instantly regret the celebratory abandon as it seems to wind him up.

'Listen. I don't know what your game is but keep away from me and Cosette.'

'Cosette? Is that her name? She looks very young, even for you. But very pretty,' I add.

'I'm warning you. One step in our direction and I'm going back to the police. You might have fooled them but not me.'

Scott knocks back his water, coughing violently as he drains the glass, and stands up. He glowers down at me, using his height and vantage point to increase the threat level.

'Are you okay?' I etch concern on my features. 'Listen. Don't worry, Scott. I promise I'll not bother you.' A deep breath. 'Actually, I've met someone else. A really nice guy who lives in London and I think he could be *the one*.' I hold up two fingers on both hands and wiggle them like inverted commas. 'You don't need to worry any more,' I repeat. It's a minor victory. The tension slips a fraction from his broad shoulders.

'Whatever. I've got to go. Look after yourself.'

'You too. It was great to bump into you.'

Without a second glance, he heads off the way he came. I watch his retreating back, in its blue striped work shirt, slim fit and clinging to his muscled torso. He'll have left his jacket at the bank. Barclays in Cheapside.

He still works on the third floor in mergers and acquisitions. I used to tell him perseverance would one day propel him up the building. The chairman of the bank has an office on the top floor, glass windows encircling a large private sanctum and affording panoramic views all around London.

'That'll be you one day,' I said. 'Top floor. Head of management.' I lied of course. Scott's too lazy. I could have helped him but on his own he'll always hover around the middle of the banking world, mediocrity swallowing him up.

I spend another half an hour watching the world go by and savour the moment of victory. It's a good start and it couldn't have gone any better. Scott's discomfort is only the beginning; after the discomfort and unease there'll be the doubts and fears. Finally, I'll bang the nail firmly in his coffin and destroy any chance he might have of a happy ever after. It's the least he deserves.

Ms Evans keeps hinting that I need to let go, but I wonder why? Turn the other cheek. Why? It doesn't work. It needs to be an eye for an eye, only that will give me comfort. She doesn't really understand how deep it goes.

I finish my drink, settle the bill and pick up the cheeses before heading back towards the Tube. My head is light from the drink, the sun and the rendezvous. I sway like a listing ship but soon surge forward, full throttle, euphoric from the lunchtime events.

However, I need to sober up and down a gallon of coffee when I get home before my date with Travis tonight. He is my project for the future and will never be allowed to treat me badly. Scott has certainly taught me a few never-to-be-repeated lessons. I smile, knowing Ms Evans would approve of my determination to move forward although I'm certain she won't approve of Travis. Married men are definitely not going to be on her list of the best ways forward for troubled patients and I'm certain they'll not be recommended in the rule book.

As I step onto the train, a warm thought tickles my imagination. I don't need to worry about not being able to have children any more. Travis has two, a young boy and girl, and a ready-made family is becoming ever more appealing. As the doors slide shut I realise that if everything works out as planned, I won't need to be defined any longer by a sterile womb.

4

Travis picked a seat in the corner and loosened his tie, pulling the tightened red knot to one side and running a finger inside the rim of his damp collar. The surgery's call, telling him his blood pressure check was overdue, had made him edgy.

He ordered a bottle of white wine, a cold, crisp Sauvignon Blanc, and let his body sink into the cushioned armchair. Twenty minutes early. He'd have time to pop out for a quick roll-up before she arrived.

The bar was a couple of streets away from his office. He'd been coming here for years, wining and dining clients through the boom times. The room was packed, buzzing with young dynamic businessmen getting up close and personal with their secretaries. Like he used to, when selling marbled penthouses to fat oil sheiks teased him with possibilities. He had imagined one day he'd be ensconced in such luxury; the playboy bachelor. But marriage had sucked him in and now he barely earned enough to pay the mortgage.

'Boo. Guess who?'

Beverley's voice cut through the air, crisp and sharp, and made him squirm in his seat.

'Shit. Don't do that. You scared me to death.'

Her hands covered his eyes from behind and a strong stench of perfume made him cough.

'You been here long? Jeez, it's busy. Don't you fancy somewhere quieter?' Beverley scanned the room, peeled off her jacket and pulled a chair up close.

'Ten minutes, give or take. Here.'

He handed her a full glass of white wine and watched her take a large swig.

'Cheers,' she said, clanging their glasses together.

Beverley could drink. In fact she could drink him under the table. This had been their common ground in the early days, when her boundless energy and passion had intoxicated him. Now her suffocating intensity felt like a pillow was squashed against his face.

'I thought we'd have a couple here and go the French place next door for something to eat. It's quieter in there,' he said.

'Sounds like a plan.'

But Travis didn't want quiet. He twiddled his thumbs in the office all day and by evening was chomping for excitement. But arguing with Beverley wasn't worth the effort, certainly not now that he wanted to move on. She kept trying to pin him down, nail his apathy with sharpened tacks.

Beverley's short black skirt rode up over her thighs but he no longer felt the urge to slide his hand underneath and excite her below the table the way he used to. He'd prefer a cigarette.

'Top up?'

Beverley's cheeks flushed as she downed her glass. 'Yes please.' She wiggled her glass in the air like a winner's trophy in some speed-drinking competition. He lifted the bottle from the ice bucket.

With his arm stretched out along the back of her chair, Travis watched as she quaffed the liquid and wondered where the allure had gone. The ducking and diving had only lasted a couple of months and now Beverley was hanging on the end of a phone, the chase over.

Then there was the matter of his wife, Queenie,

whom he had no intention of leaving. At first he thought she was strong, a woman of substance, dealing with his peccadilloes in a mature and grown-up manner and putting the children first. But recently he'd twigged it was because she didn't care; most likely never had.

He took a sip of his wine then asked, 'How's the house coming along? Did you get your new carpets?'

Beverley's recently acquired wealth, however, caused Travis a dilemma. The detached house in Southgate was worth over £2 million; her father's guilt money apparently. He'd crawled into his grave trying to buy salvation and forgiveness through the hefty bequest and Beverley had willingly accepted. She wasn't one for scruples. Choked by his own mortgage, Travis viewed the wealth like a dangled carrot.

'It's taking forever, but what fun! When are you coming round? I'm getting it ready for us.' She held her breath, stared him down. 'What about one night next week?'

Beverley's bust strained against her red shirt and he felt a sudden urge to pull the sheer material apart, the wine egging him on.

'I'll check the diary tomorrow. Come here, you tease.'

Beverley pushed him away and stretched out her legs. 'Any night except Wednesday. What about Saturday? You promised.'

Early on he'd promised a weekend date but that was when he'd been desperate to get her into bed. Travis leant over and kissed her on the lips, slithering his tongue round to wet her earlobe. 'Let's see. I've other things on my mind at the moment. This is what we both want for now.'

She leant her heavy breasts in towards him and as he clenched his teeth and closed his eyes, her hand landed near his crotch and slid back and forth.

'Come on. What about that meal?' She suddenly sprang up, uncoiling like a taut spring, and shook the empty bottle. 'Look it's all gone. Let's go.'

In frustration he straightened his trousers, keen to come up with a way to bypass the expense of a meal and go straight to the hotel. He stood up and helped her on with her jacket. 'Whatever you say, boss.'

They pushed past the increasingly drunken workers, cheek by jowl at the bar, and made their way out onto the street. The summer night felt warm and balmy but a smell, like smoking ham, hung in the air as a thick blanket of pollution furred the atmosphere. Travis coughed, his lungs thick with toxic deposits. He craved fresh air.

'Don't you just love London at night? The bustle and excitement.' Beverley bounded along like a baby kangaroo, as if oblivious to the deadly poisons. She took his hand, interwove their fingers like a couple of young lovers. Travis suddenly pulled her into a small alleyway and pinned her up against a wall.

'Why don't we go straight to the hotel and eat afterwards? I don't know about you but the food can wait. I've got much bigger things on my mind.' He took her hand and guided it down to his crotch. 'See what I mean?'

'The bigger the better.' She squealed, took his hand and led him hurriedly back out onto the main street. 'I'm game. Vamoose.'

They walked briskly across London Bridge and Travis felt light-headed, his dull mood lifting. He'd worry about things later, but for now he'd go with the flow and one more night couldn't hurt.

On either side of them, the Thames rumbled along past superficially lit banks.

The sleeping behemoth snored gently, the dark menacing undertones hidden from sight.

* * *

'I think I met your wife today.'

Travis had reknotted his tie and tucked his shirt back into his suit trousers. It was only 9pm but he was ready for bed. Weariness had set in after climax and the alcohol had induced a post-coital downer, leaving him with a dry mouth and a gurgling growl in his stomach. It had been a long day and he was ready for home, especially now the kids would be in bed.

His open mouth choked back a lazy yawn. The fan clicked and whirred in the tiny bathroom and Beverley's outline was visible through a crack in the door. Her pouting lips, like those of a puffer fish, were blood red where a steady hand had applied a thick coat of colour. Travis, his hands slick with sweat, sat on the edge of the bed as he struggled to tie the short laces on his hard leather shoes.

'What? Where? How did you know it was my wife?'

Beverley's face was pinned in close to the glass as a steady hand worked her make-up. Eyeliner. Lip liner. Blusher. Finally, she fluffed her hair with a weird spiky metal comb. Travis got up, now fully dressed, and moved towards the bathroom, adrenaline pumping in his veins, and pushed open the door.

'Smell the perfume. Remember? *Poison.*' Beverley upturned an outstretched wrist. They'd chosen it together and he'd laughed when he first squirted it, whispering in her ear that she was its namesake. That was only six months ago, Christmas shopping on Oxford Street.

'My wife. You said you met her. Where?'

'Waitrose. I took a trip there. You told me that's where your wife went and, right enough, there she was, by the fresh pineapples.'

'How did you know it was her?'

'You told me she liked pineapples.' Beverley laughed, deep and throaty.

Travis froze. He felt a sharp pain sear across his chest. 'Seriously?'

'You didn't think I wouldn't google her, surely? That's what girlfriends do. Check out the competition. You don't mind, do you? I didn't speak to her, just followed her around to see what went into the trolley. Get a few tips.'

He closed his eyes against the stabbing pain, holding a hand to his chest and leant against the door jamb. 'You definitely didn't speak to her?'

Beverley zipped up her make-up bag with one final check in the mirror and then turned to face him.

Christ she was baiting him, taunting him. She thought it was funny.

'The only thing I don't get is how she walks in those skyscraper heels. And no, I definitely didn't speak to her so you can rest easy. You don't think I'm that stupid.'

Beverley's villainous chuckle followed him back into the bedroom.

'I'm starving. What's the name of the restaurant? French, I think you said. Hope it's good.' Without waiting for a reply she lifted her bag and clicked open the door. 'Come on, let's go.'

Travis followed her out, dragged along like muddied water in the wake of a ship's churning propellers. Beverley's gait was determined and he suddenly remembered her lack of scruples; it mightn't be that easy to walk away.

Tomorrow he had two things to do. One, get his blood pressure checked and two, work out how to get shot of Beverley.

5

Scott watched Beverley look up and down the street. He had piled the pizza boxes high on her doorstep, stacking them neatly one on top of the other with a gruesome surprise in the top one. Beverley was curious, nosey and wouldn't bin the boxes without checking the contents. She'd open them in order, the top one first, and work through methodically. Scott would stay and watch, hoping her discomfort might make him feel better because he couldn't feel any worse. The nightmare was starting all over again.

After Danielle's accident, which the police couldn't pin on Beverley due to lack of evidence, Scott was like a caged lion with an immovable blade in its paw. He was unable to function and took extended sick leave from the bank. Mental health issues had been cited, and he hadn't lied. Danielle didn't hang around and after she left, an impotent rage led him to the brink of insanity.

Cosette, his new girlfriend, sweet and innocent, had coaxed him back from the edge. It had only been a few months but he was slowly moving on with his life. It was still difficult to relax but he was starting to enjoy the simple things again: breakfast in bed, candlelit dinners and a girlfriend who made no demands.

But Beverley was back, a ghoul not done with haunting. She had become a stalker in broad daylight. The police assured him it was all under control and that Miss Beverley Digby could no longer touch him, but Scott knew better. No restraining order or enforced therapy sessions were going to keep her away; she knew how to play the system.

He slunk down in his car, sweat lathering his body. His armpits exuded a rancid odour, wet globules of perspiration staining his shirt and his fists were clenched like balls of iron. He had forgotten how to loosen up, how to get release from the anger and tension which had engulfed him again. If he wasn't careful he'd find himself in therapy, sectioned for insanity, evil deeds, or both.

He watched Beverley walk down her front path and come out onto the street. Leaving the front door ajar, she walked right, then left and right again before ducking through a gap in the neighbour's hedge at number thirty-seven. It was another similarly large detached house, 1930s, leaded windows and fancy chimney breasts. Savagely clinging ivy trailed the walls of number thirty-seven whereas Beverley's house was bare, void of adornments.

Ring. Ring. Ring. Her finger stubbed furiously. She peered through the window to see if there was anyone looking back out, wondering why no one came to answer the door. She was going to have a long wait because the O'Connors had gone out about an hour ago, shortly before Scott had made his delivery. Beverley would be trying to find out if they had seen anything and who had left the pizza boxes.

Scott's car was parked directly across the road in total blackness. The only street light came from an overhead lamp outside Beverley's house and its ghostly beam shone onto her porch. Beverley hovered by the gate, waited a couple of minutes, then went back up the path.

As she counted the boxes, twenty-four in total, Scott wished he had the courage to finish her off. If Beverley thought of inviting friends round for a party, there wouldn't have been any point. It wasn't because the boxes were empty but because she didn't have any friends.

The cartons *were* all empty except for the first one which contained a margarita pizza with stringy mozzarella cheese, a few basil leaves, garlic and a chopped-up mouse. There was enough olive oil squelching over the top that she wouldn't at first recognise the meat ingredient.

Her scream was slightly delayed and, even from across the road, it made Scott jump. He had been counting to ten but wasn't prepared when she let rip on number eight and her screech tore through the night air. The intensity of the reaction for such a tiny mouse made Scott suspect she knew someone was watching.

Beverley's eyes hit on his car. If she was keeping tabs on him, it was possible she recognised his new vehicle. Scott fumbled with the keys and as soon as Beverley went back inside, he started up the engine and pulled away.

As he filtered into the sparse late-night traffic, he felt a dreadful sense of anticlimax and his dry eyes made it hard to focus. The memories ricocheted back and forth across his line of vision and a couple of times he swerved out of the way of oncoming traffic.

Short of killing Beverley, he didn't think he'd ever be free of her. Winding her up with a taste of her own medicine no longer seemed such a wise move; schoolboy tit for tat was never going to cut it. She'd probably see it as attention; flattery. It might even spur her on to hound him more. Shit. What was he doing? What could he do? His mind skittered.

Then there was Cosette. He had to keep her safe, and he didn't dare tell her what a mad, sad, evil psychotic monster his ex-girlfriend was. No one knew Beverley like he did. She had seemed so likeable and innocent which didn't make it easy, his fears falling on deaf ears. The therapy which she'd been forced into after Danielle's accident didn't seem to be working and he had no idea how to make her back off.

As he parked up outside his flat, he slumped back and let his face fall into his palms. One thing he knew for sure. The meeting in Covent Garden had been no accident and Beverley had used the coincidental angle once too often. She was one clever, scheming, conniving bitch.

6

We're like a group of alcoholics, seated in a circle, perched uncomfortably on the edge of red plastic chairs, and each of us waiting our turn to speak.

Addicts have the most unattractive personalities. Secretly they feel cleverer, superior to everyone else and use well-rehearsed storylines to cover their deadly neuroses and addictions but they kid no one but themselves. I scan the group and know I don't belong. I've nothing to own up to as I'm here under duress, legally obliged to attend, all my sessions paid for by someone else. For the life of me, I can't help wondering who is footing their bills as the Abbott Hospital doesn't come cheap. A five-star hotel in Majorca could match it, same price, less hassle, and a swimming pool thrown in.

There are six of us in the circle, including, of course, Ms Evans, whose hands tap up and down on her thighs in time to a restless right leg. She's wearing navy linen slacks today and a starchy buttoned-up white shirt, the epitome of bureaucratic efficiency although I'm not sure the see-through fabric was a wise choice as her lacy pop-up bra leaves little to the imagination.

This is my first inclusion into a group session at the Abbott Hospital. Bob Pratchett assures me such sessions are less intense than the *one-on-one* probing and much more fun. I'm hoping that by listening to other patients' stories, my own sanity will stand out. To be honest, even before we've started, I think the small group of participants look quite mad but I must remember to use the word 'sick'. Ms Evans stares me down when I use the 'm' word on purpose, she's that easy to bait.

'We'll go round the circle in turn and each of you can tell the others why you're here,' our leader begins, her hands and legs steady now the ship's about to sail. This will be fun, like a day trip to the seaside.

Bob smiles at me and winks. I raise my eyes heavenward while he silently runs the side of his hand across his throat in a knife-slitting gesture. We're careful though that Ms Evans doesn't see as our irreverence might be construed as disrespectful. We smother our giggles like naughty schoolchildren.

'Bob. Perhaps you'd like to begin. Give us your background.'

I've heard his story first-hand, but I'm intrigued to hear how he'll tell it to the group. The other three patients watch him intently, keen to forget their own torment for a few minutes, in the hope of finding comfort in a story worse than theirs.

'There's not much to tell,' he says. 'My wife has thrown me out and won't let me see my daughter unless I take my meds and come for counselling. She says I'm sick.' He smiles, a broad comforting grin, in an effort to assert his sanity. I do wonder, though, if he's trying to reassure us that he isn't hiding a shotgun under his belt. His eyes have it. The iris is indistinguishable from the pupil, the black moon eclipsing the piercing sun and the blue rims have completely disappeared. The blackness matches his madness and the next comments don't help.

'Problem is, she doesn't believe me when I tell her our neighbour is trying to kill me.' No one moves. 'About a week ago I caught him in the back garden holding a garden spade. When I approached him he wielded it high in the air. It was well past midnight. Now is that normal?'

We all simultaneously shift in our seats as if about to participate in a Mexican wave, but embarrassment gives way to stony silence. A nervous cough breaks the deadlock.

'Bob. Why do you think he's trying to kill you? Last month it was the local shopkeeper. Is there a pattern here?'

Cool, calm and collected. Good old clichéd Ms Evans; always one to 'hit the nail on the head'. Patterns. She's always harping on about behavioural patterns.

Bob laughs a little too loudly for such a quiet ensemble, lashing his wet lips, top and bottom, with a slithery tongue.

'You might find this hard to believe, Justine,' he says, daring us to admonish him for the use of her Christian name, 'but I have this effect on people. People walk past me with hatred in their eyes. I don't mind. Jesus was persecuted in the same way and rose to tell the tale and people sense my power.' This time the hush is even more acute. Christ, he's a lunatic, certified, and I realise I'd be wise to keep a wide berth. I've googled his issues and he has the textbook characteristics of a paranoid schizophrenic.

'Thank you, Bob.' Ms Evans calmly moves on. 'Tamsin. It's now your turn to tell us why you're here.'

Tamsin's gaunt, skeletal appearance makes it obvious why she's here, but we listen. Tamsin is a young anorexic who hasn't had a meal for three weeks but is soon trying to convince us that she had a full English breakfast this morning: bacon, eggs, sausage; the works.

Our leader, Ms Evans, times the session nicely. Five patients, one hour. That gives us all about ten minutes to speak. Actually, the time's passing quite quickly and I'm starting to look forward to my turn as I have a few clangers to share with the circle.

There are exactly ten minutes to go when all eyes and ears turn in my direction.

'Beverley. In your own words tell us why you're here.' Ms Evans nods encouragement.

'In a nutshell? I fell in love. Scott was his name, actually it still is. His name I mean,' I say, raising quiet appreciative laughs. 'The problem is that he met someone else and I still don't get why he preferred her.'

Danielle was slightly older than me, but only by a year. She was pretty, but nothing special, with an amazingly flat chest and, at five feet five, a couple of inches shorter. 'Also I got pregnant and he forced me to have an abortion.' I swallow. It's tougher than I thought to regurgitate the facts.

'Did you not want to keep the baby?' Tamsin asks.

'Of course I did, but he lied. Scott said if we lived together for a year or two longer we could start a family when he was more financially secure. We would buy a house together. Ha. I believed him. How stupid was I?'

'When did he meet his new girlfriend?' Bob asks.

'A couple of months before my abortion. He never intended for us to have a future together but I didn't realise it at the time. Danielle was her name.' I lower my eyes, lending my story gravitas. Although I'm not after sympathy, it's hard being so honest and the concerned looks make me falter.

'Tell the group why you're here,' Ms Evans prompts.

I let my eyes work the circle; I'm ready.

'My name is Beverley and I'm a stalker.' I pretend to own up to having an obsessive compulsive disorder and reintroduce myself like an alcoholic determined to come clean. This will impress Ms Evans and hopefully will go some way in helping convince her of my determination to beat the demons. The sooner the better.

'Danielle turned out to be pregnant at the same

time as me and also lost her baby. She fell down a concrete flight of stairs and nearly bled to death. I happened to be in the vicinity at the time and Scott tried to link my beady vigilance to her accident. You see, I couldn't help following Scott and Danielle around. I didn't think of it as stalking but I couldn't let go. I think lots of jilted lovers would do the same.'

'That's so sad. I'm really sorry,' says Dave, the nervous chain-smoking alcoholic sitting between Tamsin and Bob. Dave clutches a packet of tobacco, scrunched tightly in his hand like a security blanket, and his thumb is red and bulbous from incessant sucking. Childhood has beckoned him back.

Manuel is the fifth patient in our circle, and he just *tuts*. He's been excused from sharing on the grounds that his English makes storytelling difficult. Ms Evans likes to keep him involved though, drip feeding him little titbits in Spanish. We learn today that she has multilingual skills that complement her astute powers of deduction.

'Yes. But there'll be other times. I don't think kids with that guy would have been a good idea,' Tamsin says. Her jaw creaks, bone on bone.

'That's the problem. I now can't have children. There were complications with the abortion. Anyway, I'm here to try to change my behaviour. The therapy is to help deal with my stalking issues.' I make a final nod as my lips snap shut.

I don't mention the endless grilling by the police and the lack of evidence that narrowly kept me out of prison. There was nothing directly to link me with Danielle's tumble down the stairs and the subsequent loss of her unborn baby. But, in case the police got it wrong, and because of Scott's absolute insistence that I was somehow culpable, someone with clout felt it best I get treated for a seemingly unhealthy inability to move on. Only Ms Evans can sign me off, and only when she is convinced that I'm no longer stalking Scott, will I be released from therapy.

There is a sudden loud knock at the door. Everyone sighs, relieved to have somewhere else to look other than at me.

'We're coming!' Ms Evans glances at the clock to confirm that our time is up. 'Just rounding off.'

As we all stand up and push the chairs back against the wall, Ms Evans says a big collective 'well done'. She's like a primary school teacher, savouring the pleasure over her charges' achievements. Dave lingers, unwilling to face the world again, his thumb stuck fast between his lips. His front teeth protrude slightly, buck teeth we used to call them.

When I reach the door I smile at Ms Evans.

Didn't I do well? I'm hoping to get an extra pat on the back and she doesn't disappoint. Encouragement with a capital E is her mantra.

'Well done, Beverley. I know it's not easy telling everyone about what happened but I think you're making good progress. I hope opening up to the others helped.'

Ms Evans is pleased that I owned up to stalking habits, although I'm a bit annoyed with myself that I didn't use the past tense when talking about my vigilance as I don't want her to think it's still going on. But it's too late. I can't take it back. 'I was a stalker' might have been more astute. I need to measure my words more carefully.

'Thanks,' I say as I close the door behind me.

I know she'll soon push me to talk about Travis, or Terence as I've called him to protect his identity. I don't want to name him, in case. Southgate isn't a very large place and you never know who might get wind of our affair if I use his real name. Travis is the new man in my life and we're moving forward nicely. I won't mention the fact, when I start to open up, that I'm already working on a plan that will help make his decision to move in with me easier. That's none of my therapist's business.

Travis and his wife, Queenie, sleep in separate

bedrooms, a fact he hasn't yet shared with me. I don't like secrets but I'll give him the benefit of the doubt as he's probably trying to protect my feelings by not discussing his marriage. Queenie's bedroom is at the back of the house and she keeps her window open every night, the slightest chink letting in fresh air. She goes to bed on work nights at ten sharp, ever the consummate professional but indulges at weekends by staying up until eleven and drinking a couple of glasses of Merlot.

Travis is a late-to-bed person and climbs the stairs much later, finishing off the weekend Merlot long after his wife has retired. I do wonder though why he sometimes sleeps downstairs when they have four large bedrooms upstairs.

I head back home, still feeling slightly edgy after the pizza incident. When I awoke this morning, in the cold light of day, I wondered what I'd been so afraid of. It was probably a childish prank by someone who got the wrong address, or Scott making an ineffectual attempt to wind me up. If it was Scott, it was a pretty imaginative ploy by his standards. Perhaps he has a spine after all.

When I'm within sight of my front door I see a black cat sitting astride the bin bag into which I stashed the empty boxes. It's scratching furiously.

'Shoo. Shoo!' I yell, running the last few steps flapping my hands in the air. The animal shoots off but not before I spot the slimy rubbery length hanging from its mouth. It has managed to find the fried tail of the dead mouse.

7

E

Everyone I meet asks me what I do for a living. Where do I work? When they hear I'm taking time out from being a teaching assistant, a TA, they ask me when I'll be going back. I tell them I'm not sure as I'm busy gutting and renovating the house. Truth is, keeping tabs on Scott and Travis, maintaining control, takes up most of my time. I experiment with colour co-ordination and room layouts while I plan coincidental meetings. Ms Evans calls it stalking, but for me it's a way of life.

Like Dave's tobacco and Tamsin's diet plan, surveillance has become my security blanket. A comfort, something to cling to that reminds me constantly that I'll never be ignored or treated badly. I do it for Mum and me, something to help me stay afloat and it helps keep her memory alive. It's not the caresses and bedtime stories that I want to remember but rather her weaknesses and inability to fend off violence. You see, I don't ever want to be like her as she took the beatings lying down.

And of course there are now the Spanish lessons. Adding positive activities into my schedule is turning out to be very therapeutic.

* * *

I stare at diamond rings and gold necklaces in the jeweller's shop window, pressing my nose hard up against the glass in feigned concentration as I wait for the small group across the road to disband. The ongoing action is reflected in the window. As a shop assistant approaches me I notice Cosette's friends get up and start to move away and I'm in luck, because she stays put and in the shimmering reflection I see her reach down for a mobile phone.

I must say she's a pretty young thing, the emphasis definitely being on the young. She's all giggles and curls, and as she talks into the handset her spare hand swishes hair from one side to the other, skinny little fingers tousling the ends. I wonder if the caller is watching her too. Maybe they're FaceTiming.

'Can I help you, madam? Is it the rings you're interested in?'

I jump and narrowly miss bumping into the smartly dressed sales assistant who has appeared alongside.

'No, just having a look thanks.' I hesitate and throw her a bone. 'But I've made my choice.' I smile and point at the obscenely large diamond and sapphire ring glittering in the centre of the window display. As I move off I add, 'I'll be back.'

I won't be back, of course, as I much prefer West End jewellers, but the small shop is the best Edmonton has to offer. Also the covered entrance has provided the perfect lookout location as the language college is directly across the road. I'm soon making my way over towards the wooden bench where Cosette is sitting.

'No, I won't be late,' I hear her say into the phone.

I hover by the end of the bench but am near enough to listen in. Cosette's legs stretch out along the bench slats. She's been looking forward to the phone call; the way I used to. Scott is probably checking where she is, keeping tabs on her and she's flattered. The rapt attention of a well-heeled older man has sucked her in and she doesn't know yet that he's a control freak. More to the point, she doesn't yet know about me.

'What are you cooking?' she asks.

Scott is good in the kitchen, it's his thing. His specialties are all things Italian. Bolognaise, lasagne and spicy gnocchi. The tiramisu and panna cotta had been my downfall and a knot tightens in my stomach when I remember the comments.

'I think you need to cut back on the calories. The wine's giving you a spare tyre.'

He thought his teasing was fun but it soon hurt as our relationship became less intense. The wild passion seemed to abate too suddenly and his words played havoc with my insecurities.

But it hadn't been the wine. It had been the obscene portions he had piled on my plate and I didn't like to refuse after all his effort. That's the thing about Scott; he likes to blame other people. Perhaps I tried too hard to please him. I threw up the desserts into the toilet bowl on more than one occasion, like Tamsin still does, clearing out the stomach to cleanse the soul but instead it only left a gnawing emptiness.

'Sounds lovely.' Cosette simpers into her pink sparkly mobile which is stuck over with small silver stars. 'Yes, it's free,' she whispers, covering the mouthpiece and nodding at the other end of the bench. Her long legs unravel.

'Thanks,' I mouth back. I set my phone down, close my eyes and breathe deeply. The midday sun is high in the sky and I feel the welcome rays on my face but am soon itching to sit up straighter.

Ms Evans has suggested 'mindfulness' to help me unwind. Or yoga. I don't think she understands me at all. Even after all the soul-searching, down and dirty little secret sharing, she hasn't worked out that I don't need 'mindfulness'. I need to keep busy, keep on top of things and settling old scores is much more therapeutic than the holistic arts.

I'm surprised my therapist hasn't yet connected my restless activity to the trauma of my father's abusive habits, my mother's suicide, and all the negative implications. It's a pretty simple algorithm for a psychoanalyst.

'Great, see you later.' Cosette's mobile phone is switched off and put aside while she reaches for her bottle of water.

'Hi. Are you at the college?' I ask.

'Yes, I'm doing English. You?'

I lay my Spanish conversation textbook down along with a small dictionary. I've come prepared. 'Yes. I've just started Spanish classes for mature students.' I laugh. The word 'mature' is a nice touch. 'Back to school.'

A few seconds pass before Cosette gets up and throws a rucksack over her shoulder. 'Sorry, I need to get going. Class starts in ten minutes. It's been nice to meet you.'

'You too. Maybe bump into you again,' I say.

The words 'bump into' make me smile. As we get to know each other better she'll remember that our meeting was coincidental. It was on a sunny Thursday lunchtime in June that we 'bumped into' each other. The only vacant seat had been on the end of the bench where my ex-lover's new girlfriend happened to be sitting. No crime there.

'Beverley, by the way.'

'Cosette.'

With that she is gone.

8

It was only 7.30am. But Travis still got to work early, a lingering habit from the days when he cared about what he did, from the days when he pursued sales leads with a deep conviction that he was the best. Nowadays it was the kids, noisy and demanding first thing in the morning, that propelled him out the front door, work an excuse to escape the mayhem.

Queenie and he now led virtually separate lives, the children being the flimsy binding that held the marriage in place. Freddie and Emily were like delicate cotton threads impossibly trying to bind together a heavy worn tarpaulin disintegrating round the edges. In his wife's favour, she turned a blind eye to his affairs and her indifference no longer hurt. Apathy trailed in its wake like stagnant sludge in a slow-winding riverbed.

The first thing Travis did every morning when he reached the office was to head for the coffee machine. He craved his caffeine fix. One strong espresso would be followed by a second and a third until his brain kicked into gear and mid-morning he would refuel until the shakes forced him to stop.

In the centre of the small reception area adjacent to his office, the sight of the smooth glossy brochures, stacked like Jenga bricks on the coffee table was depressing. The pile used to excite him. Selling up-market properties to the obscenely rich, Travis used to play-act that he belonged; but he never would. It wasn't lack of desire, rather lack of drive as middle-age offered up mediocrity rather than wealth.

Now the only thing the stack offered up was a sickly synthetic smell which irritated his nostrils. In the last couple of years, as the commissions dried up, the demands of the mortgage and marriage had piled on the pressure and he lived with an albatross round his neck.

He pushed the papers aside, finding a small slot for the espresso cup on his desk, which was as cluttered as his life. As the computer and printers booted up, whirring and gurgling, he stared out the window at the early-bird commuters. Confident young men and women walked with purpose, the men with full heads of hair and the women shimmying along in miniskirts caressing firm backsides.

Tarte Tatin, the small café across the street, tempted him every couple of hours with a visit. Gigi would wave up at him and her bouncing cleavage would lure him down with the tease of a creamy French pastry. His waistline was ballooning but his visits quelled the boredom.

He got up to crack the window a fraction and let in some air. His hand hovered, willing Gigi to look up. The cloudless sky and warm sun, which pierced through a steamy heat haze, were helping lift the early morning blues. Gigi was serving a young man who strolled up and down the counter, deliberating on choices. When he finally left the shop, Gigi glanced up and wiggled her arm, beckoning Travis to come down. He grinned as she swayed her hips and clicked her fingers in time to some silent beat.

'Come on,' she mouthed.

'Okay.' He pointed at his watch and turned the dial towards the window. He threw his ten fingers out three times and mouthed 'half an hour'.

Back at his desk, Travis made a couple of phone calls, left messages, and then checked his Twitter and

LinkedIn accounts. As an afterthought he googled 'city breaks'. He owed himself a treat, a trip away; Prague or Bruges perhaps. Who knows, maybe Gigi could join him.

As he went to log off his phone pinged.

You about later? Drink maybe? B x

Before he finished reading the message, a second ping followed.

Are you there? X

Followed by a third.

Hope you're not ignoring me? Ha ha. Popping to Waitrose later... fancy some pineapples?

It still wasn't even eight. What the hell was Beverley doing texting this early? He turned his phone off and stuffed it in his pocket.

His stomach growled, desperate for sustenance and the three cups of espresso had given him the tremors. He was sweating under his tight shirt, and dampness circled his neck and coated his armpits. Raising an arm, he sniffed and recoiled before extracting a small cologne spray from his desk drawer.

On his way out, he paused and clutched the back of a chair, willing his rapidly pulsing heartbeat to subside.

* * *

Travis had been itching for months to ask Gigi for a drink. She was fun, and a few beers with an attractive woman, no strings attached, was what he needed. Having decided to tell his wife that he'd a property viewing and not to worry about supper, he finally picked up the courage.

'Listen. What are you doing after work? Fancy a drink or two down by the river?' he asked, as he handed over cash for two croissants and leant gently on the glass counter. 'Might as well make the most of the great weather.'

'Of course. I'd love to have a drink with you. Why has it taken you so long to ask?'

'Brilliant. I'll be finished around six. Shall I pop by then?'

'Perfect. I look forward to it.' With that, Gigi turned away to serve another customer. 'Two baguettes coming up.'

With a spring in his step he headed back to the office and tentatively reached for his phone. He turned it back on to find there were another ten texts from Beverley. He typed.

Sorry am with clients. Will get back later.

No sooner had he pressed 'send' than a reply bounced back.

Great. What time? Xx Where were my xxxs??

How the hell did he know what time? Beverley was worse than his wife used to be. If he'd hoped Beverley might get the message from subsequent lack of contact after the evening in the hotel, he was well off the mark. She was like a tick under his skin. He was about to turn the phone back to silent when the screen lit up again.

Don't ignore me. Just like to keep my diary up to date! Say 5?

Jesus. Now he had to tell her *when* he was going to contact her.

OK. I'll call at 5.
Perfect. Have a great day. I'll be waiting
xxxxxxxxxxxxx

He'd definitely call at five but it would be the last time. He'd arrange to meet up with her once more, tell her face to face that he was staying with his wife and that they should call it a day. His heart raced again, the palpitations like a distant drum roll as searing hot flushes, like scorching furnace flames, burned up his neck.

9

At four, Travis found himself in Canary Wharf. The riverside apartments had the best views in London and the location alone meant they commanded million-pound price tags. His client, Mr Keverne, wandered through the sleek black-and-white living space, padding across the marbled floors and running his fingers over the shiny angular worktops.

Travis headed outside to the corner wrap-around balcony, pulled the glass doors behind him and glanced down from the first-floor terrace. Small speed boats shot up and down the Thames, haring past leisure cruisers which ferried tourists along the river. He held his hand up and felt a slight skiff of rain, the cool welcome against his skin.

Travis wasn't hopeful of a sale. Mr Keverne was elderly, probably mid-seventies, with a heavily lined forehead and leathery skin. A deep suntan hinted at retirement and time spent in the sun, but still Travis doubted he was in the market for such an expensive bachelor pad. These were the sort of properties Travis coveted, the sort he'd once dreamed of owning.

The glass doors behind slid open and jolted him out of his reverie. Mr Keverne stepped out and smiled, displaying dazzlingly white implants.

'What's the asking price again?'

'£1.5 million. Cheap at half the price!' Travis joked. 'It's only just come on the market so I can't see there'll be much leeway in the price.'

Mr Keverne moved alongside Travis, rested his hands on the railing and looked straight ahead. A couple of minutes lapsed before he spoke. 'I'll take it.'

Travis stood up straighter, his eyes widening as a large beam spread across his face.

'Wow. That's brilliant news. I don't think you'll regret your decision.'

'I hope not.'

Travis offered his hand. 'Congratulations.'

His eyes were drawn to the heavy gold bracelet

round the elderly man's right wrist and the expensive Rolex watch on the left.

'Come on, young man. Let's go and get this deal moving.' Mr Keverne gripped Travis' hand tightly until he got a response.

'Yes certainly, sir. I'll take you straight back to the office and we can start the ball rolling.'

Never judge a book by its cover. Mr Keverne was no weakened old-aged pensioner grasping at life's fading pleasures, this guy probably had a few million in the bank. With a final cursory glance around the apartment, Mr Keverne followed Travis into the corridor where they hopped into the glass-fronted lift. In the foyer a uniformed concierge ushered them out through a heavy set of glass doors.

As they hailed a taxi, Travis felt buoyant, his mind racing with exciting new possibilities. It wasn't only the commission, but the thought that perhaps such a lifestyle might not yet be beyond his grasp. If home life didn't improve, and if he worked harder, he might be able to put himself first again. Other than the adjoining apartment, there was only one left; the penthouse. Travis pictured himself on the roof terrace, festooned with exotic plants and cooled by the granite cascading water feature. This time next year he could have a cocktail in one hand and a pretty girl or two on his arm.

'After you,' he said, opening the door wide for Mr Keverne as a black cab pulled alongside. Things were definitely looking brighter.

* * *

Travis and Gigi ended up in a small bar on the riverbank, Travis buoyed from the agreed sale and bubbling with renewed energy. Gigi's bare arms shimmered in the evening heat.

'Yes, I'm married. What about you?'

Travis liked the early days of relationships when personal questions weren't misconstrued and expectations were limited. Having fun was what mattered.

'I was. A long story,' she said. 'You men are not to be trusted.' Gigi's smile was like a beacon in a towering lighthouse. Travis leant across and pushed back a stray wisp of hair that had fallen over her brow and flicked away a speck of bread flour stuck to the ends.

Gigi smelt of freshly baked bread and roses and Travis breathed in the heady scent, letting the tension slip from his body. He lifted the beer to his lips and took a long swig but, as the drink hit the back of his throat, he coughed violently.

'Shit.'

'Are you okay?' Gigi leant forward. Travis blinked several times and coughed again.

'Yes. I'm fine. It went down the wrong way,' he spluttered, patting his chest.

* * *

Over Gigi's shoulder to the right, he saw Beverley heading in their direction. She wore headphones, singing as she walked.

'You look as if you've seen a ghost. It's not your wife, I hope.'

Perhaps he had seen a ghost. He now remembered he was supposed to phone Beverley at five and it was nearly seven. For some reason this suddenly seemed important, as if this fact alongside the vision up ahead were somehow connected.

'No, it's not but it's someone I really don't want to see. Listen, do you mind if I make tracks? I'll make it up to you, I promise.' Travis was already on his feet, scrambling to get his jacket on with one hand while knocking back the beer with the other. 'I'm really sorry.'

'Of course not, but I was enjoying myself. You go and I'll see you tomorrow.'

He didn't kiss her but instead extended a hand.

'Oh, I see. It's another woman but not your wife. You're sealing our business deal with a drink. Nice to meet you too.' Gigi smiled, shook his hand and winked.

'I'm really sorry,' he repeated. 'It's been lovely but...'

'Go on. No worries.'

He turned to leave, watching as Beverley took a right into Conduit Street. Perhaps she hadn't seen him and it was a strange coincidence. But Travis didn't believe in coincidence.

'Bye, Gigi. See you later.'

Travis strode off, eyes peeled straight ahead, and didn't look back.

10

The phone calls are proving to be very time-consuming. For maximum effect I need to keep up the silent heavy breathing every few days and try to fit a call in when I have a free moment.

'Hello? Who's there? Hello?'

Her tone was reasonably tolerant at first, with some minor swearing and irritation, but it soon heated up. Today she's very bad-tempered, not ladylike at all.

'Listen, you pervy shit. Hang the fuck up. I'm warning you.'

I wonder why she's warning me and what she intends to do. She knows that you can't trace withheld prank calls. She withholds her own number often enough.

The phone snaps off at this point and she goes and

pours herself a drink. I can't see her but imagine it will be a strong red Burgundy, or Malbec from a box in the fridge. She likes her red wine chilled!

I won't start on her mobile yet. There's no hurry. Increasing the pressure slowly will give her time to mull but she'll be mortified when she discovers she has a stalker.

She blocked my calls for two whole days by unplugging the landline. The engaged tone really grated and I was about to give up, when the ring tone came back on and I finally got through.

'Hello.' Her voice had been light, expectant, as if she'd already forgotten the reasons for disconnecting the phone. My persistence is really winding her up.

'Hello.' No answer. 'Hello. JUST FUCK OFF.'

I'm really getting to her and it serves her right. She's starting to understand what it's like to lose control.

11

'Take another step down. The staircase is long so take one step at a time.' Ms Evans' voice is coaxing, cajoling. Her tone is low and soothing with a long drawn-out drawl at the end of each sentence. 'Everything here is safe, calm and peaceful. Let yourself relax. One more step and your body will feel as if it's floating blissfully away...'

Ms Evans has been very persuasive about the hypnotherapy route. She's done courses and gained qualifications in putting people under and assures me that I'll only talk about things that I want to. She won't be able to tease me into revealing or doing anything I'm uncomfortable with and I must say, she's done quite the sales pitch. Also, it'll be worth it if it helps pass the time.

I'm being led down an imaginary stairway, slowly, steadily, one step at a time. When I reach the bottom I'll leave conscious thought behind. Letting go doesn't rest easy but the blackened room and eye shades are helping to block out the world.

Soon I'm in a large room with ripped pink-and-yellow patterned wallpaper but it's warm and quiet.

'Where are you?' Ms Evans' voice is distant, but chirpy, like early-morning birdsong.

'I'm at home.'

'What are you doing?'

'I'm looking out my parents' bedroom window. I can see into the hospital grounds across the road. People are walking in and out, and there's a man in striped pyjamas but it's not a concentration camp. It's a looney bin.' A little giggle pops out.

'Oh. Why do you think it's a looney bin?'

'Dad calls it a looney bin.' A slight tic makes my eyelid flicker. 'But Mum says it's a place to make people better; people who are sick in the mind.'

In my trance I see Mum staggering towards the Abbott grounds, clutching her pale blue handbag. I'm gripping the windowsill and can, if I stand on tiptoe, see over the top. Her bag contains all manner of pills. 'My sweets.' She smiles through cracked lips and swollen black eyes whose lids are stuck together.

'Can I have one?'

'No. These sweets are for grown-ups. They help to make us happy.' She was lying of course; she was never happy. Dad saw to that and I couldn't make her happy, as I only got in the way, so I left her alone and didn't complain. The misery flows through me, thick sludge clogging my arteries.

'Is your mum sick?'

My left leg jiggles up and down. I put my hand on top.

'No. It's because Dad hits her that she comes here. But she doesn't tell because he'll only hit her more. She says she's feeling blue. I'm alone. All alone.'

I used to wonder what shade of blue she meant. Her dark mood made me plump for navy. I put my forefinger to my lips, holding it close, and say, 'Ssshh. We mustn't tell.'

We made a pact, Mum and me, to let Dad knock her about when he fancied and no one need ever know. She never told, protecting him, not herself, and mine were silent fears.

I'm suddenly afraid. Dad has grabbed the rolling pin. There's a half-kneaded pizza base on top of the work surface but it's the spilt flour on the tiles that has caught his eye.

Suddenly a damp trickle weeps between my legs as urine seeps through my sweatpants. I'm now upstairs, outside the closed bedroom door and have slithered to the ground. Angry incoherent words are muffled and Dad thinks I don't know what he's doing. I need to talk to someone but I'm not allowed in. Huge silent sobs rack my body.

I want to take my trousers off but instead I say, 'Sorry, Ms Evans. I should have stayed in my bedroom like I was told.' I'm not sure what I'm saying but my body's trembling. Hypnosis was meant to make me feel better.

'What mustn't you tell?'

I can't remember. I think back to my parents, rewind the cogs in my brain.

For a long time I didn't realise what was going on. I was so young. The smiling, strong, handsome man, who swooped me up in his arms and twirled me round as I squealed in delight, couldn't possibly be the same person screaming at Mum behind closed doors. At first I thought Mum had a 'fancy man' whom she let in after Dad went out. This fancy man, for some reason, beat her up and I decided one day I'd kill him.

'I wanted a sister.' I change the subject. I'll worry about the damp legs when Ms Evans walks me back up the staircase. 'Someone to talk to, someone to explain what was going on. "I'm sorry you're on your own," Mum said. Instead she bought me dolls to keep me company. Frozen Charlottes.'

'Frozen Charlottes?' Ms Evans' low monotone is soothing. Although the dolls couldn't speak, their staring glass eyes and icy cold cheeks kept me company while the banging went on. Like dead babies, I clung to them and shared my deepest darkest fears, telling them my tormented secrets.

'My little sisters.' It sounds ridiculous even to my own ears. 'I chat to them. They tell me not to worry, that they'll always keep me company.' At night I would dream that they were alive and dancing round the room. The hallucinations were so real that Mum locked them away. 'They're very valuable,' I boast. After I accepted they weren't real I learnt their worth.

'Do you still have these "little sisters"?'

'Yes.' They're displayed neatly on the new IKEA shelving unit. Not such a macabre presence but they still egg me on. I was going to let my kids play with them one day, but I don't share that. I need to get up and change my clothes.

'Okay, Beverley. Let's walk back up the staircase

now. When I count to five you'll be here with me. With each number take another step until you're at the top. When you walk through the door you'll be wide awake again.'

I'm a bit hesitant and deliberately take my time, treading carefully. I walk through the door on number five and try to open my eyes, momentarily forgetting the eye mask which I yank off. It's been witness to secrets which I've tried to forget. I stretch out my neck and gently move my head from side to side.

'Okay?'

Instead of feeling refreshed and better from the experience, I'm aware of dampness in my legs and am mortified at having wet myself.

'Oh my God. I'm so sorry.' A very small blot has landed on the couch and the sight of the newly up-holstered furniture makes things worse.

'Don't worry. No harm done. A clean cloth will sort it.' Ms Evans' melodic voice contains an irritated edge.

I try consciously not to cry but as Ms Evans hands me a tissue, I realise it's too late. Tears stream down my cheeks as my misery surfaces.

12

Cosette's gurgling laugh could have come from a child watching a clown take a tumble. Lack of sleep had made Scott impatient, edgy, and his girlfriend seemed to think it was all a bit of a joke.

'The silent calls aren't some random mobile phone salesman. How many times do I need to tell you?'

'I think you're going a bit over the top. Okay, so Beverley is your ex but I'm cool with it. She never even mentioned you.'

'You've no idea what she's like, what she's capable of. Listen, it's no coincidence you're at the same college.'

'Don't be ridiculous. She's learning Spanish and I'm doing English. We just happened to get talking.'

'And I just happened to bump into her last week in Covent Garden. I didn't tell you that. Yes, some co-incidence.' Scott gritted his teeth. He remembered the first time Beverley had bumped into Danielle, at the opposite end of some random café in Shoreditch.

'How bizarre is that,' Danielle had said. 'She seems pleasant enough, if a bit weird. She even asked if I'd any holiday plans.' It was only some time later, when Beverley turned up at the same doctor's surgery, that he began to worry as it was one coinci-dence too many.

The floor in Scott's front lounge was strewn with tools: screwdrivers, nails, and pliers and a large elec-tric drill was set to one side. Scott dipped in and out of the toolbox while he talked.

'Can you hand me up the drill? This fixing's still a bit loose.' Scott jiggled furiously at a lock, trying to coax it away from the window frame. He gripped the top of the ladder with his spare hand, fighting off an attack of vertigo.

* * *

Cosette handed him up his tools, one after another, feeling more and more anxious by his intensity. It was as if another Scott had appeared out of nowhere; someone she didn't recognise who rechecked fittings, over and over again. He'd been working all afternoon and hadn't even started on the upstairs doors and windows.

'You don't seriously think she's going to break in?'

Scott glowered down from his perch. 'Please don't speak to her again. Say you'll not. Steer clear. Actually forget the "please". Don't go anywhere near her.'

'Okay, I promise. But she didn't even mention you.'

Scott stretched up and drilled the final nail into a new set of blinds. 'Make sure to keep these shut tightly at night-time. Perhaps it would be a good idea to keep them partly closed during the daytime as well.' Scott turned the wooden slats up and down. 'The lamp'll give us enough light.'

Cosette perched on top of a stool and took a swig of water. Scott was acting like a mad man on a mission. She didn't know who he was and was more scared by his behaviour than of some random ex-girlfriend with a grudge.

'Scott. She told me she's got a steady boyfriend so I don't think she's still pining after you if that's what you're worried about. Don't you think you're over-reacting?'

Scott clambered down from the stepladders, tested the mechanism again and snapped the blinds shut.

'Look, Cosette, I've got stuff to tell you and probably now is as good a time as any.'

Scott lifted a bottle of wine from the fridge, uncorked it and poured out a couple of glasses. 'Let's go into the lounge and I'll tell you all about her. All about Beverley Digby.'

* * *

'We'd only been together for about six months when things started getting very intense. She became more and more demanding, phoning me at all hours of the day and night, checking where I was, who I was with. I felt I was being stalked.'

Cosette, stretched out along the sofa, speared the ends of some dried-up olives with a stick.

'It was only when I tried to break it off that she got really paranoid. When I started to ignore her calls, let her down gently, she became more and more persistent. She'd turn up at the bank or ring my door-bell in the middle of the night. The phone calls wouldn't stop.' Scott took a long gulp of wine and shifted in his seat, eyes firmly directed at Cosette. His fury simmered like a dormant volcano.

'It was only after I met Danielle that things became unbearable.'

'Why? Where did you meet Danielle?'

Scott wasn't sure how much to tell Cosette. He didn't want to hurt her, make her feel second best, although as he closed his eyes he remembered meeting Danielle for the first time. After that evening he knew she was special. 'The One.' She became his soulmate, together forever. But Danielle had slammed the proverbial door shut when she left and he'd had to move on. He left these thoughts out of the telling.

'I met Danielle at a banking seminar. It was a weekend thing in Brighton. We sort of hit it off.' Her smile had lit up the room, her earthy laugh bouncing off the walls. Dressed in a skin-tight black satin dress, golden hair cascading over her shoulders, Danielle played the room. When her chocolate-brown eyes gazed at him, Scott was lost.

'What did Beverley do when she found out you were seeing someone else?'

'Sorry?' Cosette's question jolted him back. He leant over and took her hand, relieved that she didn't seem jealous. She still had the confidence of youth, the belief in a happy ever after.

'I don't know how she found out, but she did. She wouldn't accept we were over and when she learnt about Danielle she wouldn't back off. I didn't realise, when Danielle got pregnant, that Beverley was also pregnant.'

It sounded like he was some careless fly-by-night gigolo but Beverley had told him she was on the pill and he'd believed her.

'She miscarried,' he said. 'Beverley, that is.'

Cosette set her glass down, her face powdery white in the half-light. Scott thought of an abandoned puppy, all watery downcast eyes and droopy ears.

'I'm sorry. I didn't want to tell you any of this but if we're going to make a commitment, you need to know about Beverley. This isn't about Danielle, it's about Beverley. Unless I tell you, you'll not understand the reason for all the security.'

Cosette got up from the sofa and wandered towards the kitchen. 'Let's get a takeaway. Here, I've got the menu,' she said over her shoulder, waving a piece of card in the air.

Rain hammered against the windowpanes and a break in the heatwave was being heralded in by a clattering of thunder which rumbled through the flat and shook the walls.

Cosette jumped as Scott came up behind her and wrapped his arms around her slim body, leaning his face into her hair. She smelled of freshly squeezed lemons.

'The future's about us. It's not about the past, but I need you to know why I'm so paranoid. I'll not put bars on the windows, if that's what you're thinking.' His smile was weak. 'But I think it's time for you to move in.'

Silent tears flowed down Cosette's cheeks as Scott hugged her close.

'Have you got your case packed?'

Cosette stood on tiptoe, kissed him on the lips and clung on, as if to a life raft tossing on choppy seas. A sudden flash of lightning streaked through a rogue gap in the blinds, like an accusation piercing through the lies. The abortion had been his idea but miscarriage, in the telling, didn't sound accusatory.

As Scott looked over Cosette's shoulder towards the slightly off-kilter blinds, he felt no guilt at the second lie. It wasn't true that he wouldn't put bars on the windows, they were being delivered first thing in the morning.

13

I've held the small purse close to me for over a week. Cosette has been skirting round me with aplomb, changing direction whenever I get close, and tripping over a paving slab, not looking where she was going, was divine justice. The graze on her shin was nasty and the blood flowed, the blame pointing its finger firmly at Scott.

I spot her squirrelled away in a corner of the library, head down. She's hedged in between laden bookshelves, skyscrapers that tower towards the ceiling and the only way out is past me. My eyesight's good and I can see she's holding aloft Mary Shelley's *Frankenstein*. It must be part of her syllabus as she's far too young to be intrigued by the monster angle of human creation and Scott hasn't squashed her innocence quite yet.

I snake in and out past the wooden chair ends, carefully negotiating rogue legs that jut out from students who lean forward.

'Hi,' I whisper. 'Is it free?'

Cosette freezes, stares at me, and after a second makes a reluctant little nod gesture. '*Don't talk to her. Ignore her. Just walk on past.*' She'll be replaying Scott's words, but she's too polite to make a fuss; it's partly an age thing. I sit down before she can tell me the spare seat is for a friend.

'I'm leaving soon so you'll be able to spread yourself out,' she says with the merest upturn of lips.

'It's okay. I'm not staying. Only I've got something of yours.' I slowly unzip my handbag.

'Shit. It keeps catching,' I mumble. It doesn't catch of course, but I'm enjoying myself, keeping up the suspense.

Her angst is apparent. Scott has done a good job with his storytelling. I spend a few seconds searching around the bottom of my bag for the purse. I could be reaching for a handgun, loaded and ready to fire; that's what Scott would have thought. Instead, I produce a small bright-red purse containing a twenty-pound note, a ring holding a single key, of which I've made a copy, three first-class stamps and a student railcard. Her eyes widen.

'Where did you find it? I've been looking everywhere.' She forgets to be wary and her face lights up. I like the word 'find'. She lost it. It wasn't stolen.

I sit down, crowd her exit and keep my voice reverently low.

'You dropped it in the café last week. I picked it up after you'd gone and I didn't dare bring it round.' I raise my eyebrows in mock exasperation. She knows Scott wouldn't have let me in. 'I've been looking for you to give it back.'

'Thanks so much. There's not a lot in there but it's got sentimental value. It was Mum's.' She thumbs through the contents, lifting out the railcard and reinserting it into the slot. I've taken a picture of this as well in case it might come in handy.

I've regained some ground as Cosette has no idea I lifted the purse out of her bag when she popped to the toilet. It was the last time I saw her before Scott must have had 'the talk'. She's been sidestepping round me ever since, weaving in and out as if in a minefield loaded with live ammunition. Anyway, I have the slick-fingered touch of Oliver Twist, a magician's sleight of hand which can be useful.

'I thought you'd be missing the railcard. You've

also got a twenty-pound note in there. I hope there's nothing missing.' I continue to reel in her trust like an angler with a wriggly fish hooked on the spike.

'I leave my bank card at home to stop me spending,' Cosette says and zips the purse back up.

An exaggerated tutting sound comes from behind the bookshelves and it's hard not to share a silent giggle.

'Can I get you a coffee? To say thanks. I'm nearly done here.'

'Yes. Why not?' The first battle in my favour. One–nil.

We walk out of the library, Cosette a couple of steps ahead but I let her take the lead. It's the best way because she'll remember it was her idea.

The café is located at the front of the building, near the entrance to the street. It's bright and sterile, an unthreatening place to rendezvous, and quiet, with only a smattering of students dotted around the room.

'Here,' says Cosette, emboldened by her invitation, and plops her rucksack on one of two vacant grey plastic chairs. 'What would you like?'

'Cappuccino, please. Thanks.'

I watch as she heads towards the counter and stands patiently in the queue. I wonder if she'll tell

Scott or keep the bold invitation to herself as he'll definitely ask if there have been any random sightings of his ex-girlfriend.

Cosette returns with a large milky coffee for me and a tall glass filled with a thick green gunge that resembles caked pond weed.

'Kale and spinach smoothie.' She stirs vigorously and offers me the straw. 'Have a taste. It's really refreshing.'

It's not the poisonous mix that makes me hesitate, rather the fear of leaving rogue traces of DNA. My paranoia would give Ms Evans a field day.

'Thanks but I'll stick to coffee. A bit too healthy for me.' I laugh.

It takes a good five minutes until the elephant in the room is addressed. Scott. I'm delighted that she's the one to broach the subject, in fact seems keen to talk.

'Scott told me what happened between you. I'm sorry.'

I don't answer because I want to hear her version of events. Scott's unlikely to have gone into detail, and even more unlikely to have come clean.

'He told me about the miscarriage and how things weren't the same afterwards.'

Her dainty lips sip delicately at the green mixture. Suddenly, loud laughter peels out from a far corner of the café where a mammoth frothy coffee has splattered across the linoleum, dotting it with pink and white marshmallows. A group of young girls stare, wide-eyed at the mess but continue to snigger behind their hands. I feel my age.

'An abortion, actually,' I say.

Cosette, momentarily distracted, turns her head back. 'Sorry?'

'I had an abortion. Not a miscarriage. Scott paid for it as he wasn't quite ready to be a dad.'

'Oh, I'm really sorry. I thought Scott said you miscarried but perhaps I misheard; misunderstood,' she lies. I've scored another point. Two-nil. I keep my lips tight, giving her time to register the fact that miscarriage and abortion are completely different accounts of the same event; the loss of life. Scott will have told her how sad we both were after the event and how it tore us apart. But he won't have mentioned how he whistled over supper after the deadly deed was done.

'Scott had a doctor friend who arranged the termination. All expenses paid.' A puff of disgust at this point does little to hide my bitterness but my jokiness should lessen the threat. Cosette's trust is essential. 'He promised me that when he was more financially secure, a little further up the banking ladder, that we'd start a family. Lots of kids.'

The waitress, gripping a mop and bucket, glares at the gaggle of students who slink away. She scrubs the floor, like the doctor who scraped and cleaned away my baby, with efficient purposeful hands.

The activity jolts Cosette to action. 'Listen, I must get going.' She stands up and fiddles with her hair. 'I've got a lecture in five minutes.' She's not a bad liar, little white lies flitting like flies round a candle, but she'd better watch out as Scott's mantra is honesty. Well, honesty from all around if not from himself.

'No problem. Thanks for the coffee.' I lift the mug firmly in both hands and clench until my knuckles whiten. She has no more lectures until tomorrow.

'Thanks again for the purse.' With her rucksack over one shoulder, she marches off.

For Cosette, the doubts will fester. I'd love to be a fly on the wall this evening when she confronts her boyfriend with the lie, as it's not a little fib but a great big whopper. I'm sure, after a few more revelations, she'll realise what a complete bastard her boyfriend is and get out before it's too late.

Scott will never be able to rest easy again, I'll make sure of it.

14

I

I'm in the mood for something soothing, mellow. I look through the CDs and pick out Chopin. I like to listen to music. I used to play the piano and listening helps me get a better grip on rhythm and style. Waltz in C sharp minor kicks off the concert and the clink of ebony and ivory helps me concentrate on work I have to do.

Googling has made me consider how my stalking will be construed. There are many possibilities. Perhaps I'm a rejected stalker unable to let go. Perhaps I'm trying to draw the eye, get her attention in weird and wonderful ways without daring to reveal myself. Intimacy could be the motivator with sex high on the agenda. She certainly rates herself.

The cadences in the background rise and fall as the melodies invade my senses.

I won't be the incompetent or resentful stalker. I let the mouse hover over the predatory stalker and read on. This is much more interesting. Control and power are the drivers but it will require quite an input of fear and violence. I definitely have the unemotional traits to put me in this category and I'm up for the challenge.

As the rattle of the piano keys reaches a thundering crescendo, I pound my fingers along the desktop, flitting from one end to the next as I work imaginary scales up and down the surface. Practise makes perfect.

I check my Hotmail accounts with their bland, forgettable addresses. Today I use whoami@hotmail.com to begin the cyberstalking. Who am I? That's the question indeed.

I spend over an hour Photoshopping the pictures. I have several of my target and I crop them down, keeping only the head and shoulders. I slide the images onto a series of different naked bodies. The overweight torsos display obscene defining features: inverted nipples, festering birthmarks, swollen abdomens, disfiguring stretch marks. There's plenty of choice.

I then work on sending the line-dancing crab viral. It'll not appeal to everyone but she'll be shocked, mortified at the image, especially as her head is sitting atop the naked mover. I include a Chopin polonaise as the sound-track. Predatory stalkers aren't by nature cultured so it's a nice touch, shows substance.

The mock-up is soon slotted into thousands of Facebook accounts and within half an hour there have been 500 hits. Whereas a predatory stalker might not be particularly cultured, I reckon they would have a reasonable level of computer know-how. Wizardry in hacking should be top of their CV.

15

I'm enjoying the Spanish lessons. As I swish the paintbrush up and down the walls, a bright azure, I conjure up images of sunny romantic destinations. A Barcelona city break springs to mind.

We could take in the Picasso Museum and the stunning architecture of the Sagrada Familia. Travis likes bike riding, so a trip to Carretera de les Aigues is on the list along with shopping at the Els Encants market. We could round it all off with a romantic stroll through the labyrinth of Horta, the city's oldest garden and perhaps this is where he'll propose.

A loud bang at the door makes me jump and it soon becomes a mad hammering. The bell mustn't be working.

'Coming!' I yell. I carefully set the brush aside, making sure that it doesn't drip onto the reclaimed parquet flooring and climb down the ladder. The banging continues and I creep up to the window in the lounge and peek out from behind the curtains. Shit. It's Scott.

I used to watch out the window, praying that it would be him, that he'd come round to beg my forgiveness and plead with me to come back. But he'd become adept at ignoring my texts and phone calls and keeping out of sight. Ha. My new more subtle approach seems to have worked.

I pull back the chain and open the door wide. 'Scott. What a surprise. Come in.'

'I'm not here for a bloody social call but to warn you to keep away from Cosette.'

Scott barges into the hall but not before he has pushed me out of the way and slammed the front door. The noise is like a thunderclap. His face is bizarrely red and puffy, his hairline damp and his receding head of hair is like an ebbing tide.

'I know what you're up to. Don't forget, Beverley, I've been here before. If you go within ten yards of Cosette again I'm going back to the police.'

'Why? What are you going to have me charged with? Sharing a drink?'

I move as casually as I can towards the kitchen, sidling past his large body, careful not to skim against him. Touching him, even unintentionally, could lead to accusations.

'Listen, let's have a coffee and talk like civilised human beings,' I suggest.

'I don't want a bloody coffee.' He spits, which doesn't look too attractive from my standpoint. 'This is my last warning. Don't you dare speak to her again. Did you think I wouldn't find out?'

'I don't care if you know or not. I'm not doing anything wrong and I do know what I can and can't do. Last time I checked, making friends wasn't on the taboo list.'

He's sweating, panic kicking in. I can't believe he thought I'd move on, accept what happened without payback. He takes a step towards me and for a moment I think his raised hand is heading in the direction of my face.

'Are you going to hit me now? I dare you.' I egg him on, sticking my chin out, willing him to cross the line. A slap would be good. It would give me fodder to make his life even more unpleasant and I'd relish the pain, the sharper the better.

'God I'd love to but I'm not that stupid. I know you, Beverley. You're one mad, sad bitch. Don't kid yourself. Everyone has their breaking point and so help me if you push me one step further you'll be sorry.'

'Why? What are you going to do? The only thing I wanted you've already taken from me. There's not much left to take.' The abortion, the infection, the sterile womb were all down to Scott.

He pauses for a moment as if he's going to add something but decides against it and instead turns his back and heads towards the door.

'Cosette tells me she's moving in. I suspect she'll soon be after a marriage proposal. Hope you're now financially secure enough because she's feeling broody. But I forgot. She told me all this before I shared your confusion over the words abortion and miscarriage.'

I spurt my venom loud and clear and only recoil my forked tongue when he's gone. The front door slams harder than when he came in and the whole house vibrates. I can hear the wrath in his retreating tread and out of the window I watch him stomp away with steam billowing from his nostrils.

16

Facebook. Not my thing but I signed up a few days ago to gather witnesses to my ballooning waistline. It's a good way to drip feed people information that they're not remotely interested in. I feel duty-bound, as a member, to randomly scroll through the postings. Everyone seems to be smiling, faking happy. Familiar faces beam out from hip locations all round the world: cable cars, Trans-Siberian railways, and underwater shark cages. There's even a picture of some random person on top of Mount Everest. OMG. It's Harper Holland, Head Boy of '85.

Taking up Pilates at the same studio as Queenie mustn't look contrived. My daily postings, cleverly edited to show bogus rolls of flesh, have gained plenty of likes, smiley faces and encouraging comments about the benefits of core conditioning. Khloe Jacobsen, one of my old classmates, has even suggested the health club where I'll be going. How cool is that?

Adverts keep popping up teasing with moisturising products and financial advice. There has been a very magnetic quiz selling the belief that only one per cent of the population will be able to answer all the questions. I feel bizarrely chuffed when I get 100 per cent even though I know it's a scam for something.

Then all of a sudden my face pops up. Not just my face, but my whole body. I enlarge the screen. My swollen belly is criss-crossed with angry stretch marks running all the way to a vile patch of pink and purple pubic hair. Even as I watch aghast, two likes appear along with a random message from someone I don't know. I click on the message.

Hi Beverley. Like the picture? Fun, isn't it? Have you checked out the background? Zoom in. Twenty-four pizza boxes there... a clue to what might have caused the spare tyre! Our little secret.
Anyway, enjoy the notoriety. Everyone is famous for fifteen minutes. Laters.

I spend the next half hour frantically deleting all traces of myself from Facebook and finally manage to close down my account. It seems the safest course of action as I can't see any way to track down the culprit. I'm already twenty minutes late for my appointment with Ms Evans and I'm not allowed to miss appointments except with a validated note from a doctor.

* * *

I lock up and dash across the road and down the drive towards the hospital entrance. I'm breathing heavily when I knock on the door, aware that I'm looking flustered and unkempt.

'Come in.'

'Sorry I'm late. The dishwasher sprung a leak and I couldn't find the stopcock.' I gently close the door behind me.

'No problem, Beverley. Better late than never.' Ms Evans is welcoming but probably secretly pleased to have been given an easy afternoon. Same money. Less work.

The couch has been moved out of the therapy room for repair, something to do with the wind-up mechanism. It won't go up or down and has stuck apparently in an awkward halfway position. Instead I find myself sitting in a plush Queen Anne Belvedere leather armchair directly facing Ms Evans. It's going to be hard to avoid her beady stare and it couldn't have happened on a worse day. I try to put the Facebook taunt to the back of my mind.

'Perhaps today you'd like to tell me a bit about how you're moving forward. About your new home and I think you mentioned a new man. Terence, if I remember correctly.'

Over her shoulder I can see out the window. Someone is standing a short distance away from the building, hovering beside the large oak tree, and wielding a paintbrush. It takes me a minute to register it's Bob Pratchett. When Ms Evans follows my gaze he jumps behind the thick trunk and I can't help but giggle. His fingers wiggle into view every now and then, flicking up and down on opposite sides of the trunk to keep my attention.

'I met Terence at a property show in Eastbourne. He was selling villas in Spain. He thought I was really interested in buying and at lunchtime followed me into the bar and offered to buy me a drink. I'm a bit wicked when it comes to salespeople. The commission had him salivating like a slobbering Labrador, but we sort of hit it off.'

Bob has started doing funny little dance moves

but keeping well out of Justine's eyeline. I have an urge to burst out laughing but am worried Ms Evans might jot down that I'm suffering from schizoid illusions. The urge gets worse when Bob starts painting the tree with bold white stripes, ducking out of sight at regular intervals.

'In what way did you hit it off?' Here we go again, more questions.

'We have the same sense of humour. He makes me laugh and says I understand him in ways his wife doesn't. I mean, didn't. They're separated,' I lie. I don't mention our shared love of Bollinger or the slightly kinky sex.

'This sounds promising, Beverley. However, there is something I now need to discuss with you.' Her voice loses its lightness of tone as she consults her notes, as if referring to a prewritten after-dinner speech at a fundraiser. It must be important.

'Yes?'

Bob waves goodbye, holding the paintbrush aloft and before Ms Evans continues, he has disappeared from view, pocketing the light relief.

'I received a phone call earlier this morning from your case officer, Damien Hoarden. Mr Scott Barry has lodged a new complaint against you.' Ms Evans is reading her speech verbatim, without looking up. 'He says you're harassing him and his girlfriend, and he's in the process of obtaining a fresh restraining order.'

I decide not to jump up and act incensed as this might make Ms Evans think I'm feeling guilty and it might also encourage her to think I am guilty.

'You must be joking. I bumped into Scott by chance in Covent Garden. I was at the market, for goodness' sake, minding my own business. How can that be construed as harassment? I've been going there for years. Mr Barry also knows that, as we used to go there together,' I say calmly.

I don't mention the Spanish lessons or meeting Cosette but I guess Scott will have gone the full hog with his vitriol.

'Mr Hoarden says that, according to Mr Barry, you have deliberately befriended his new girlfriend in order to get at him.' Ms Evans watches me.

'I'm at the same college as Mr Barry's girlfriend and we had a coffee together. Once. You've got to be joking.'

I sit up and lean forward out of the chair. I'm not surprised by the turn of events as Scott was fuming when he came round, and he certainly wasn't going to let things rest. It was most likely him posting the scarred images of me on Facebook as a childish attempt to scare me off. He's got enough spare time on his hands to fiddle on the computer now that he's on a three-day working week due to stress leave. The silent phone calls, the pizza boxes and the dead mouse. It adds up. He's trying to turn the stalking issue back my way.

'Are you sure it was coincidence, Beverley? Meeting Cosette, I mean.'

Scott seems to have gone into detail about my relationship with his girlfriend, and appears to have officially named Cosette as his significant other.

'Of course I'm sure. Learning Spanish has always been on my "to-do" list. Now that I've got a bit of money, Goldmeyer College is the obvious choice. It's the best language school in London.' I pout and let out an audible sniff.

'In light of the request for a new restraining order, I've been asked to recommend to Mr Hoarden if this will be necessary. Are you to be trusted to keep your distance? They're looking for a recommendation based on our progress.'

What role is Ms Evans now playing? Court prosecutor? Judge? Police officer? This isn't any of her business and yet she seems to have been handed a rather pivotal role in making monumental decisions pertaining to my life.

'Does the report mention that Scott, I mean Mr

Barry, barged into my house the other day brandishing threats? He even tried to hit me.'

The clock on the wall reaches the hour. When Ms Evans doesn't respond, I put on my shoes, sparkly new white designer trainers with wedges. I tie a double knot in the laces, pump my feet up and down and get out of the chair. A long jog round the lake will wake me up, help me work out a way to deal with events. I can't take any more interrogation.

'Do you mind if we call it a day? I'm off to sign up for a Pilates class and registration is at five. But I promise I won't go within a hundred yards of Mr Barry.' I'm not sure now if I'm up to any new classes but it sounds a positive move on my part.

Ms Evans stands up and I note she's a good bit taller than me in her high-heeled work shoes. In flat sensible pumps, she'd give me an inch or two.

'Okay. I've made a note of your comments and hopefully when we meet next week there'll be nothing more to report. As long as you keep away from Mr Barry and his girlfriend I can't see there being a problem.' Her smile seems genuine, encouraging.

But I can't promise anything of the kind and if Scott is the one posting obscene Facebook pictures then I'll have no option but to keep at him.

'Thanks,' I say.

As I head outside I have conflicting emotions. It feels good to be under Scott's skin again and back in his life, but I still feel the need to punish him. It's the only way I'll be able to stop picking at the scab. The destruction of my womb comes at a very high price and the therapy keeps my anger simmering rather than helping calm it down.

I jog back through the park which skirts the hospital grounds and take the longer route home. As I build up speed I realise I'm really freaked out by the online attacks. If it is indeed Scott, I've probably done him a favour by jolting him out of his inherent lethargy. My persistence as far as Cosette is concerned has certainly fired him up.

I pound on faster and faster until my brain is ready to explode, letting the pain suffocate coherent thought and bury the demons till tomorrow. After all, tomorrow is another day. I'll worry about the day after that when tomorrow comes. One day at a time.

17

Travis caressed the cream leather seats, running his fingertips along the fine-grained upholstery. Queenie hadn't put up too much of a fuss when he'd casually thrown into conversation that he was treating himself on his birthday and that she needn't worry about getting him a present. A couple of jumpers, a smart pair of slacks and a Barbour jacket had originally made up his wish list and his wife had been pleased enough not to have to make the choices. Instead he'd torn up the list.

'A fucking Mercedes? You must be joking. It's your first sale in months.' Hailstones of disbelief rained down on him. 'Is this some pathetic mid-life crisis?'

She wouldn't ruin his birthday. Mr Keverne's

friend had offered on an adjacent apartment and the cash was rolling in. Business was on the up so why shouldn't he treat himself? A fresh property boom was forecast.

He lounged back, slid down the visor and checked his appearance in the mirror. His fringe refused to stand up, young dude style, despite the latherings of gel. He and Freddie would drop by the barbers on the way home. Freddie was thrilled with the new car, begging to be taken for a spin after school. Like father, like son.

Travis readjusted his sunglasses, closed over the sunroof and turned the music up, closing his eyes and bobbing his head to the beat. Life was definitely on the up, money coming in, Gigi chomping at the bit for some serious fun and...

'Jesus. Fuck me.' There was an explosive bang on the glass. His eyes shot open as if from a nightmare to be confronted by an axe-wielding murderer.

'Beverley. For Christ's sake.' Her face was pressed hard against the driver's window and her fist was raised for another blow.

'Wake up, sleepy head.' Without blinking she stared down at him. 'Open up.'

His finger hovered before he pressed the button to let the window slide down.

'What the hell are you doing here?'

'Waiting to see the principal. I can guess why you're here. Can I get in? Fab car, by the way.' She stroked her hand across the glossy black paintwork and walked round to the passenger door.

He reluctantly opened up and she slid in beside him. 'Listen, this isn't a good time. Freddie will be out in ten minutes.'

'Why ever not? Haven't you told him about me yet? Perhaps now might be a very good time.'

The group of milling mothers was growing by the second. His plan of attracting attention in the school playground with his new car was going horribly awry. Through the window he could see Katy McCarthy standing alone by the playground entrance. Her prick of a husband had recently walked out and Travis had been planning to offer consolation, a shoulder to cry on. The sight of firm buttocks in skinny jeans and pert breasts poking through a white T-shirt were egging him on.

'Told him what? Listen, Beverley, you need to back off. I'm taking Freddie straight home. Now's not a good time.' He pushed his sunglasses onto the top of his head and faced her.

'You've already said that but now seems as good a time as any to me.'

'Look, I know the timing might not be ideal, but I've decided to stay with my wife and kids. I'm sorry, but seeing as you're here, perhaps it's best to get it out in the open. I've been waiting for the right moment.' He'd been dreading it but now he'd said the words, a weight lifted.

'I'm here for a job interview,' she said, ignoring his pronouncement. 'I used to be a classroom assistant, many years ago. I love working with kids and they're looking for someone to help out with Year 6. What year's Freddie in?'

'Why here? You could teach anywhere.'

'Why not here? Anyway, when you get fed up again with life at home, I'll be waiting. I'm patient and let's face it, we're good together.' She leant across and ran a finger down his cheek.

'What are you doing?' He frantically scanned the car park and playground.

'Also, it'll give me a chance to get to know Freddie. Not such a bad idea, is it?'

'Beverley. We're over. There's no future for us, no happy ever after. I've got responsibilities, a wife and kids.'

Beverley glanced out the window and opened the door. 'We'll see about that. Oh look, there's Mrs Pepper now. Must dash. Let's catch up soon. I'll call you.' With that she leant across and planted a kiss on his cheek. He swiped her away, pushing her backwards at the same time as he heard another rap at the window.

'Hello. You must be Freddie?' A small, dishevelled boy in a yellow shirt and grey shorts stood by the car. Beverley stooped down and extended a hand for him to shake. He glanced warily at his father who shook his head.

'Hi. Hop in, young man.'

'Bye, Freddie. I hope to be your new teaching assistant, by the way. Bye, Travis. Lovely to bump into you.'

With that she turned round and walked up the path towards the head teacher.

18

There it is again. Yes, it's a definite rattle. I can't open my eyes because of night dryness, my lids sewn together. I reach for the water by my bed and flick it over them until they peel back.

My phone screen shows it's only 2am. Through the crack in the window I can hear the tread of footsteps, quiet but unmistakable. Someone is scouting round the side of the house towards the back garden.

I get up, pull my dressing gown tight and move towards the pane, inching the curtain back. Down below is a shape, an indistinct outline. They're wearing a dark hoodie, like a Crimewatch suspect and trampling on the flower beds. A bin topples over and I stiffen as a cat lets out an almighty squeal. All of a sudden they've gone, disappeared. Perhaps I'm dreaming in the darkness. Little shards of sleep irritate my eyes and my finger finds the corners and scratches furiously.

Five minutes pass before I go back to bed. I settle on top of the duvet, wide awake, and turn on the lamp, making a mental note to buy security lights for the garden, the ones that come on and off with movement. I feel better knowing that next time I'll have a better view of rogue strangers, consoling myself that it was probably some drunk watering the plants, or an opportunist casing joints for open windows.

Ms Evans asks about my dreams and raises a questioning eyebrow when I say I don't dream, or if I do, I can't remember them. I'm not sure why I lie to her because I have the most horrendous nightmares.

Before the rattle woke me, I was being chased along a beach. It must have been a flashback to the beach in Cornwall where I walked every day after Danielle lost her baby, and where I went to escape Scott who hounded me incessantly to find out if I'd been involved. He was so certain, and at that point he was the one who needed a restraining order, not me. He's as avid a proponent of *an eye for an eye* as I am.

A smattering of trees along the beach soon turned to forest, thick, gloomy and airless and my pursuant forced me to snake in and out between the towering trunks. When I collapsed, my heart ready to explode, Bob Pratchett appeared out of nowhere and leant over me wielding a huge brush. Scott and Cosette stood behind him, egging him on, but they turned and drove off, leaving me to my fate. Their getaway car was dark, shiny with pink stripes running along the side.

* * *

Instead of snuggling back under the bedding, I get up and head downstairs to put the kettle on, sleep now a distant hope. As the water boils, I wonder if I should share my recollections in therapy. If nothing else they might give Ms Evans a good laugh.

I sit up on a bar stool and swivel, letting the relaxing movement calm me down. I then spot something stuck to the window, a large piece of white paper. Automatically I do a three-sixty manoeuvre and scan the kitchen for an intruder, checking that no one is hiding behind the cupboards or standing over me with a meat cleaver.

I scurry across and switch on the lights, bathing the room in fluorescent white, and see that the notice is stuck to the outside of the window. No one has been in the kitchen, but this offers small comfort. I inch open the glass door, reach my hand round and rip the paper away. There's no noise, no laboured breathing of a predatory stranger. The neighbourhood is asleep. As I bang the door shut again, I double check that the key has turned securely in the lock.

The words are written in bold black ink, childishly scrawled.

Welcome to the world of stalking.
  Watching you watching me.
  SEE HOW YOU LIKE IT

My legs weaken and I begin to shake. I'm not sure what's going on. The world of stalking? Who is watching me? Why? What's going on? Scott can't possibly be so pathetic and childish.

As the trembling abates, my first thought is that I've managed to suck Scott back into my web. The only thing worse than being cast aside is being ignored and if he wants tit for tat, then bring it on. But if he thinks I'm going to back off from Cosette, he's got it completely wrong.

I turn off the main lights again, but leave alight a small unit above the oven. The camomile tea is soothing but as the screen on my phone flashes, I splutter. A new message has pinged across from a weird numbers-only Hotmail account.

Not much fun getting night-time messages, is it? Now you know what it feels like.

19

The temperature had risen and hit the mid-thirties. Travis turned the fans up but the whirring noise made it hard to concentrate.

The cramped two-room office space was suffocating in the summer and like a fridge-freezer in the winter. He dreamt of larger premises with air conditioning and proper heating and now with work picking up and his personal life back on track, the dream might well become reality.

'What's global warming, Dad?' Freddie had asked him over breakfast. 'Miss Digby says that's why it's so hot.'

'Do you like Miss Digby?'

'Yeah, she's fun. We're drawing pictures today. She says I'm very talented. What's talented?'

'It means you're very clever. Just like your father.'

They laughed in unison.

He hadn't seen Beverley since their meeting in the school car park, and Freddie hadn't reported back anything sinister about his new classroom assistant. She seemed to be quite the hit. All's well that ends well, Travis thought. He took out a handkerchief and wiped the sweat from his brow and glanced down across the road.

Gigi seemed to float about her work and he was amazed at how easily she was reeling him in. Images of her naked body would pop into his head all hours of the day and night, her white apron conjuring up all manner of lurid imaginings.

He had booked a restaurant for after work, Bella Roma, taking a punt on something upmarket and expensive. Consummating their relationship couldn't wait any longer.

A couple of times he waved down to catch her attention but she didn't respond. He decided to pop down, buy a couple of pastries, and firm up the arrangements. He moved to the window, leant his face out and tilted it towards the scorching sun, but Gigi still didn't look up.

It was only ten. He had toyed with keeping his head down all morning and ignore her waves, play cool, but for some reason she was ignoring him.

Mind games. They did his head in. He gathered up loose change from the ashtray on his desk, counted out the coins and headed down the fire escape onto the street. The humidity was suffocating and a searing heat blanket enveloped him the minute he stepped outside. Tarte Tatin was busy so he hovered outside until there was a lull in customers.

'Morning, gorgeous. How's tricks?'

'Okay. We're very busy. Everyone's out and about.' She kept her eyes averted.

'Anything up?'

Gigi went and lifted up her handbag and extracted a large brown envelope. 'See for yourself.'

He gingerly took out a single piece of card that was inside. His whole life flashed in front of him. A glossy A4 photograph of Queenie and him with the kids slipped from his grasp. He bent down, picked it up, turning it over in his hands looking for clues and noticed on the back the date had been pencilled in.

'What the heck? Where did you get this? Shit.'

It had been taken in Majorca a couple of years back. Queenie and he were each holding a child's hand and they were racing along the water's edge. It was one of his favourite photographs.

A stabbing pain, sharp and piercing, shot through him and he visibly winced.

'You okay?'

A minute lapsed before he spoke.

'Not really.'

Travis sat down on a seat to the left of the counter. The envelope was addressed in bold black handwriting to Gigi Moreau c/o Tarte Tatin. Across the front of the picture, in neat small text, were written the words '*He's happily married. Back off.*'

Travis reached into his trouser pocket for the Gaviscon tablets and popped one into his mouth to settle the queasiness. Queenie kept telling him that he needed a full medical check-up and that it wasn't heartburn.

'Angina more likely,' she insisted. But she'd stopped nagging him long ago. Nowadays he was at the back of her 'worry' queue, well behind the kids and her job, but as the pain persisted he thought she might be right. This was more than indigestion.

'I think it's best we leave it tonight, don't you?' Gigi asked. It was a rhetorical question. Her smile sagged as she leant across and lightly touched his shoulder, pulling away when a customer entered.

'Listen, I must get back to work. Stay there till you feel better,' Gigi said as she slid behind the counter.

Travis forced himself to get up and, putting on a brave face, he bade a hushed goodbye and made his way across the road, slowly climbing back up the stairs. At the top he took out his phone and scrolled down recent calls. He pressed redial and waited as it went to voicemail.

Hello. Beverley's phone. You know what to do. Leave a message.
Beverley. We need to meet. I'll come round tonight. Make sure you're in. It's Travis, by the way.

20

I'm upstairs in my parents' bedroom. I still think of it as their room, and a couple of coats of paint haven't washed away the stained memories. It feels lonely, as the screams and smacks have left a gaping silence. I was like a stranger living in the same house as my parents, an incidental bystander watching the bloodied battles. There was nowhere to turn so I swallowed up the trauma, buried it deep.

But today is about moving on, about the future. On the end of the new king size bed I bounce up and down, running my palms over the shiny quilted cover. Travis phoned. At last he's coming round, so I've prepared the room. I'll give him a guided tour and finish with the master bedroom.

I can see the entrance to the Abbott grounds from where I'm perched and suddenly the little therapy group appear through the main gates. Ms Evans is on sick leave so I asked them to come over anyway. 'It's not too far and I've got freshly ground coffee,' I said, 'and biscuits.' I need to talk, find answers. The group won't judge me, they'll listen when I tell them the anonymous phone calls continued all night and, even with the handset turned to mute, they played havoc with my mind. Twenty-seven calls in total.

Bob reaches my front door ahead of Dave and Manuel with Tamsin dragging along behind. She'll need more than coffee. She's like a walking skeleton, her tight jeans showcasing the bones. Bob is the big fish in a small pond, the self-appointed leader. In therapy we humour him when he talks of standing for parliament, confident that one day he'll run the country. Even Ms Evans nods encouragement and I wonder why. She needs to set him straight, tell him a few home truths.

'Come in. Coffee's on.' I fling the door wide as Bob's finger hits the bell. 'I thought we'd sit in the kitchen. The table's not round but don't tell Ms Evans.' A collective laugh and they shuffle in. Apparently, sitting in a circle is more conducive to conversation. I lead them down the hallway towards the kitchen like the Pied Piper leading the rats.

I've decided to head up the session as if I'm Ms Evans, sucking out personal poisons with a cajoling tone. I'll share last, getting their full attention once their own unburdening is complete, and talk about the pizza boxes, the phone calls and the Facebook incident as well as the late-night messages. It'll be good to share and, unlike Bob, I can at least provide physical proof of my paranoia.

After small talk about the weather, Brexit and my exciting house revamp, we're ready to start. Not a care in the world. I rattle coffee mugs, milk and sugar and pass round the neatly arranged biscuits while the party gets under way. The discomfort only returns when the questions begin.

'Tamsin. Would you like to go first?'

She's still firmly in denial about everything. She doesn't diet, she eats well, and she has a rigorous exercise regime and feels just wonderful. Bob dares to confront her.

'What brings you here then?' He smiles through wet slits of lips, a slithery little snake's tongue lapping up the moisture.

As she goes to speak, justify her inclusion, there's a sudden ring at the front door.

I turn my head as if I can see along the hallway and outside. For a moment, edgy and anxious, I toy with ignoring it. Perhaps it's more pizza, but it's early in the day and random deliveries are best made under cover of darkness. My nightmare of a dead cat with its throat cut splaying blood on the doormat seems ridiculous in the light of day but it's fresh in my mind. I get up.

'Sorry. Won't be a minute. I've no idea who that'll be. Help yourselves.' I head towards the front door and peak out through the glass panels. My face comes right up against Travis' on the other side which makes me jump. I wasn't expecting him until much later, after the group had gone.

'Open up. We need to talk.' He raps loudly on the glass, his image distorted by the frosting. 'It's urgent.' His voice is distorted too, irregular and rasping.

I'm not ready to see him; my lips are dry, my appearance unkempt. I check the hall mirror and smooth down my hair. My face is pale, dark rings testament to the insomnia. I glance back towards the kitchen, wondering how I'll keep Travis away from the random group of weirdos as he might question my inclusion into such an odd circle of acquaintances.

But he's seen me and I've no choice but to pull

back the chain.

'Travis. You're early. I thought you said this evening?' My voice is sing-song. I fiddle with my hair, realising that he's not seen me in leggings and T-shirt before. Our clandestine dates have thrived on short dresses and stockings, the lush red lipstick a thing of the night.

'This can't wait. Can I come in?'

'Sure, but I've got company. We're having coffee but you're welcome to join us.' I point down the hallway, knowing he'll decline as we're not yet part of an accepted social couple.

'No thanks. This is important.'

I open the door to the dining room and he follows me in, pushing the door to behind him. It's not a social call, that's for sure. He hands me a photograph, folded in two. I wonder why he's made such a mess of the picture, marring it with fold lines. Seems a pity.

'Did you send this?' He's angry but not in the way Scott gets angry. There's a lack of bite; venom. There's a softer side to Travis' character, his nature non-confrontational. It could be that he's weak but either way he'll give me the benefit of the doubt; innocent until proven guilty. Scott would have dragged me by the hair straight to the gallows.

'What is it?' I can see what it is, the image very

clear. There's no doubt about the happiness of everyone involved. It's Facebook perfection; buckets and spades in the sun. Majorca most likely, as I don't think he's taken his family anywhere else since he got married.

'It's my family.'

'So? What's it got to do with me?' I open my hands wide, palms upwards and shrug.

He hesitates, doubt clouding his reaction.

'A friend of mine received this in the post today. I know it's from you.'

'A female friend? I assume it wasn't sent to one of your male buddies.' I stare at the photo as if looking for clues. 'Although it's not the sort of thing to send to a male friend unless you're selling Spanish time-shares.' I keep it punchy, light. He's easier to fool than Scott but perhaps that's what having children does for a man and it's part of the appeal, the reason I work so hard on him.

'Yes, if you must know. A lady friend.' He's trying to deny romantic involvement, a token gesture to save me hurt.

'Where would I have got such a picture? You've got to be kidding.' I daren't tell him I spotted the picture on Queenie's Facebook page, where she's been showcasing her perfect life, a few days ago.

A crack appears in the doorway behind Travis. One of my mad friends is listening. Shit, I should have locked them in. We're like members of a secret sect and I'm not keen to expose my involvement.

'I've no idea how or where you got it. But we're over, Beverley. I've no intention of leaving my wife and kids. Whatever you think you saw is all in your imagination. My family is everything to me.'

Travis is not a very inventive liar. He'll deny intimacy with Gigi with his last breath, but his childlike manners have their appeal; he's like a little boy sucking a sweet while denying its theft. A little more guile and I'll get him on side.

'Travis, you've already told me that. I'm cool with it. Doesn't mean I don't still love you. Gigi's a pretty lady, but do you really want to be a stepdad? Isn't two kids enough?'

His puckered face tells a story. It's the French in Gigi, all words and emotional gesticulations; full of bullshit. He doesn't know she has a child.

'You okay?' I'm a bit concerned when he goes quiet. I'm used to violent tit for tat with Scott but Travis is going to slope off. He takes the picture back, folds it over again and turns to go. Footsteps outside the dining room door shuffle off.

'I'm fine, but please keep away. You need to get on

with your life and let things go. I'm sorry if I led you on.'

It's as confrontational as he can get. Travis blames himself for everything that's wrong in his life, smoking, drinking and womanising masking and compounding the problems. I'm tempted to ask him to join our circle and let me look after him, and to reveal Freddie and Emily's rooms with their first coats of paint.

As we walk back to the front door, I ask, 'What did you think of Freddie's drawings? He's quite the little Van Gogh.'

'Sorry?'

'He's got them in his schoolbag. Have a look. We're working on family pictures and he's put me in the background. Although I'm not part of his family he wanted to include me so it made his picture stand out.'

'Bye, Beverley.' Travis has heard enough. I wonder if Queenie will ask who the random lady in the picture is, but I doubt she'll care. In fact, I know she won't.

'Bye, Travis. See you soon.'

He wanders off, looks left and right, unsure of which way to turn.

21

While talking to Travis, I momentarily forgot about the group in the kitchen. My life is split into very distinctive but disparate parts. There's the part that Ms Evans is trying to sort out, the deep-rooted and troubled persona that makes me act in compulsive, intrusive ways; the stalking is what she's trying to understand.

Then there's the side of me that has nothing in common with the random gang in my house. They're like a band of prison mates willing me back to the cells, to keep them company. Discussing their depression is a masochistic pleasure which they hold close like dirty security blankets but when I need a break, they don't let up.

'All okay?' Bob speaks first and I guess he was the one listening in. 'Want to talk about it?' He doesn't wait for me to reply. 'Was that Travis? Sorry, I meant Terence.' He laughs.

'Who's Terence?' Dave asks.

'The alias of Travis. Beverley's boyfriend.' Bob thinks he's hilarious but all he's doing is winding me up.

'Sorry I'd rather not talk about it.'

'Was he the one who sent the pizza boxes?'

'What?' I didn't tell anyone this, or did I? I threw the boxes away and binned the memory. They only seem important again, now that Bob has brought them up.

'How do you know about those?' Everyone looks at Bob, confused, me included. Perhaps I let it slip.

'You must have told me. How else?'

I sit back down opposite Bob, who has stretched his legs out on top of the table, willing me to reprimand him. His unpredictability is unnerving. One minute he's laughing like a hyena and the next, silent as a lamb; constantly play-acting, using personas too numerous to count.

'Do you mind not smoking inside? I'd prefer it if you went into the garden.' Dave looks up when he realises I'm talking to him. It's a good distraction, turning the conversation away from myself, but I'm irked that Dave didn't ask. He fidgets with a roll-up, licking the paper back and forth.

I've read somewhere that people with mental disorders still have personality traits that aren't linked to their problems. Selfish people are still selfish. Egomaniacs never change despite the suicide attempts. Alcoholics are arrogant, insecure and not very likeable except after the first drink. Four or five down the hatch they're deathly dull, irritating, aggressive and painful to be around. Before they fall unconscious, they're likely to kill themselves or anyone who gets too close.

Dave has tried to kill himself half a dozen times. I wonder why he's never been successful. If he tries to smoke again I'll help him tie the noose. His wife left him for another man but he's no balls to fight for her, not a plan in sight, whereas I'll fight to the death to get what I want.

The group misery is infectious and I want them all to leave.

'No worries. It'll do me good to wait,' Dave says, setting down the carefully constructed death stick.

'Listen, guys. I've got a bit of a headache. Do you mind if we call it a day? I'm really sorry.'

'Did that prick get to you?' It's Bob again.

'No. Honestly, I'm fine. I just need to lie down.'

'I bet you're not the only girl he's mucking around.'

'Why do you say that? You don't even know him.' I stand up and push my chair firmly under the table.

'I saw him having a drink with a lady in The Bull pub on the High Street last week.' Bob wraps his sweater round his neck. 'I wouldn't worry though, it didn't look serious.'

The other three look at me.

'It was probably his wife. It's complicated.'

I walk with them to the front door in silence. Dave pushes the cigarette behind his ear, triumphant that he's lasted an extra five minutes. Tamsin has drunk three strong black coffees which will act as stringent laxatives and pocketed three biscuits for the walk back to the hospital. She's been sectioned and is not allowed home until she's gained a few pounds. Manuel knows more than he's letting on and I suspect he's bilingual but maintaining the secretive, mysterious façade.

'Bye. Thanks for coming. Another time.' I give a weak wave, like the queen pretending to connect with her subjects from inside an ivory tower.

'Bye, Beverley. Love your house, by the way. Travis

is a fool. Oh and it wasn't his wife, Queenie. She's a friend of mine, you know. We go way back.' Bob winks and hops off, a rabbit on the move, bounding down the steps two at a time.

22

Damian Hoarden is moulded to his chair, the blubber folded into tight confines. His complexion has the oily sheen of a whale and his chins are made up of four sections. Worse still, his character matches the revolting appearance.

I'm perched opposite on a small upright chair, jiggling my leg up and down, my nervous agitation in stark contrast to Mr Hoarden's lethargic demeanour. I suspect an underactive thyroid might be an excuse for the inability to burn off the globular mounds but whatever, it's not obvious if his size is the result of a lack of energy and enthusiasm or if it's the other way round. In my favour, his obesity may have helped him understand obsessive cycles and how hard they are to break.

'Beverley,' he says. The one word starts the ball rolling, echoing Ms Evans' motto of 'less is more'. 'As Ms Evans has already told you, Mr Scott Barry has lodged an official complaint that you've been following him and his girlfriend again. He used the word *stalking* and is now after a new restraining order.' Mr Hoarden doesn't close his mouth, letting his red blubbery lips hang down and he runs his tongue round towards his back teeth as if trying to release a bit of food. A thick forefinger, its nail edge ragged and sharp, enters the fray.

Watching awakens the same sensation as when our teacher would scratch the blackboard with his fingernails. Mr Hoarden has my complete attention.

'Please tell me your side of the story, Miss Digby, because his claims sound familiar.' He's not that interested but needs to get the forms filled in.

I can trace the earliest onset of my obsessive behaviour towards Scott back to a particular night when I phoned him, begging to meet up. The pregnancy termination had already taken place, all expenses paid. Scott thought I was going to merrily move on after the lifeblood had been sucked out of me but he didn't know about the complications, as he hadn't been in touch since April first, the date of our baby's murder. With a light kiss on the cheek, he strolled away from the clinic, unconcerned about the light bleeding, relief written large. After a final meal together, to drown phoney sorrows, he kept his distance.

'Why not tonight? I can come round and we can talk things through,' I'd pleaded. Of course, there was nothing to talk about as far as he was concerned as he'd already bolted.

'Listen, I'll call you tomorrow. I can't really talk now.'

I should have known Danielle would be there but for some reason, I didn't think he was such a bastard; brushing me and the baby under the carpet as if we were dirt from his shoes. I could hear soft music in the background.

'I want to talk now. I have to tell you something.' He needed to look into my eyes, feel the despair when he heard that my womb was irreparably damaged. 'I'll come round.'

'No. You can't come round now. I promise I'll call you tomorrow and it'll be easier if I come to yours. Look this isn't fair on Danielle.'

'What's not fair on Danielle?' That was the moment I flipped. His ex-girlfriend talking to him on the phone wasn't fair on his new girlfriend. He was worried Danielle might get jealous, offended that his attention was taken up, even for a second, with thoughts of someone else. His death knell was putting the phone down at that point.

'I don't know what Mr Barry has been claiming, but I have no idea why he thinks I need a restraining order. What has he told you?'

Mr Hoarden refers to his notes, running his chubby fingers along the sentences as if reading braille.

'He says you're following him and his new girlfriend, Co... Co...'

'Cosette. Cosette is the name of his new girlfriend. We're at the same college, that's all.' It hadn't been as easy as I'd hoped enrolling as a mature student, course choices were limited and the French and Italian classes had been full. 'I'm doing Spanish. It's purely a coincidence that we're both there. I've been planning to go for ages. Cosette just happens to be there too, learning English.'

'I see. Mr Barry also claims that you've been tailing him to work. He's seen you three times now in

Covent Garden where he regularly goes for after-work drinks.'

'So? I go to the market, what's the crime in that? I've been going there for years.' I've been careful when tailing Scott, all encounters meticulously planned and all taking place in broad daylight and in busy places. I've been building the pressure slowly and steadily. It's now time to turn the tables, tell Mr Hoarden what Scott is up to. I'm still assuming the pizza boxes, the phone calls and the online pho-tomontages are Scott's pathetic attempts to get his own back; tit for tat, so I spill the beans.

'Have you reported any of this? It's not in your notes.' Mr Hoarden flicks through the pages, per-spiring from the exertion.

'No. Unlike Mr Barry, I wouldn't want to waste yours or police time with trivial name calling. He's just playing games, trying to get his own back. But I'd like these incidences noted.' Two can play.

'I see,' is all Mr Hoarden says. 'No, there's nothing in here.' He scrawls across the pages with small black spidery scribbles.

'When can I stop the therapy sessions, by the way?'

'Ms Evans has suggested another month. She says

you're making good progress.' A half-hearted smile reveals a glimpse of ragged yellowing teeth. It looks as if his apathy for action is going to play into my hands.

'Okay, Miss Digby. I'll not recommend a restraining order at this juncture. But I do suggest you keep your distance and I've noted your concerns regarding Mr Scott's behaviour and would suggest you keep a note of any other odd incidences. It sounds a bit like he's now the stalker.' Mr Hoarden guffaws, tickled by the sudden realisation, all four chins wobbling and he coughs from the effort.

'Thank you. Is that all? Can I go?' I stand up, not waiting for him to extricate himself from the chair.

'Yes. Hopefully I won't have to see you again any time soon.'

* * *

As I leave the main entrance of the hospital grounds, I spot Ms Evans approaching. Another month should give me plenty of time to unload all my neuroses and for me to tell her why I chose her as my therapist. She must surely have wondered, as there were hundreds to choose from in the area.

'Good morning, Beverley.'

'Good morning, Ms Evans. Another lovely day.'

We stroll on past each other like a couple of acquaintances. Thing is, we're not casual acquaintances. We both know far too much about each other for that to be the case.

23

'Predatory stalkers use stalking to gratify their need for dominance and control and ultimately to gratify sadistic sexual desires.'

Browsing case histories, I'm fascinated by the characteristics I'm meant to portray. I want to be convincing as a predatory stalker and it mightn't be a bad idea for her to fear the possibility of sexual deviance. I don't want her to only experience sleepless nights, edginess and anxiety. I'm aiming for nightmarish. When she's terrified, fearful for her life 24/7 with no response from the police, then I might take my foot off the pedal. But then again I might not. It takes one to know one and I'm starting to enjoy myself.

'Cold and calculating, on the surface the predatory stalker is often able to maintain the façade as a devoted husband, or in rare cases, wife, caring professional or kind-hearted neighbour. Underneath, though, lurks an underbelly of twisted sexual desires and predatory violence.'[1]

I can relate to this.

I'm standing over the hob, stirring rhythmically to mix up the ingredients. I like cooking, trying out new recipes. It's a calming, therapeutic hobby. Occasionally I have a disaster in the kitchen, but the smell from the rich dark meat makes me close my eyes and devour the aroma. Tonight's offering is a success.

Roadkill has been on the news recently. There's a local community group in Enfield which runs a roadkill programme and, as I cook, I reread a flyer that came through the letter box. There's a number listed which you can phone and one of their 'do good' members aims to be at the scene within thirty minutes. They take away the dead animal and promise that the carcass will be put to good use. I'm not sure whether they use it to feed the starving millions or if they stuff it for posterity, as I'm sure at least one of their members is likely to be a taxidermist. Either way, if you're lucky they might offer you a finder's fee. 'Waste not, want not' is their motto.

When my back wheels skidded across the road, I knew I'd hit something. The glare of headlights had drawn the eye of the night-time scavenger. It was tempting to drive on, swerve round the bloodied carcass but instead I pulled over and had a look.

It was a struggle, hoisting the weakly pulsating badger into the boot of my car but I spread out an old torn dust sheet across the boot and managed to lay the animal down. It surrendered to its fate and stiffened quickly.

Instead of a finder's fee, I opted to cook it myself. Badger chasseur, served with tomato sauce and croutons sounds good and the recipe is pretty simple.

'There are five tastes and textures in there, including the tongue, the eyeballs, the muscle... The salivary glands taste quite different. And of course, the brain. You get that by putting a teaspoon in the hole in the back and rooting around.'

It's good having the kitchen to myself, spreading out over all the surfaces with gay abandon. As I pick and choose which bits of the badger to use, poking through its innards, I realise there is blood and gore everywhere. It's dripping from the work surfaces, into the sink and a fine red slippery trail coats the floor tiles.

I sip at the juice from a teaspoon, seasoning with a little more salt and pepper, and then start to clear up. I bag together the unrecognisable remains of bones, striped pelt, and corded tail. Finally, the elongated weasel-like head, with its miniscule ears, is stuffed in on top.

The vegetables in the simmering pot are well past

their sell-by date; softened carrots, limp celery stalks and browning onions. A healthy measure of rich red wine tops the mixture and, as the cauldron bubbles back to life, I pour myself a well-earned glass from the bottle.

It's ten minutes before midnight when I venture out to my car and heave the bag of motley body parts into the boot. Her face will be a picture when she opens it up but I wonder how long it will take her to work out what's inside. The little pebble eyes will provide the best clue.

Cheers!

---

1. The Predatory Stalker, A Wolf in Sheep's Clothing (Dec 2012) - by Joni E Johnston Psy.D

24

Cosette is nearly as dogged as I am. Scott's childish attempts to freak me out have left me more irritated than afraid and have fed the determination to keep at him. My befriending of Cosette is definitely putting a strain on their relationship.

She's fed up with his 'little white lies' which are starting to morph into whoppers. Old habits die hard. The niggling doubts, fed by my negative throw-away comments about her boyfriend, are festering.

'He thinks I believe him,' she says slurping through the straw and making glugging sounds as she reaches the bottom of the glass. She's like a petulant child. It must be her contrary nature that appeals to Scott or else he really has a child fetish.

Perhaps if he'd moved on to her, rather than to Danielle, I wouldn't have got so jealous and angry because Cosette's hard to dislike.

'What's he up to now? Jeez. I'm glad he's not my problem any more.' I gulp my wine.

'His ex-girlfriend is back in London. Danielle. He lied when she phoned and he made up some story about a disgruntled client. He must think I was born yesterday. What disgruntled client phones a banker at home after ten at night?'

The white wine has an acid bite, sharp and stinging. It's like paint stripper attacking the delicate coating at the back of my throat, and it's a battle to keep down.

'Danielle? What does she want?' My tone is mildly inquisitive but my insides are like pig swill.

'That's what I don't know. Scott doesn't talk about her much except that she's an ex. They split up after she lost their baby in some freak accident.'

She doesn't know. He hasn't told her that he tried to blame me, put me in the frame for Danielle's tumble, and I doubt Cosette knows I'm in therapy because of his accusations. I need to contain the vitriol, play her carefully, and make her choose to leave of her own accord.

'I thought she'd gone, left him. I wonder why she's back.'

'He's met up with her. I'm certain because he's acting weird. He bought me a necklace and I'm sure it's like a "guilt" present. Look.'

The tiny silver chain has a heart clinging precariously to the thinly welded rope. The fact it's not gold speaks volumes.

'Have you moved in yet?'

'Sort of. Although I haven't unpacked properly. I'm not certain how committed Scott is. He says he wants us to move forward but I'm not sure. Now that Danielle is around, I don't know what to think.'

Danielle has a way of hanging about, getting her kicks with someone else's boyfriend; all the fun and none of the shit. Scott was seeing her months before my abortion and now she's back. Poor Cosette, so young and starry-eyed.

'I'm sorry. But don't let him treat you like a doormat. He tramples all over people to get what he wants. I should know.'

'I thought he was *the one*.' She wiggles her forefingers like inverted commas to stress the point. I smile at the familiar gesture.

'Yes. So did I.' I can't help my air of condescension. It's not that I want her to feel foolish or gullible or even second best, but I want her to see what a complete prick Scott is. I'll have persuaded her to move out by the end of the month.

'How're things going with Terence?' Her French accent puts the stress on the 'ence' and I wonder at first who she's talking about. It rhymes with ponce.

The change of subject tells me she's had enough and needs time to digest our conversation, bury the feelings of disloyalty. She's got the stubborn belief that accompanies first love, that all will work out in the end and that their relationship is uniquely special.

'Really well, actually. I'm getting the house ready for him to move in. At last I've found my Mr Right.' I convince her with my smile but resist the finger wiggling. She doesn't need to know about the wife, the kids or Gigi. Travis is already becoming worn down by the pressure and it'll not be long till he's over my threshold. Queenie doesn't seem to care and is probably packing his bags as we speak but she'll hate me for the inconvenience.

'That's great. Listen, I've got to go, but thanks for the drink. And the chat,' she adds as an afterthought. She's playing down my influence, doesn't yet realise the effectiveness of subliminal suggestion. Snide comments here and there are hitting the spot.

As she walks away, I decide to miss my Spanish class and catch up at home. I open my phone and go to *planner*. Classroom teaching, Spanish classes and house renovation have turned into a full-time job. Only after Travis has moved in and Scott's punishment has fitted the crime, will I be able to start completely afresh and perhaps find time for some real hobbies. But for now, I'm a woman on a mission.

I study my *weekly planner* and realise I need to free up some time slots for Danielle. I'm not sure what's going on but she's a definite threat. I insert a red *high priority* tag next to her name. The idea was certainly not for Cosette to walk away and leave the door open for her predecessor to come back in. Over my dead body, if not someone else's.

25

Scott hovered, took a few deep breaths before hanging his jacket up on the peg in the hall and prepared for confrontation. Wobbly broken sobs were coming from the kitchen but quieter, less hysterical than earlier. He hoped Cosette had calmed down since her frenzied incoherent phone call.

'Hi, babe.' He pushed open the door and reeled backwards from the stench, his fingers clipping shut the end of his nose.

Cosette's face was smeared with blood and her hair, coated in a red congealed gunge, stuck out as if from an electric shock.

'What the fuck?'

The macabre contents of a bin bag were strewn

across the kitchen floor; dark, viscous blood coating the tiles. An animal's head, its mouth dismembered, had rolled into the corner, its upturned snout smiling back. Cosette was whimpering, crouching on the floor.

Scott's feet squelched their way through the entrails.

'I opened the box. It was addressed to you and there was a black bag inside.'

He put his hand out and helped her up, choking back the fumes whose cocktail was a mix between an egg farm and a sewage plant. He threw open the back door and heaved over the flower bed.

'That fucking bitch. Look, I'll put on my boots and let's clear this lot up. Would you do me a favour first? Take some pictures. We need this on record.'

'Who'd do something like this?'

'Isn't it obvious? That bitch, Beverley.'

Cosette gingerly moved to the sink and scrubbed her hands raw. Struggling to hold the phone, which had avoided the fallout, she snapped the scene from several angles. Scott took out a pair of yellow rubber gloves from under the sink and pulled them on.

'She doesn't forgive me for what happened. She'll never let it rest. Don't you see?'

'She's moved on, Scott. She's happy, got a new

man. Why would she waste time on you?' Cosette's tone was clipped as she got down on hands and knees and scoured the floor, using sheets and sheets of kitchen roll to sop up the mess.

* * *

Scott wondered if Cosette's grim determined silence might be connected to what happened the other night, when Danielle had phoned out of the blue.

'A drink. Old times' sake?' His ex-girlfriend's husky voice had wafted through the handset, a ghost from the past.

It was late and he and Cosette were already in bed. When he heard Danielle's voice, Scott had slipped out from under the duvet and padded towards the door, closing it gently behind.

'Danielle? Is that really you?' For a moment Scott thought he was dreaming, that she would hang up and be gone. 'Okay. Text where and when and I'll be there.'

'Who was on the phone?' Cosette, shivering, appeared behind him, encased in one of his extra-large T-shirts like an underfed street urchin. Scott swiped his phone off and took her hand.

'No one important. A disgruntled client. Sorry, I tried not to wake you.'

Now as he watched Cosette scour the tiles, forwards and backwards, backwards and forwards he suspected the purposeful angry actions might be linked to something other than the slaughtered badger spread out in front of them.

* * *

Scott got to the wine bar early, butterflies in his stomach. Danielle had disappeared after she'd lost the baby, the final nail in the coffin of their relationship. He'd clung on long after their relationship had gone sour, hoping that a baby would make things right; make her stay. The day before Danielle fell down the stairs they'd argued. She told him she was going to bring the baby up on her own, that she didn't need a man.

His explanations about Beverley had been brushed aside.

'I haven't been seeing her behind your back. She keeps phoning me, turning up at weird places, forcing me to talk to her. Whatever she's told you, it isn't true.'

But Danielle didn't believe him. Beverley had made sure of that by feeding lie after lie, sending pictures of them together, putting recent dates to old photographs; photographs taken when they'd first gone out. There was one picture, though, which had been impossible to explain away. It was of Beverley and him walking along a seafront. He had an arm around her shoulder with his other hand on her stomach, the bump faint but distinct.

'I should have told you she was pregnant. It wasn't planned and she didn't want to keep the baby, so it didn't seem important.' He had lied to Danielle, a big mistake. He should have told her the truth, about the botched abortion which he'd arranged and Beverley's depression and subsequent desire for revenge. Instead, he'd carried on, falling more and more in love with Danielle, assuming Beverley would disappear and he and Danielle could live happily ever after. That was until Beverley confronted Danielle with the undiluted truth.

The wine bar was half empty but he still hardly recognised Danielle when she walked in. At first he'd looked away but slowly dared to turn back. The skin-tight dress of his night-time fantasies had been replaced by baggy slacks and a loose-fitting blouse. High heels had given way to flat pumps and the hourglass figure was hidden under the layers.

'Scott.' The familiar eyes crinkled at the corners. 'It's good to see you.'

She smelt the same, although the heady fragrance was more subtle.

'Danielle.' He kissed her on the cheek, stifling a nervous cough. 'You look great.' What else could he say?

'Thanks, although I don't believe you.' If it was meant as a light-hearted dig at his past lies, he wasn't certain.

The moment had been a long time coming. He'd clung to memories of their wild throbbing passion, fearful that he'd never see her again and had finally succumbed to the pull of contentment. But there was always the 'what ifs?' and 'maybes' at the back of his mind.

* * *

'Pass the black bags. You *can* help you know.'

'Sorry. I was miles away. Here.' Scott handed Cosette the roll of sacks and stuffed away the red sodden papers.

'Thanks.'

'Cosette. I've got to go to the police with this. This isn't some late-night phone time prankster. A badger today, God knows what it'll be tomorrow. If it didn't come from Beverley, someone still sent it and we need to find out who. Don't you think?' He wasn't considering anyone else but needed Cosette on side.

'You're probably right. I'll come with you but I still don't think this is Beverley's work. Can you really see her killing a wild animal, slicing it open and packaging up the innards just to wind you up?'

'Someone did. It's got my name on the box, so who else could it have been?'

26

Ms Evans is definitely not so chipper this morning; maybe it's the rain beating at the windows or perhaps she had a late night, hung-over like the rest of us.

'How did your meeting go with Mr Hoarden?'

'Fine, I think. Another four weeks and I'll be out of your hair,' I joke.

'It's just he's had another complaint from Mr Barry.' Her tone is serious. I'm guessing this is about what was in the box, the box my neighbour was curious about this morning. Mrs O'Connor had poked her head through the hedge and commented on the sizeable package she'd spotted on my doorstep.

'Hope it's not more pizzas.' She whistled through lips cut through her face like slits in a melon.

'I've no idea what's inside. How exciting,' I replied, not touching the box until she'd disappeared.

'What am I supposed to have done this time?' I suddenly sneeze. I'm not one for prissy sizzling sneezes but instead blast out the irritants like a trumpet-heralding fanfare. It seems to distract Ms Evans and she waits while I drain my nose into a tissue. 'Sorry, it's hay fever. I get it every year.'

I gently poke a finger into my eye, deep into the corner and itch. It's a daring move and gives momentary relief; but the problem with daring is that you pay later as nasty bulbous styes have marred my appearance more than once.

'He received a parcel containing some very nasty contents. It was serious enough for him to go to the police.' Ms Evans pauses as the mention of *the police* is meant to make me sit up, take note but she's forgotten I'm an old hand.

'What was in the parcel?' I say I have no idea what was inside and that when I found it on the doorstep I didn't bother opening it, but instead scribbled Scott's name on the front and dumped it back from where I assumed it had come. He still has an axe to grind, there's no doubt about it and deserves what he gets. This is what I tell her.

'Let's just say it was something pretty gruesome. A dismembered dead animal.'

Her concise delivery of the facts makes me wonder if she's enjoying the moment, the imparting of a macabre story.

* * *

When Mr Walters, our neighbour from three doors down, was murdered in his bed one night, my mother relived the tale, over and over, exaggerating events with every telling. The story brought all eyes and ears her way. She kept trying to find someone new who might be interested. At first she reported the perpetrator to be a random stranger, then a family member and finally, in hushed conspiratorial tones she whispered that the wounds were so deep that it would have taken a man's strength to have done the deed. The son, she thought.

* * *

'Shit. You're joking. He can't really think it was me?' Christ. 'What sort of dead animal? I hope it wasn't my neighbour's cat!'

'A badger, I think.' Ms Evans hands me a grainy

photograph and the image is so red I think at first it must be a developing error. I peer closely and see that the blood flow has been captured close up. Cosette likes to snap, so I reckon she's taken the shots.

'Fuck me. You're not serious.' I tell her I'm shocked at the contents and even more shocked that Scott would go to such lengths to wind me up. 'I'm now glad I didn't open the box.'

'Before we start our session, I need to tell you that the police are involved and will be popping round to speak to you.' The words *popping round* make it sound like a friendly visit; that they'll be dropping in for tea and biscuits.

'Can't wait.' Another sneeze dilutes the moment but the blast seems to wind Ms Evans up, as if it's a deliberate attempt to distract her.

'This is serious, Beverley. With your previous history the police are likely to look into it. If you did send the box it might be better to own up.'

If I'm going to own up to anything it certainly won't be to Ms Evans. She's one nosey cow. Four weeks and I'M... OUT... OF... HERE. She waits for a reply but I manage to manufacture three false sneezes in a row to throw her off kilter. If it's a police matter then it has nothing whatsoever to do with her.

'I'll take my chances, thanks.' I blow loudly, shutting down the line of questioning.

'Okay. Let's move on. Today I'd like to talk a bit more about your father and your relationship with him.' She's running out of things to talk about but I lie down, glad to be back on the mended couch, and sink in, letting it suck the tension from my body like a deflating valve on a tyre.

The rain has got heavier, thick pellets of lead ricochet off the glass, and with my eyes closed, the downpour sounds even louder. But it's helping to drown out the tone of Ms Evans' voice which has a definite raggedy edge today.

'How did you feel about your father when you discovered he attacked your mother?'

'Sad, confused, angry, and afraid.' I wonder which adjective she'll home in on.

'Did you still love him, despite his actions?' Of course I did. He was my father.

'Yes. I think so.' Although I've recently started to ponder this particular question. 'You don't just stop loving someone when they do bad things, do you.' I wait but the silence prods me. 'I loved it when it was only him and me. Until I wound him up that was.'

'Oh. How did you wind him up?'

I still don't know. I loved him, kept trying to

please him but when he had a drink he became aggressive. He attacked me with words but never his fist; that he kept for Mum. The harder I tried the worse he got.

When I don't reply, Ms Evans carries on. 'Did you blame yourself?' Of course; that's what kids do, isn't it? It comes with the territory. When Dad got cross I'd beg him to swing me round in the air because he smiled when he did and all was right with the world again. As I got older and the swinging stopped, the smiles dried up.

'Yes,' I answer. Who else was there to blame?

'Are you attracted to men like your father? Do your boyfriends remind you of him?'

What a ridiculous question! Jeremy, Scott and Travis are nothing like my father. 'No, of course not,' I snort.

'If they treat you badly have you learnt to walk away?' She knows I haven't. After all, that's why I'm here. I squirm on the couch as she starts digging for shit.

'I find it hard to let go. When something has been so good, you can't just give up.' But I did eventually walk away after Mum successfully overdosed, death removing the blindfold.

The clock chimes the hour and I open my eyes.

Thank goodness. The sun has popped out from behind a cloud; like the policemen who will be popping round for tea and biscuits.

Ms Evans has gone quiet. She's staring at her phone, her mind elsewhere and reading a message with a grim set to her jaw. Her legs are uncrossed and her right foot is tapping up and down.

'Okay?' I'm the one to ask a question.

She types, fast angry taps with a finely manicured finger, before pressing the send button.

'Sorry. A minor emergency.' She sets her phone down. 'Well done, Beverley. I think we got somewhere today, don't you?' She hasn't written anything down but is going through the motions like a well-programmed robot.

'Whatever. We didn't manage to solve the mystery of the parcel though.' Light-hearted humour is aimed at levelling the playing field. 'Bye. I'll see you next week.'

'Bye, Beverley.'

* * *

I walk out through the grounds and pass Ms Evans' room again on the way. She's standing by the open window, eyes closed, gently breathing in and out.

Probably trying to relax. Listening to other peoples' problems must be exhausting and I wonder if I'm to blame for today's stoop in her body. Perhaps it was the random text message, but there's definitely something bothering her.

Through the open window, music blasts out from deep inside the hospital and Ms Evans lips mime the words from Carmen's 'The Toreador'.

> *Le cirque est plein, c'est jour de fête*
> *Le cirque est plein du haut en bas,*
> *Les spectateurs, perdant la tête,*
> *Les spectateurs s'interpellent, a grand*
>   *fracas!*

As she sings along, oblivious to my attention, she looks slightly deranged and I smile to think that I'm the one telling her my problems. Perhaps it should be the other way round as I know she has plenty of problems of her own.

27

I think at first my phone's ringing, but the screen is blank. My dry eyes and the rancid taste in my mouth remind me that it's Saturday morning. I reach for the paracetamol, using my fingernail to slit open the capsules, and dig out two. My mouth is so dry that I drink a whole glass of water before I can swallow them.

As I slink back down under the duvet the doorbell rings again. It's only 10.03. My stomach is in revolt from the end of week excesses and I suddenly remember the cheese, chocolate and toast. The pounding in my head is the red wine. On the third ring I struggle up and scoop out my dressing gown from under a heap of discarded clothes.

'Coming. Hang on.' My voice echoes off the bare walls like a volley of shots in a rifle range but a sudden explosive bang at the door shocks my eyes wide open.

'For Christ's sake. I'm coming.'

At the front door I can make out, through the frosted glass, two callers on the porch. Despite the distorted images I know they are policemen from their outfits. The man is dressed in a suit and the woman in a black-and-white uniform. I pull my dressing gown tight and open the door.

DCI Colgate hasn't changed much, his sharp little teeth not as white as his name would suggest. A sprinkle of grey now feathers his short back and sides but the eyes are still fierce and intense, and I know he means business.

'Miss Digby. Good morning. It's been a long time. Do you mind if we come in?'

'What's this about? What's happened?' There's no one in my life who would make me the first port of call in an emergency so I can't work out a reason for the visit. Then I remember Ms Evans said they'd be popping round. I'd been in such a heavy sleep I'd forgotten.

Colgate's colleague is a pretty young woman who looks to be fresh out of school. Her polished black shoes cover weirdly small feet and her hair is swept back under the tight fitting cap.

'If you'd let PC Lindsay and myself in, we'll tell you.' He forces me to step aside as he indicates for Lindsay to enter. 'After you.' The charm's still in place, along with the concrete smile and the viper's tongue which flicks in and out.

'I'll go and put some clothes on if you don't mind.'

'Be my guest,' he says. 'We're in no hurry.'

I leave them in the kitchen and race upstairs. My sweatpants are tangled up in the duvet and I recoil from the smell of the T-shirt, stuck with telltale remnants of crisps, but slip it on anyway, anxious to get back downstairs. In the bathroom I pull a brush through my hair and clean my teeth, spitting violently to expel the dregs.

'Nice house you've got, Miss Digby. Have you moved in recently?' When I reappear, Colgate is holding up a paintbrush and running his fingers across the hardened ends of the bristle.

'It's my family home.' None of his business. 'Can you tell me what this is about?' He'll try to confuse me with small talk, aiming to trip me up by moving quickly from one subject to another. He's like a snake in the grass, slithering this way and that.

'We need you to take a look at these.' He extracts a couple of photos from his jacket, sets them down on the table. Memories come flooding back of other photographs.

Last night's cheese, curdled Stilton, regurgitates near the back of my throat. I daren't look. I remember the pictures of Danielle lying on the hard grey slabs of the stairwell, her right arm twisted back at a weird angle. She'd landed on her side, her protuberance like a Swiss exercise ball which probably saved her life, but not the baby's. That was the last time DCI Colgate shared his snaps.

His beady hawk eyes bore through me and he guesses that I'm remembering.

'Go on. Have a look.' PC Lindsay stands back, visibly uncomfortable, as her boss thrusts the pictures under my nose. I wonder if it's his confrontational nature that makes her uneasy or sympathy at my sickly appearance.

It's the red pictures, the dead badger snaps; the ones I've already seen. Did Ms Evans hand them to Colgate or did he give her copies? Perhaps Scott took them directly to the police station, Cosette by his side, but my head's too fuzzy to work things out.

Colgate knows I'm in therapy after the Danielle incident. He hounded me till the end, insisting that prison was a more apt punishment than lying on a couch. But without proof, all he was able to pin on me was a blatant disregard for authority. 'Lock her up. She's a lying bitch.' Colgate's courtroom outburst had warranted a caution and played into my hands, forcing him to slink off with his tail between his legs and for the case to be dropped. He's been sharpening his claws ever since, furious at being made a fool of, especially by a woman. 'I've already seen these. Ms Evans showed them to me. She's my therapist.' I make it sound as if she's my significant other, trying to ignore the knot in my stomach.

'Do you know what they are?'

'Ms Evans told me. A dead badger or something. What are they to do with me?' I clench my fists.

'You tell me.' His sarcastic smile brims with innuendo.

I could tell him about the pizza boxes and show him the scribbled warning an intruder left on my own back door, but I don't. The more I tell him, the more time he'll have to spend with me, digging and delving and he'd not believe me anyway if I try to turn the tables; that's what hardened criminals do and he'd latch on.

'I'm sorry, I can't help you. I've no idea what you're on about,' I say. I tell him I don't know where the badger came from; only that Scott would have been the most likely sender. I was only returning an unwanted package which appeared on my doorstep. 'Ask my neighbour if you don't believe me,' I add.

Colgate glances across at his blushing colleague. 'Lindsay. Please can you read out the other accusations Mr Barry has made against Miss Digby.' He wanders round the room, running his fingers across the marbled surfaces, looking for dirt.

'Mr Barry claims that you're still following him and his new girlfriend,' she begins.

'Rephrase that, please, Lindsay. Stalking, not following, was the word he used.'

'Mr Barry says you are stalking him and his girlfriend. He's kept a careful note of the dates and times of the incidences.' The evidence has been jotted down in a little black book and Colgate interrupts his colleague as she goes to read on from the notes.

'That's okay for now, thank you, Lindsay.' Colgate prefers the sound of his own voice. 'Suffice to say, this is a warning, Miss Digby. Given your previous record, I would advise you not to go within five miles of Mr Barry and his girlfriend. Any more dead badgers and you're looking at a stint inside.'

Colgate nods at Lindsay that proceedings have come to an end.

'Enjoy the rest of your weekend and a couple of raw eggs might help with the hangover. Might make you throw up but perhaps a clean-out of the system would be a good thing.' He smirks.

As I follow them down the hall, my bare feet suck up dirt from the dusty floorboards. Colgate unlatches the door, ushers his colleague out in front of him, and leaves me to close it in their wake. I flop down hard against the wall, my heartbeat pulsing in my head.

Scott is a snivelling little weasel. I know the pizza boxes were from him. The badger does appear a bit extreme for someone with his inherent apathy but I'll not be taking the blame for the bloodied animal. Two can point fingers, and he shouldn't keep winding me up.

28

Travis turned and twisted the key, this way and that, jiggling it carefully so as not to break it off. He pulled it out and tried again before peering into the hole of the lock, looking for a clue but the key was intact, no tiny shards having sheared off.

He shivered in the heat, wiping the back of his hand across his brow and scanned the empty cul-de-sac. His eyes rested on their own front garden which was raggedy, parched. Queenie's pot plants were bare, no sign of the bright colourful arrays. Sticky green weeds with serrated edges clung stubbornly to the topsoil, the red geraniums having disintegrated into straggling pieces of string. Funny he hadn't noticed before.

Although he knew Queenie was at work, the kids at school, he peered through the ground-floor window.

'All okay?'

His neighbour's voice startled him.

'Mrs Walker. Yes, everything's fine.'

Mrs Walker stood by the gate, her skeletal fingers, like stiff wiry pipe cleaners, rested on top of the metal frame as rust flaked to the ground.

'Be careful of the gate. I need to mend it,' Travis said, eyeing the one hinge that held it weakly in place. Mrs Walker's wet rheumy eyes looked down as she lifted her hand away and Travis wondered when Queenie had stopped nagging him to mend the gate.

'I thought you might need this.' His neighbour dangled a spare key, tagged to Freddie's Mickey Mouse keyring. Travis coughed as the old woman's gaze challenged him.

'Thanks. Brilliant. You shouldn't have come out though, I could have called round.' He took the key, jangled it in the air before popping it in his pocket and moved back towards the gate where Mrs Walker stood firm.

'Do you want to try it? Make sure it fits?'

Bitch. She'd been watching. She knew Queenie had changed the locks, probably knew why and had more than willingly accepted a new spare key, like a winner's medal. The first time a suitcase had landed at his feet, Mrs Walker had looked away but he'd seen the sly smirk, comeuppance written bold.

'Don't worry, I'm sure it'll fit fine. I've got to pop to the shops. Thanks again and enjoy the sunshine.'

Wrinkles circled the old crow's neck and crevices round her mouth were like weathered striations in hardened rock. Lines in her forehead reminded him of an old school jotter. 'But don't fall asleep again,' he joked, remembering the sunstroke Mrs Walker had suffered after a snooze in the midday sun the previous summer.

His neighbour shuffled away along the pavement, her movements not so cocky and when she disappeared from view, Travis headed towards Southgate Tube station, and back to the office.

* * *

It was rush hour, but in reverse. The smattering of people on the platform was relaxed, heading up to London for a fun night out. There was no sign of uptight commuters weighed down by mortgages and responsibilities and the gentle buzz of conversations lacked urgency; work clothes replaced by softer lines and easy fabrics.

Travis stood uneasily in his grey pinstriped suit. He stuffed his tie into a pocket, took off his jacket and slung it over his shoulder. A hoot of forced laughter rang out from a group of young people, bursting with noise and energy, and one of the girls caught his eye, a pretty brunette in skinny jeans and leopard-print top. He smiled back but, without his glasses, it took a minute to register that her eyes were focused on the approaching train.

'Come on, guys. All aboard. First round's on me.'

Travis moved to the end carriage, away from the partygoers and chose a seat by the window, his back against the wall. He'd call Queenie later, not let on he'd got home early and let her tell him about the locks. He'd been married long enough to know that not asking questions was the best way to get information.

The doors hissed closed, latecomers filling up vacant seats. Everyone was clutching a mobile phone or wearing earphones. If their lives weren't full of meaning, at least no one would be any the wiser. An elegant woman took a seat across the aisle and her eyes stared past Travis out the window, as her head, encased by dangling wires, nodded rhythmically. Travis used to engage with strangers, in an easy way. Queenie called him a charmer, a man whose smooth words slipped easily off the tongue. He used to pick seats next to pretty women and brush his hard thighs against their legs, alleviating the boredom of the daily commute. But nowadays he was more hesitant, concerned his friendly smiles might be misconstrued.

Yet it was hard not to be drawn to the sheer black stockings which caressed the woman's shapely legs, tightly crossed and closed for business. He forced his gaze away and dug out his phone. Gigi still hadn't picked up and he'd not been able to get hold of Queenie, despite the messages and even Beverley was unusually quiet.

As the bleak tunnels of the Piccadilly line swallowed him up, mobile screens went blank and eyes collectively closed. The dank, filthy cables that ran along outside the window confirmed they were deep underground and suddenly he became engulfed by panic. Everything went dark. What if Queenie had thrown him out? Changed the locks for good? Perhaps she'd found out about Beverley and this time wouldn't let him come home? He had nowhere to go; no backup plan.

If Beverley had sent the happy family snap to Gigi, perhaps she'd sent something similar to Queenie? He tried to think of pictures Beverley and he had taken together, a couple of selfies on a night out. He'd been careful but Beverley, sneaky and determined, could have taken pictures when he wasn't looking. He had dozed off more than once after lovemaking and she could easily have snapped them lying naked, side by side.

'Can you hear me? Are you all right? What's your name?'

A light flickered on and off overhead. There was a hushed silence, like the aftershock of some catastrophe as the train ground to a halt. Perhaps there'd been an incident.

'We'll be at the station in a minute. Here, have some water.' It was a man's voice; deep, husky. A water bottle was thrust towards Travis' lips and he sipped but someone else's hand guided it. He wasn't sure if he was shivering or shaking. Perhaps he was in shock from an explosion or terror attack.

'Do you think he's had a heart attack?' She spoke in a refined foreign accent, French or perhaps Swiss. It was the lady with the sheer black stockings, holding her earphones to one side and standing over him. Her bosoms dangled above his face and before he blacked out he imagined leaning a bit further forward, raising himself up and nestling his cheeks between their naked warmth.

29

A rustle in the trees, it's the wind. That's all.

Superstition keeps me on the right, the dark woods to the left. Hide and seek. Boo. Now you see me, now you don't.

Watch the pavement cracks, take off my shoes; lighten my tread. Move carefully over the ragged lines. I speed up, suddenly, but it was only an owl. Stop. Listen. I feel foolish, childish. It was nothing. What a hoot. Breathe in. Breathe out. Relax. Take another breath. You know the ropes.

Then he's walking towards you. Tall, straight backed, Caucasian. Or is he? It's too dark to be sure under the dull watery street lights.

'Hi. Can you tell me where Willian Street is?' He looks

nice, pleasant, and his voice is cultured. You know where it is but should you tell? Engage? His hands are covered but it's much too hot for gloves and the soft leather grain gives you doubts. The observation might come in useful later on. Note it down. Times and dates. Anything you can think of. Facts are key.

'Sorry. I'm not from around here.' Fear draws out the lies and survival instinct kicks in.

'I'm here.' He points at the map, a small A–Z. Why no phone? Google Maps? Perhaps there's a tracer out on him already. He wills me to look, help him get his bearings. But I don't. I'm void of trust.

'Sorry, I'm in a hurry but good luck. Hope you find it.' I'm off. Not too fast. Not too slow. Polite. No trace of fear. Tuck that tightly away under your skin. Follow the rules.

Is he watching me? Has he noted my bare feet moving fleetly across the pavement? My fists and jaws are clenched. Has he turned and gone the other way?

I think I've done it; lost him. A foolish flush burns me up. But then I hear them. Footsteps. Right then left. Left then right. The hard-soled beat of well-heeled shoes. The tread of nightmares.

They're speeding up, louder, sharper, heavier. And then he's closing in. It's a race against time. Run rabbit run. Run rabbit run.

There's a brick wall up ahead; nowhere left to go.

Then maybe, just maybe, I see a way out. There's a small road on the right; a dead end but lights are on. People are at home. I swerve wildly round and turn the corner. The street name looms large. Willian Street. But it's too late.

* * *

It's just another dream. Another nightmare. Different faces, different streets. But the terror is the same. There's no let up. Day and night. Night and day. There's no pattern, only one theme. A stalker is on my tail.

I try to wake up but my body is rigid, my limbs numb and I'm unable to move. It's always the same. The sleep monster sucks me back down and won't let go.

Coffee. I need coffee. I need to be awake, wide awake to make my escape but I still can't move. I can't get up. There's no escape. The wall ahead is solid, too high to climb. I'm like a coma victim, hearing, knowing and seeing but unable to tell; to impart the horror.

A small hole high up in the wall catches my eye. It's near the ceiling. If I can reach it I might make it, slither through. It's my escape. I scale the wall, fingers gripping hard against the brick. And then I'm there. If only I can get through I'll be safe. I'm certain.

I slide my head in first, and then wriggle round, body

oiled from top to bottom, until my head pops out. The doctor's there to catch me. The soft white towel wraps me up and I'm safe at last. My cry is deafening, heartbeat strong. The doctor's wearing gloves. They're made of fine-grained leather.

* * *

Suddenly I sit upright, jerked awake. My nightwear's soaked and stuck like cling film to my body. My ears are pinned back, my eyes agog. The bedside clock shows 3am. It's the same every night, the buried demons won't let me rest. They torture my night and fuel my day.

I get up and quietly pad downstairs, closing the bedroom door behind me. In the kitchen I flick the lights on; white and glaring they stun the nightmares and dissipate the images. The outside light flickers and through the back window I take in the plants, rich and lush in summer bloom. They remind me that deadheading wasn't enough.

I have one more thing to do. One more person who needs to pay.

I close my eyes and remember. Once again I'm walking down the hall, slowly scuffing my feet. I glanced sideways but you averted your eyes; snapped your gaze away.

The remote control was clenched in your fist as you

clicked and clicked, turning the volume up; higher and higher. My eyes made impotent silent pleas. You knew where I was going. The garden shed held no mystery and you were just the lookout; there to keep an eye. Doing your job.

You weren't his type and you pretended not to see. You turned a blind eye.

But I know who you are. You still don't recognise me. Not yet. But soon you will.

When I peel back my skin, layer by bloodied layer, you'll see what's underneath. It's carefully hidden, buried underground for now. But soon you'll see me and then you'll pay the price.

Not long to go.

30

Freddie had been hard to calm down; well-nigh impossible. 'Want Miss Digby, want Miss Digby,' he wailed. His little shoulders huddled in so close I could smell the sweet-scented shampoo in his hair. I closed my eyes and breathed in but Miss Altringham shook her head suggesting I move back a bit.

'My car is outside, I could take him home? Look after him until Mrs Lowther gets back from the hospital?'

'Can I go home with Miss Digby? Please, miss. Please, miss.' Watery little eyes pleaded but to no avail. School policy won over and I left Freddie to his fate but he screamed my name all the way down the corridor.

As I crossed the playground I got out my key fob and clicked open my new car. The shiny paintwork glistened in the sun. A bright metallic blue Mini Cooper convertible; ample room for four. Freddie had whooped in delight when he spotted the bold white stripes running along the sides.

'Cool,' he said. 'Cool.' Queenie didn't do cool. A point to me. The heat was on and things were definitely hotting up.

With the ignition running, I rolled the roof down and turned up the radio. Freddie's little face was pressed to the window of his classroom, a small hand slightly raised. I waved back, smiled, put my foot down and drove out. He'd soon be mine, part of the package. The perfect ready-made family would be my future: Travis, Freddie and Emily. Queenie should have worked harder, given them more attention.

* * *

Bob Pratchett and Queenie are walking out together. The palm of his hand is flat against the small of her back, offering soft assurance. They could be a couple, similar ages, but their outfits scream their differences. Garish red trousers skim Bob's snake hips and a Hawaiian flowery shirt covers his pigeon chest whereas she's dressed top to toe in navy blue. I can't work out why they're here together.

I jump back behind a wall and wait for them to pass. It's a close shave. As they walk across Barnet hospital car park, away from the entrance, I wonder who drove here. Then I spot Queenie's car some distance away. How did Bob know Travis had taken a turn? Did Queenie phone him when she heard, ask him to come with her? Were they that close? I need to keep an eye on Bob. How did they become such good friends?

The corridors inside the hospital have the clinical stench of bleach and sickness. Smiles are turned off inside, along with mobile phones. I wonder why there isn't a red circle with a black line through a smiley face; but it's not necessary. Deference towards the infirm keeps mouths downturned and visitors glum.

'Mr Lowther? Let me see.' Amber, her plastic name tag giving her identity but not personality, checks the list. 'Are you family?' It's on her 'to-do' list of questions but she's unlikely to check or ask for photographic evidence.

'I'm his sister.' The *no-smile* rule helps here.

'Ward 10. First floor, along on the right. Ring the bell and they'll let you in.'

'Thanks.'

Everything in the hospital is square, straight edged. Illness is treated with efficiency, no sugar-coating. I think of the plush carpeting of the Abbott Hospital, the corniced ceilings, not a hint of death in sight, where suicides are smartly brushed under the luxuriant piles. The money rolls in and helps cover up the blood.

In the stairwell I take the concrete steps two at a time, trying to quash the flashbacks of Danielle's distorted and twisted body. At least I'm going upwards, away from the memories.

Ward 10 is directly opposite the exit from the stairs and I soon find myself peering through a narrow glass slit in a thick fire door. I ring the bell, glancing left and right but there's no one about. Perhaps the good weather keeps visitors away.

A petite pale-faced nurse opens up, lets me in and points to a room on the left.

'Mr Lowther is by the window.'

I clutch the grapes, looking down at the brown paper bag and wonder whether Travis will set them out or give them to a nurse to take away and hide from view. They could be misconstrued as evidence of some illicit wrongdoing. I'm not sure if Queenie has a soft enough heart to take Travis back but a rogue bunch of grapes might help her decide and it's worth a shot.

'Travis?' I'm not sure if it's him, if I've got the right bed. His face is ashen and he's lying on his back, eyes tight. I've never seen him lying down before. Our sex has never been followed by sleep apart from the occasional post-coital five-minute shut-eye. He gets up and dressed within ten minutes of climax.

There's no reply. 'Travis? Is that you?' I lean in closer, unsure of why I'm asking the question because I know it's him, but he's so unrecognisable.

'Beverley?' His intonation is similarly questioning.

'How are you?' I bend down and kiss him on the forehead, a waft of the clinical having replaced the familiar reek of aftershave.

'Shit. How did you know I was here?' He's not accusing, rather resigned.

'Freddie. They told him at school. I've brought you some grapes.' I fiddle with the bag and tear it apart.

'Thanks.' He's too weak to argue.

'What happened?' I pull up a lone chair and squeeze it in behind the curtain.

There are six beds in the ward, four occupied. The one beside Travis looks like it has been recently vacated and it's stripped bare, like in a movie when the relative arrives to find their loved one gone. Dead. Taken away on a trolley, somewhere out of view. There's little evidence of life anywhere and even Travis is struggling to stay awake.

'Angina. I passed out on the train.' It sounds better than a heart attack, more encouraging, but nevertheless bad. There's still the possibility of a future together, albeit a weakened one.

'Were you going home?' I'm curious. Travis doesn't usually catch the train back until round about now. Six at the earliest.

'No, back to the office.' His breathing is laboured, his eyes heavy. 'Queenie threw me out. I got home early and she'd changed the locks. I'd nowhere else to go except back to the office.' His voice is disjointed as he pauses after every couple of words.

'Why? Not because of Gigi? Surely not.'

It's a mean trick; kick a man when he's down but I don't want to miss my chance. He can't run away, turn off his phone. He's not certain how much I know about Gigi, and spotting me by the river will have fed his doubts.

'What?' His mind is fuddled.

'Why has she thrown you out? That's dreadful.

Where will you go?' Make hay while the sun shines. The master bedroom is ready.

'She warned Gigi off. We'd only had a drink together and then she sent Gigi a picture of us, as a family, telling her to back off. I've no idea how Queenie found out.'

I'm delighted he hasn't connected the photo to me and he hasn't even asked. He doesn't seem to have considered the possibility that the picture was taken off the internet, picked out from his wife's array of perfectly orchestrated family portraits. Queenie seems unaware of the nausea they cause; the tuts and raised eyebrows from people she hardly knows but has 'befriended'. Unintentionally, she's put a nail in her own coffin.

'I'm sorry.' I take his hand and rub it gently, his usually manicured nails raggedy, his skin dry.

An old man, two beds down, lets out a loud moan. I'm the only one who seems startled and I pray it's not the precursor to a death rattle but it breaks the silence, gives me a moment's respite. I haven't come prepared for sickness and have to avert my eyes from Travis' face. Yet, after all these months of vigilance and planning, I've got my chance to take control. If Queenie won't have him back, he'll have to move in with me as he's nowhere else to go.

I stay a while longer and ask some random questions which he tries to answer. There's no anger or irritation in his voice as the near-death experience has killed his fight if not his body. When he dozes off again I make a move.

* * *

I wander back out into the sunshine, but feel deflated. Travis was meant to look after me, and me him. We were to form the perfect team; the Stepford couple with a model family. Travis ticked all the boxes but being nursemaid wasn't part of the plan. Although there's the bonus of Freddie and Emily, happy families is looking less likely as the possibility of death has taken hold.

At the far end of the car park, well away from careless parkers, the white stripes on my new car shine boldly. I remember Freddie's excited face and smile. Only as I draw close do I notice the red. There's a thick smear across the wing mirror which makes me think a bird has miscued, blinded by the sun, and ricocheted off the glass.

But as I circle the car to have a better look, I see it; bold and accusing. **BITCH** has been sprayed in deep red paint along the side which is hidden from view.

There are plenty of empty spaces nearer to the hospital entrance where the regular visitors park, but not me. I know how easily wing mirrors can get clipped.

I look up. Of course I'm well out of range of the CCTV cameras; it's automatic. I learnt, when Scott accused me of stalking, never to leave a trail of evidence. Big Brother is watching you and I've been careful ever since.

Yet this time my caution has played into someone else's hands. Someone has been watching me and seen where I parked. This is no random act of vandalism, it's deliberate. All around, other cars gleam spotlessly in the sunshine.

I wonder if Queenie could be that vengeful. She always seems in control. A strange thing for a responsible mother to do though. Perhaps Bob did it for her? I scour the car park, shielding my eyes against the sun, half expecting to see Scott close by, hiding behind a wall, enjoying a prank of childish vengeance.

I open the car door, collapse into the hot cream leather seats and straighten the rear-view mirror. It could have been anyone but someone's got it in for me. I'm not sure Mr Hoarden, Ms Evans or even DCI Colgate would believe I'm no longer the hunter but the hunted; the prey, not the predator. Perhaps I should accept the damage to my car as a random act of vandalism and let it go.

As I turn on the ignition and click my seat belt into place, I breathe deeply. I need Travis to get better and stick to my original plan. I want company round the house; a healthy, noisy group will keep the bogeymen away and only a proper family will help me forget my own dark past.

31

'Of course we can still be friends. But I've moved on, Danielle. I'm with Cosette now. We're happy.' Scott's voice was hesitant, unconvincing and he wondered at the fickleness of relationships.

With Danielle beside him, sharing drinks like old times, Scott felt the warm familiar stirrings. Her dishevelled appearance didn't matter. It was Danielle after all, his soulmate, and he'd been easily persuaded to join her for a drink when she'd called.

'That's not why I'm here. Listen, Scott. Can we talk about Beverley?'

'What about Beverley?' Scott drew back.

'She turned up at the hospital, you know. The day

I lost the baby. It didn't seem important at the time, just a random sighting, but I'm certain it was Beverley at the far end of the corridor, walking the other way.' As she sipped her gin and tonic, Danielle's hand shook and Scott laid his on top.

'Go on.'

'I didn't think anything of it until recently. Last week I was up in London and she walked past me in the street. It seemed coincidental, like everything about Beverley. Among the thousands roaming around Piccadilly Circus she strolled past me. Just like that.' Danielle sucked the lemon, squeezing her eyes against the bitter taste. 'Have you seen her recently?'

'Yes. She's still hanging around like a bad penny.' He didn't want to expand, tell her too much, and it didn't seem fair on Cosette. 'Strangely enough I bumped into her in Covent Garden a week or so ago and she's also studying at the same college as Cosette.' He decided to leave the badger saga out.

'Scott, I know you humoured me when I lost the baby, telling the police that you thought Beverley was somehow involved although you didn't really see, at the time, how she could have been. There was no evidence. Call it instinct, but I know she killed our baby.

I tripped on something in the stairwell. An invisible string or something, I didn't just tumble.'

Perhaps the past doesn't let anyone move on. It's always there, picking at the sores and building scabs that never heal. Scott thought Danielle had moved on, finally accepted what had happened, but he was wrong. Beverley, on the other hand, wouldn't let anyone move on.

'She's crazy, Danielle, but there was no proof that she did anything criminal. The police found nothing, no trace of anything at the site. It was my baby too. It's been really hard but you've got to try to put it behind you.'

'Seeing Beverley brought it all back. It's not so easy to move on.' Light tears dotted her cheeks. 'I thought I could, back to work and all that, but it's still so fresh in my mind. And the other day I had a flashback. It's happened before.'

'Go on,' he coaxed, leaning forward in his seat.

'You remember the day I fell, tumbled down the stairs? There was someone at the top, standing behind the door. The person was wearing dark flat pumps but the soles of the shoes were light coloured; beige I think. I saw them move away as I lay twisted on my side. The memory's only recently come back but I can't shake it.'

There had been no proof of anyone around at the time. Scott had tried hard to put Beverley at the scene, more to placate Danielle than through any deep-seated belief that Beverley had been there. Danielle had mentioned none of this before, claiming at the time to remember nothing.

'I'm sorry,' he said. There was nothing to add. To go to the police now would most likely be construed as a conspiratorial effort to put Beverley back in the frame, get revenge for recent events.

'It doesn't matter. I wanted to get it off my chest and no one else understands.'

Scott took Danielle's hand, pulled her off the chair and put his arms around her. Time stood still for several seconds as they melted into each other.

Danielle finally pulled away. 'I've got to go, but it was great to see you and thanks for listening.' She slipped her jacket on and lifted her bag off the floor. 'And I hope it works out with you and Cosette.'

Scott watched Danielle walk away, her shoulders straight and determined. He then slumped back down into his seat and ordered another drink.

* * *

By the time Scott reached the train station, he was looking forward to getting home. Cosette had texted to say supper was ready and the wine on chill. Domestic simplicity and contentment nudged away the unsettling feelings. His relationship with Cosette was simpler, less complicated than the all-consuming passion he'd shared with Danielle and he needed to move on, grow up and put down roots.

Back soon. Sorry about the delay. Drinks with clients. Very hungry! Xx

As he put the phone back in his jacket and stepped onto the train, he promised this would be his last lie. He would bury the ghosts of Christmas past and wouldn't tell Cosette about meeting Danielle. Time to move on.

He whistled all the way back to his flat, the night air warm and balmy. On impulse he'd picked up a bunch of flowers from the corner shop and tucked them under his arm as he turned the key in the lock.

'Hi. I'm home.'

Inside, he unlaced his shoes and set them neatly by the door. It was only then that he became aware of hushed voices in the kitchen.

'In here, Scott. We've got company.'

He had his own flashback. *Fatal Attraction*. Dead rabbits. As he pushed open the door, a warm wafting smell of roast dinner invaded his nostrils, but he stopped short when he saw the two police officers.

'Good evening, Mr Barry. Sorry to call so late but we need to ask where you've been all evening.' The detective's voice pierced his jugular.

DCI Colgate's long legs were splayed out under the table and his boots had left distinct black scuff marks on top of the spotlessly scrubbed tiles. PC Lindsay, rosy-cheeked, stood behind.

'I've been at work. Why? What's this all about?'

'We need to know where you were between the hours of five thirty and now. 10pm.' Colgate checked his watch.

'At work, I've just told you. I finished late and then popped into a bar for a couple of drinks.' Scott's first thought was that perhaps they had proof that Beverley had sent the badger and they were pursuing a new restraining order. But if that was the case, why did they need to know where he had been this evening?

'Were you anywhere near Barnet General Hospital?'

'For Christ's sake. I've told you. Here's my train

ticket if you don't believe me.' He tugged the ticket out of his trouser pocket.

'It's just that Miss Beverley Digby has lodged her own complaint against you. She says you've been threatening her, sending strange packages, threatening messages and tonight someone damaged her new car. Sprayed red paint across one side.'

In the background Cosette drained vegetables through a plastic colander before she put them back in a saucepan and replaced the lid.

'This is ridiculous. She's the one harassing me. You saw the dead badger. For fuck's sake. Why the hell would I want to damage her car? The last thing I want is to see her at all or have anything to do with her!'

Cosette opened the oven, letting out a hot blast of steam, and cautiously lifted out the roasting tray. The chicken was accusingly burnt on top and the flowers he held seemed to back up the guilt. He laid them down on the table.

'That smells good.' Colgate sniffed. 'A bit overdone, but better safe than sorry. Anyway, we'll let you enjoy your supper but we'll be in touch. It's all getting a bit complicated. One minute Miss Digby is accusing you, the other you're accusing her.' Colgate laughed.

The policeman extended an outstretched hand towards Cosette which she ignored, keeping her attention on the carving.

'Bye. Hope you catch whoever did it,' she said. The knife was sharp, slicing seamlessly through the carcass. Colgate stood and watched.

'She's good with a knife,' he said. With that he buttoned up his coat and turned to Lindsay. 'We'll see ourselves out. Enjoy your supper.'

Scott leant with his back to the door once they'd gone. Christ, he needed food and another stiff drink.

* * *

In the kitchen, Cosette had dimmed the lights and lit a couple of candles. The flowers were in the centre of the table, neatly arranged in a see-through cut-glass vase and had sprung back to life.

'You pour the wine and I'll serve up. Hope it's not too cold,' she said.

'Come here, you. It smells delicious, and so do you.' Scott's arms encircled his young girlfriend, encasing her slim body as he kissed her gently on the lips. 'Thanks. I love you.'

Scott sat down, filled their glasses and held his up. 'To us.'

'To us,' she said.

Cosette would help him weather the storm, deal with all the shit. As he started to eat, she seemed like the best choice he'd made in a long time. Maybe she really was the one for keeps.

32

I get up to close a gap in the curtains, check the time and lie down again. Ms Evans asks how I sleep. Am I getting eight hours every night? Early to bed, early to rise and all that. I tell her I'm in bed by ten and up with the lark. It's the shit in between that causes the problems.

'I see,' she says dispassionately and puts it in her notes. I don't think she does though, see. Her astute insight must offer peaceful slumber which irritates me. She'll not be mooching round the house at 3am.

Tonight the ceiling spins, the fancy stucco work swirling as in the eye of a tornado, round and round, faster and faster rapidly closing in on the dangling lightshade. I'll soon be sucked into its black hole, lost for ever.

But this time it's not the alcohol. The window is cracked but the fresh paint fumes are toxic, making me nauseous. I turn the bedside light on again, fed up of tossing and turning and readjust the pillow, re-straighten the duvet and take a sip of water. I know it'll not help but it's something to do. I've another six hours to kill.

I haven't told Ms Evans of the night terrors, the sudden panic attacks and waves of depression that ride over me like a thundering tsunami. Darkness is my enemy. I finally sit up and slump on the edge of the bed, mentally exhausted, limbs heavy.

Perhaps it's time to own up and tell her how jealous I was of the darkness when Scott and I were together. He would succumb to sleep within five min-utes of lights out. Sex or no sex, he was in a catatonic state for seven hours, give or take a few minutes, after a mumbled 'goodnight'.

I'd stare at the back of his head, jealous that he'd gone; angry that I'd been abandoned to the night. Scott would twitch when I touched his crown, coiling my fingers through his hair as I tried to pull him back, keep me company.

I was ecstatic when he occasionally couldn't sleep

so he would see what it was like. This happened only a few times like when he thought he had bankrupted Barclays and when his mother took sick. Only a major trauma kept him awake and then he'd turn into a rabid dog, all teeth and foam.

I want to joke with Ms Evans that perhaps I should have used the time more fruitfully and readjusted my pillow over his face but I doubt she'd see the funny side. Another black question mark in the notebook more likely.

I give in and head downstairs, padding over the bare wooden boards, gingerly sidestepping the tacks that once held down the carpet. They're like miniature landmines in a war zone.

I draw my dressing gown tight and sit down at the computer. Night-time googling differs from that of the daytime. Searches of supermarket opening hours, directions to restaurants or flights to exotic destinations are replaced by surreptitious searches of old friends, ex-lovers and random people whose names you'd almost forgotten. Was it Pat Godley or Pat Goodman? Oscar Wilson or Oscar Woodward? Even my old headmistress suddenly seems of interest.

My eyes are heavy. Perhaps I'll fall asleep in the chair, briefly cheating the insomnia which threatens early onset dementia according to recent reports. Perhaps madness is already here, thoughts flitting skittishly round in my head. I hop from person to person, subject to subject.

As I read the obituary of Freja Gough, dead at thirty-three from some rare blood disease, my ghoulish concentration is broken by an incoming email. The blue box pops up in the bottom right-hand corner of the screen.

What's up, Beverley? Can't you sleep again? I'd turn that light down a bit; dim the room. It might help but then again it might not. Whose image are you checking out? What posts have caught your eye? Come on. Share.

I leap up, push the chair back with a violent shove and rush towards the window. I trip over an empty plastic carton on the floor, stubbing my toe which sends a sharp pain through my foot. I swear loudly, pick up the container and hurl it across the room.

The road is deserted. I look left and right and scan the cars parked along the road, the colours hard to discern but the shapes and makes familiar. There's only one I don't recognise as being that of a neighbour. It's a Mercedes; C class. I know, because I nearly bought one.

I push my head closer to the glass and peer through the window but can't see anyone and the cars are all empty. I unpin the heavy curtains and pull them shut before I return to the computer screen. Suddenly the room feels very cold.

Did you see me? I'm out there, walking up and down. The dog's legs need stretching. That's all. You can join me if you like? Or perhaps not. I've already turned the corner. Another time. Sweet dreams.

Panicked, I rush upstairs, flitting nimbly past the landmines, in and out, left and right until I reach my bedroom where I grab a pair of jogging pants from the wardrobe. I pull a hooded sweat top over my head and throw on my trainers. My shaking fingers struggle to tie the laces. I tumble out the front door, grabbing my keys and mobile on the way, and slam it shut.

The night air is chill and silent, not a soul in sight. Even the owls are asleep. I turn this way and that, racking my brain for clues as to possible directions they might have taken. Right would take them back to the High Street, where the homeless guy huddled against the glass by Boots might stir.

Left would take them towards the Bourne Estate where teenage rebels loiter, all hours of day and night. I look across the road, slightly to the right and decide to try down Winchmore Avenue. It's a long road dotted with residential side streets and I reckon this would have been their most likely choice. My instinct tells me they know the area. They can't be far ahead. I jog faster, my feet pounding across the concrete, until the cold air clamps around my lungs and breathing hurts. The silence speaks loudly but the occasional upstairs light reminds me I'm not alone. I bend down, crouch over and stretch my arms out towards my toes to ease the stitch but it's futile; the knot has tightened. I've come the wrong way. My stalker must be fast, fit, determined.

I decide to go home the way I came and walk past the same houses but in reverse. The semi-detached homes are like the marriages inside; solid and respectable with their bland façades. Two point four windows mirror the number of children. I wonder at my craving for such blandness and my belief that it holds the answer.

A street lamp stands outside number twenty-one. An insipid glow is dulled by the overhanging foliage

of a mature tree, heavy branches blocking out the
light. But on the thick trunk I can make out an A4
poster, most likely an appeal for information on a
missing cat. The notice has been newly pinned, the
writing and picture clear and bold. As I draw closer, I
see the picture is of a person rather than an animal.

MISSING. Have you seen this person? Last
seen in Winchmore Avenue on Tuesday 3 July
at 3.50am.
    If so, please call urgently on…

On a phone number not too dissimilar to mine.
    I check my watch. It's exactly 3.50am and it's also
the third of July. I stare at the picture. It was taken a
couple of months back. It's a copy of my Facebook
profile picture, head and shoulders and I'm smiling
broadly at the camera. My head is cocked coquet-
tishly to one side and my lips are pouting. It's a perfect showcased selfie.
    As I rip it off the trunk I check the phone number.
The moment I realise it's my own number, my mobile
rings.

33

Lack of sleep, compounded by nauseous anxiety, makes me feel as if I've taken a cocktail of alcohol and magic mushrooms. The hallucinations have only begun to abate, inched out by the intake of four strong coffees.

The police station is deserted when I arrive. The grey square walls are as unenticing as a prison block, but without the barbed wire, and I'm tempted to turn back. Cold light of day makes me think I'm overreacting, but I've come this far and at nine on the dot I push through the heavy swing doors.

I stick my chin out and approach the desk.

'I'd like to speak to DCI Colgate, please. My name's Beverley Digby.' I recognise PC Lindsay from the house call, but opt for a respectful distant approach. Familiarity might dilute her professionalism.

I lean on the countertop, placing both hands firmly on the surface. Lindsay, neat and polished, glances up at the clock. She looks like she's about to tell me her boss isn't in when the door behind swooshes open.

'Lindsay. Coffee, please, if you're not too busy.' Colgate sweeps past with a curt nod and a loud voice.

'Sir. Miss Digby's here to see you.'

'Morning, Miss Digby. Take a seat and make yourself at home,' Colgate says as he slithers past, his left hand grazing the shadow of stubble on his face.

I sit and fidget as the clock hands clunk forward, getting up every couple of minutes to do a circle of the foyer. Impatience is nudging me towards aggression when Colgate reappears rubbing a wet finger across a razor gash on his chin.

'Miss Digby. Come through.' I ignore his outstretched hand and follow him through to the back of the station with Lindsay close behind, a junior having been left in charge on reception.

The interview room is like a fridge and cold blasts of icy air seep through the air-conditioning vent. Colgate tuts, clicks off a switch on the wall and indicates for me to take a seat.

'Well, Miss Digby. It's nice to see you again. How can we help?' Colgate pulls out his chair, drags the legs across the floor and opens the conversation with a sigh.

'It's the stalker. I'm having all sorts of threats now. Last night they were spying on me and I found this attached to a tree trunk.' I unscrunch the missing person's poster and slap it down on the table under Colgate's nose.

'I see. What time was this at?' A sarcastic twist curls his lips as he reads the notice. 'It seems to be quite a specific time that you went missing. 3.50am? And the phone number. Have you tried to call it?'

'It's my number and I've had twenty-five calls already. They started at 3.50am and have just stopped.' I check my mobile screen.

'Do you have any idea who your stalker might be?' Colgate sets the poster down. 'Take a copy, please, Lindsay. For the records.' He pushes it towards his colleague who sits alongside.

'Yes, sir.'

'I told you. I'm certain it's Scott. Mr Barry. He's still got it in for me. You know our history.'

'I do indeed. How could I forget?' Colgate links his fingers together, stretches his arms in the air before placing them firmly behind his head. 'Go on. Why do you think Mr Barry's got it in for you?'

'I'm friends with his new girlfriend, that's all. He still can't forgive me for what happened but I've moved on. I've no interest in him any more but he doesn't seem to believe me.' My fingers drum on the table, keeping time with my legs which are like pistons, moving up and down in steady rhythm. 'I didn't send the dead animal but Scott seems to blame me for everything.' I lower my eyes.

'Well actually, Miss Digby, I think you're not quite telling the truth here. Hang on.' Colgate leafs through a file of notes, before turning towards Lindsay.

'Find me the name of Mr Barry's neighbour who made the statement, please, Lindsay. It's somewhere in the pile. Reed, I think it was.'

'Rogers, sir. Here it is. He saw Miss Digby get out of a car, a blue Mini Cooper convertible, and deliver a cardboard box to Mr Barry's doorstep. The date and time is noted.' Lindsay's pink-painted forefinger points to the log.

'You see, Miss Digby, I think you've still got it in for Mr Barry. It's more likely that you're still stalking him rather than the other way round. That's the way it looks from where I'm sitting.'

'That's not true. Because I'm friends with his girl-friend he can't let it rest. I was returning the un-opened package that I found on my doorstep. He started it. I've already told you. I'd nothing to do with what was inside.'

Colgate glances at the clock, puffing into hands which cover his mouth and nose. He uncoils, scrapes his chair back across the hard floor, chalk on black-board, and stands up.

'I'm sorry I can't give you any more time at present but I suggest, Miss Digby, you make a record of all suspect activity; times, dates and keep us in-formed. It looks as if someone is having a bit of fun at your expense.' His grin makes me think of the Cheshire cat. 'If the twenty-five calls have all been from a withheld number, it's likely this was the only poster, so I wouldn't worry too much. That's probably the end of it.'

As an afterthought he adds, 'I do suggest, how-ever, that you keep well away from Mr Barry and his girlfriend. If it is him who's pestering you, then you'd do well to steer clear. I'm sure you have plenty of other friends. Lindsay, please show Miss Digby out.'

As Colgate turns to walk away, a torrent of bot-tled-up fury explodes in a screech of words.

'Is that it? Some mad person is stalking me,

calling me at all hours of day and night, damaging my property and all you can say is that's probably the end of it?'

Colgate's calm, flat response has the tone of a victory speech. Churchill on D-Day.

'Remember, Miss Digby, when you were following Mr Barry and his girlfriend, Danielle, I seem to recall you wondering what the fuss was about; when it was the other way round. I suspect someone's now having some fun at your expense, trying to turn the tables but don't worry, they'll get fed up soon enough.'

Like an usherette at the cinema, Lindsay holds the door open as Colgate marches back out into the corridor. He's not going to help me, forgiveness isn't a trait Colgate has in his armoury and my distress has only renewed his flagging energy.

Back outside, I peel off my cardigan, dropping my bunched-up shoulders, and shake my arms free to let the early morning sun coat my skin. Colgate's attitude reminds me why I stalk. It's about regaining control, stealing my life back from thieves, like Scott, who've stolen too much.

34

My appointment has been changed from late afternoon to early morning. For some reason I've been given Ms Evans' first slot of the day and am outside her room early, keen to get started, but there's no sign of her.

Her car is usually parked in the same space each day, third bay to the right of the main entrance; a woman of habit. On several occasions I've been tempted to drive, rather than walk, across the road and up the long driveway when it rains and park in her spot, curious as to how she'd react. If I apologised, saying I didn't realise it was her spot, she'd know I was lying as she tells me often enough that I'm like her, very observant.

But I don't want to wind her up. I've only three more therapy sessions left, including today, and then I'm free; free from all the interrogation and probing, so I need to behave. I sit down on the plush upholstered sofa in the foyer, and sink into the feathered cushions. The Abbott is like a five-star hotel, the luxury making the patients question their condition. It's like a placebo making us feel momentarily better and wondering what all the fuss is about. If I ever get sectioned, I'll insist on the Abbott with its fresh laundry, soft white towels and nouvelle cuisine.

I check over notes I've made for today's session. There are things I want to bring up. Ms Evans might be able to help me find some answers regarding my stalker and how best I should respond. She's certainly getting well paid to help and I've got no one else to talk to.

'Beverley. Sorry I'm late.' I don't hear her approach as she's not wearing her click-clack working heels. The grey canvas pumps are out of sync with her usual professional look and I wonder if I could have bared my soul so readily if she'd looked this casual from the outset. 'Excuse the footwear,' she says, reading my mind. 'I'll be five minutes.'

'Don't worry. It's not a problem. I'm early anyway.' I try not to stare at her off-kilter appearance. Her hair hasn't yet been swept up back from her face and I imagine stragglers in my soup from a chef's slovenliness. Perhaps she's like this every morning for the first appointment but she's breathing too heavily and it's not from exertion; there's an anxious edge to it. Maybe she'll be lying on the couch when I go in.

Ms Evans unlocks the door to her room, closes it gently behind and five minutes lapse before she flings it wide again.

'Come in. I'm ready.'

Before lying down, I take off my own shoes and leave them neatly under the recently mended couch like I was instructed the first time I came. Perhaps on my last session I'll fling them into the corner, a coming-of-age rebellion. Like a student tossing their mortarboard on graduation day.

'Okay, Beverley. How are we today?'

I want to joke that neither of us look too chipper but I don't. I'm back in character.

'To be honest, things aren't good. I hope you don't mind if I run something past you?'

'Of course. Tell me what's up and I'll see if I can help.'

I begin. She doesn't interrupt but sits quietly, lets me talk. I go into detail about the phone calls, the threat stuck to my back door, the poster on the tree, the night-time online messages and finally the damage to my new car. 'Bitch. It was plastered in red paint all along one side. It cost over £500 to get cleaned off and to have the bodywork repainted.' The cost seems important to back up my story. In the telling, cold light of day, the rest seems rather petty.

'How awful. Did you report these incidents?'

'Yes, but the police aren't that interested. They've enough to do and to be honest, I'm not sure they really believe me. I've a long history with the detective, DCI Colgate. We go way back.'

'I see. Why do you think they don't believe you?' She's turning it round, asking rhetorical questions, ones to which she knows the answers. I was the stalker once so the likelihood of being taken seriously, especially by the police, is slim.

'I think it's personal. DCI Colgate has got it in for me and, unless someone attempts murder, I don't think the police really care.'

'What do you think you should do?'

It crosses my mind that Ms Evans is enjoying this, but I need to ask the questions.

'What should I do? I really don't know.'

'Have you any idea who's doing it? That might be a start.'

'Yes. I'm almost certain it's Scott. He thinks I'm

stalking him and his new girlfriend, Cosette, and he's already reported me to the police, as you know. No doubt he thinks he's being clever turning the tables.' I exhale a puff of contempt for the pettiness, unwilling to unveil my fear.

'Why does Mr Barry think you're stalking him and Cosette, Beverley?'

It's all about her bloody job. She doesn't want to work outside her remit; she's getting paid to sign me off and needs satisfactory conclusions about my state of mind, not that of my ex-boyfriend.

'Jesus. I'm not bloody stalking him. I'm at college with Cosette, that's all.'

I'm certainly not going to own up to deliberately trying to enrol on the same course or stealing the purse as an excuse to engage in conversation. Bumping into Scott in Covent Garden might have been intentional but I'm the only one who could possibly know that. This isn't stalking. This is about being unable to let go of the past and get closure. The fact that I feel compelled to punish Scott is no one else's business.

Ms Evans sets down her pen and recrosses her legs in the opposite direction. It's an unnatural little movement and today she definitely looks uncomfortable. Perhaps her night-time experiences aren't that good either.

'If it is Mr Barry, what do you think he hopes to achieve?'

She's not going to help, give me advice or let me have measured opinions. I seriously wonder at this point whether she has opinions on anything. Perhaps she became a psychotherapist to find answers to her own deep-seated issues but it seems unlikely she'd have got anywhere.

'Oh, it doesn't matter. Perhaps I'm overreacting but I needed to get it off my chest, tell someone what's going on. It's helped getting it out in the open.'

'That's good. I'm glad talking about it helped.'

I want to say, 'It's your turn now,' get up from the couch and use an outstretched arm to indicate it's her turn to lie down. But I don't. Anyway, it's helped pass the time if nothing else as half an hour is already up, and I make a mental note that there are only another two and a half hours of inane questioning left before I'll be out of her hair for good.

I lie back again and let Ms Evans take the reins, the finishing post in sight.

* * *

Once the session is over and I'm outside again, I feel deflated, anxious. The reality that I have a stalker, dark and menacing, hits home again. It's not some made-up fantasy; the facts don't lie. Yet I'm the only one who is scared, attune to the threats. I wonder if Scott feels frightened by all my attention. He always seems angry rather than scared, but it's hard to tell. The late-night harassment aimed in my direction smacks of anger and revenge.

I hoped Ms Evans would be more helpful but she now only talks about the future. She is pushing me to tell her about Terence, my new boyfriend, and what plans I have for moving forward. She doesn't have time to help me with my phantom stalker and my past is now well and truly consigned to history; she's heard enough to make a case.

Yet I feel as if I'm on a conveyor belt and the emergency stop button has stuck. There's no way off and I'm being forced to keep moving on and leave the past behind. I think of my childhood hamster, Dizzy. He would go round and round on a wheel, faster and faster until exhaustion forced his little legs to a standstill. But it didn't take long before he had to start up again and continue his journey on the road to nowhere.

'He must be so dizzy,' I used to say. That's how I

now feel; dizzy, light-headed and exhausted. I'm fed up dealing with everything on my own and, with what's going on, it's time to move forward. The house is now ready for my new family.

My slow walk speeds to a steady jog and by the time I reach the main road I'm more buoyant, racing for home. Tomorrow I'll asks Travis to move in, confident he'll agree, now he no longer has any other options.

I'll become part of a new family, one that functions, shares and works together. It'll be the new armour to help me face the world. Also, it's definitely been worth the wait to steal Ms Evans' husband out from under her nose. It's unlikely that she's put two and two together yet, but it'll be fun when she finally twigs.

Ms Evans and Queenie. It's hard to believe they're one and the same person. Merging her roles must have been challenging, but she's proficient in both guises, successfully separating her home and professional lives. With a birthday on the fourth of June, she's a typical Gemini with two completely opposing personalities. It's a mystery indeed, as to which side of her character is in charge.

35

Travis checked and rechecked his mobile every ten minutes. But there were no messages; even the emails had dried up. He felt like a soldier, abandoned, forgotten and left in the trenches to die.

Queenie had brought Freddie and Emily in to see him but his wife had directed the kids to his bedside without following and instead disappeared off for a coffee. She wasn't going to forgive him this time and his weakened condition hadn't softened her resolve. He was going to have to beg. He needed a place to sleep, somewhere to recover while he got his strength back and the kids kept asking when he was coming home.

As he set his phone back down onto the bedside

table, it pinged. He checked the screen, expecting a LinkedIn notification or an app update.

Hi Soldier. Are you up for visitors? Planning to pop by after lunch. Thought you might need cheering up.
Bev xx

Travis sat up straighter, smiled to himself and typed.

Yes please. Am bored to death in here! X

Perhaps he wouldn't need to beg. Good old Beverley might be the one to come to his rescue.

He hoisted himself out of bed, swallowing hard to contain the nausea. He wasn't sure whether it was the drugs or hospital food that made it worse. The nurse suggested he take a shower and freshen up as they were hoping he would be well enough to go home the next day, quoting a dire shortage of beds and assuming he had somewhere to go with someone to look after him.

Travis recoiled as he sniffed the T-shirt he'd been sleeping in, aware for the first time of the sickly stench. He hauled himself up and navigated his way across the ward, like a sailor in choppy waters, steadying himself every so often on the metal bed ends. He smiled at a couple of patients but sickness hung heavy and his pleasantries about the weather wafted over leaden heads.

By the time he'd finished showering his spirits had lifted considerably. He walked more upright and when he got back to bed, he crunched up a hidden packet of cigarettes and threw them in the bin.

At one on the dot, he watched through the window as Beverley drove in. Her dark blue Mini with the white stripes was hard to miss. Freddie had pointed it out, insisting he wanted one the same when he grew up. Beverley looked bright and sunny in tight yellow jeans and matching top, a white jumper casually slung about her shoulders, and designer sunglasses shielded her eyes. She looked quite the stunner.

Travis found it hard to remember where it had gone wrong with Beverley, maybe it had been the timing. When they'd hooked up, he'd been looking for some innocent fun; something to distract him from Queenie's constant tiredness and sexual apathy. His wife's temper, usually so well-contained, had exploded several times, increasing marital pressure still further.

But Beverley had wanted more; much more. Her

impatience and persistence to hurry things along hadn't helped. The realisation that she'd been keeping tabs on him and Queenie had freaked him out; the silent phone calls, the random sightings and then the strange appointment as classroom assistant at Freddie's school. Travis had felt as if he was being stalked and there'd been too many coincidences to buy into.

He watched Beverley saunter across the car park, hips swaying provocatively, towards the hospital entrance. The sex had been great though and perhaps he had treated her rather shoddily; maybe she deserved a second chance.

When she glanced up and waved, Travis pulled away from the window and fell heavily down on the bed. Reaching for his aftershave, he dabbed a healthy blob on his chin, eyes watering as the fumes hit the back of his throat. If he played his cards right, Beverley might offer him a lifeline.

36

He so loves to fight. That's children for you. He's taken to wielding a plastic sword above his head and pointing it in the direction of anyone who comes within a foot of the swings and slides, and members of the school staff find it hard to calm him down. The more they crouch low on hunkers, trying to coax the toy weapon out of his hands, the more he swishes it around. I think it's the sharing aspect they're working on, but I'd be more concerned about brutal intent.

Either way, Freddie is a dab hand at aiming the blade. He never misses his targets. A swipe here, a swipe there; all innocent massacres of course. After all, he's only a child but his aims are carefully directed and he always man-

ages to miss the other children by the slightest of margins when he gets in close. He's quite the little warrior with the sharpest of eyes. I've been watching the playground antics from a distance.

My online purchases arrive as I get home. The postman jokes that Christmas must have come early. Little does he know. I take the parcels into the sitting room, place them neatly in the corner and fetch the gin. It's cocktail time.

I squeeze a lemon, pour the juice into the shaker before adding sugar syrup, a few chopped rosemary leaves and fresh egg whites. I then add the sloe gin and shake. Faster and faster. Harder and harder. Round and round, high in the air. Once it has frothed I pour the liquid into an iced glass and savour the nectar.

Before lifting the first parcel onto the table, I turn up the music; 'Tales from Vienna Woods' by Strauss and dance round the room. One two three. One two three. One two three. My partner is imaginary, following my rhythm but I control the steps.

I then start to open the parcels but in the wrong order. I make a mental note to number them for Freddie so that he keeps the most exciting till last; I know children's habits so well.

The sword is even more lifelike than in the pictures

and is razor sharp. The claims were true. It's come all the way from China. I'm amazed at the glint of steel, the sharp lethal tip, and wonder at the ease of purchase.

I rip open the second package and a piece of material falls out. It's the waist sash. The plastic helmet, tight black pants and armoured plate will certainly hit the spot. Freddie will whoop in delight at the samurai outfit. What child wouldn't? It will only be when he's wielding the metal blade with gay abandon that there will be concerns. It's doubtful that the sharpness of the blade will be picked up on immediately in all the excitement, but it soon will be.

Yet I'm not worried. I'm confident that he will use the lifelike weapon with aplomb. I've watched him practice. I know he'll not injure anyone but it's important that others will construe things differently. When the present, with its sharp dangerous dimensions, is questioned the finger will point in her direction. I'll make sure of that.

The parcels will be waiting when the children get home from school.

I slow my movements, dizzy from all the spinning.

Children are every parent's Achilles heel. Keeping them safe is what matters most. I know that's how it is. As I toss my head back and throw down the rest of the gin cocktail, I swallow the memories. Like the lemon, they're sharp and bitter.

That's how it is for most parents. They watch their children closely. Filter danger. Keep them safe. But not my parents. I was invisible. My nightmares were belittled as the wild imaginings of a vivid imagination. They would pass. It was all part of growing up.

37

I'm walking up and down, back and forth through the bedding plants at our local garden centre, looking for inspiration. A young member of staff with 'Seasons in Bloom' emblazoned in bright yellow font on the back of his shirt is wielding a hose, spraying everything in sight. The hose writhes like a snake, squirming furiously in his grasp. Today is forecast to be the hottest day of the year so far.

Travis is too weak to join me, happy to potter at home and wait in for the children. Queenie should have dropped them off by now. Logic tells me I should be missing him; early days and all that, but truth is I'm glad to be out of the house with its suffocating atmosphere. The early euphoria of his arrival, with a battered half-filled suitcase, has already dissipated and the realism is smothering me.

I push the trolley vacantly past the geraniums. The red, pink and white displays are the reason I came but are depressing with their cheerfulness. My back garden has taken time to perfect, the colourful beds my pride and joy, and the geraniums are for the front. I'm adept at nurturing both the garden and myself, pruning when required and digging out the weeds. Looking after Travis is a whole new ball game though. He's sapping my energy and his tears of self-pity have come as a shock. The 'good time bad boy', who seemed so appealing, so suitable for my purposes after months of meticulous planning, has drowned in the deluge.

I cram the trolley full of plants, sticking to my list and throw in a couple of trowels alongside. Freddie and Emily will help me liven up the front of the house; perhaps parenting practice will help. As an afterthought I add a couple of sets of children's gardening gloves, pink and sky blue for Emily and dark green and yellow for Freddie.

In the café, I linger over tea and scones, amazed at the pleasure of eating on my own when I've craved company for so long. Perhaps this is what happens when you reach your goal: *Anticlimax with a capital A.*

* * *

When I pull into the driveway, everything is unnaturally quiet. I've only been gone a couple of hours but it seems a lot longer. I lock the car, leaving the flowers in the boot for the kids to carry in, and tentatively put the key in the front door, half expecting Freddie to come pounding down the hall shouting 'Miss Digby, Miss Digby.' But there's no noise, not a soul in sight. When I reach the kitchen, I see the sliding doors leading out to the patio are open wide. Perhaps they're all playing hide and seek and deliberately keeping voices to a whisper. But no one is playing and the scene in front of me is like the aftermath of a nuclear bomb, orchestrated by an eerie silence.

'What the fuck?' I freeze at the sight of the decimation, every single plant has been beheaded; death is everywhere.

Emily is choking out subdued sobs, the aftershocks of a major outburst. Travis is holding her close, patting her head, his eyes glazed.

'What's happened? Travis?' My voice is calm but Travis seems to have lost his.

Brown cardboard boxes, ripped apart, have been discarded by the back door and Freddie's and Emily's names, in bold ink, are vaguely decipherable on the packaging.

'Travis?' I repeat. 'Where's Freddie? For Christ's sake what's going on?'

'It's not Freddie's fault,' is Travis' opening gambit. 'You shouldn't have bought him the sword, Beverley. It was so sharp.'

'What bloody sword? What are you talking about?'

'The outfit was fine but what were you thinking?'

The sword, its evil glint twinkling, lies discarded amongst the decimated flower heads. Coloured, shrivelling petals and clustered blooms lie defeated on the ground; dead soldiers cut down in the prime of life. The bare stalks point proudly heavenwards, a declaration that survival is possible without such colourful adornments.

I walk through the garden, picking up and dropping the flowers that have been sliced through the throat with a clean sharp swoosh of metal. The sword has small bits of green and yellow stuck to the end and as I peer more closely I make out the merest speck of blood.

'Where's Freddie?' Sweat has formed an oily slick across my skin but Travis' immobility tempers my fear. If there'd been serious injury, he'd have forgotten his limp and run to the rescue. Nevertheless my stomach is tight.

'Upstairs, I think. Don't be cross with him. Tell him it's your fault that you didn't know how sharp the sword was.'

Emily stares at me. I'm the stranger she's never met whom Travis said she would adore. From the eyes, I'm not so sure but perhaps I no longer want to be adored.

I wander through the house, in and out of rooms, upstairs and down until I finally head for the cellar. It's kept bolted but not locked. I used to hide down here or up in the attic and will someone to come and find me, but no one ever did. Instinct tells me this is where I'll find Freddie.

'Freddie. I know you're in here. I want to talk. I'm not cross with you.' There's a faint rustling noise from behind the wine rack. 'Okay. When you're ready, come on up.' I switch the light off again and go to pull the door to, leaving the cellar in darkness. I knew it would do the trick.

'Miss Digby. I'm here.'

From behind the rows and rows of red wine, a collection it took my father twenty years to amass, a small samurai warrior appears, looking like a minia-ture monster and reminds me of ET waddling out from his hideout; an ugly, threatening alien with a child's heart.

'Come on. I'm here.'

As he slinks towards me, his head downcast and emitting loud blubbery sounds I'm reminded of Travis. He's a little man on his early journey to become a big cry baby.

I hug him close and pat his soft head, free from the confines of the helmet which has been discarded near the wine bottles. 'You're not in trouble. It's okay.'

As Freddie and I ascend the steep wooden planks together, hand in hand, I'm thinking about what I'll say to Travis. His accusations ring loud and clear in my ears. I'm not sure if he really believes I would have done such a thing or if he's trying to find an excuse to blame me for the mess his life is in and maybe give him a way out if he decides to slope back home to Queenie.

The sheen has definitely come off my illusion of happy families, but whatever happens, I'll call the shots. Travis will only be given a 'get out of jail free' card if I decide as he certainly won't be walking away of his own free will. Scott is testimony that this wouldn't be a good idea.

Once we're back upstairs, cold lemonade with squeezed lemons floating on the top helps to placate

Freddie. His shuddering shoulders and heaving tear-less sobs finally abate as he ambles out to find his sister among the carved-up blooms. I can't help wondering if he'll try to locate the offending weapon, the trophy that caught the attention.

Travis is sitting on the garden wall, head in hands. He probably struggled outside with a much less pronounced limp when I was out of sight. I've seen his movement from afar when he thinks I'm not looking but he'll cling to victim status as long as he thinks he can get away with it.

'If you didn't send the presents then who did?' He doesn't look at me as I sit alongside, uncomfortable in the face of confrontation. He'll be hoping I can offer an alternative so that he won't have to make any momentous decisions about the future, at least not today.

I play along. Queenie would be my obvious suggestion but he needs to come to that conclusion on his own. He'll stick up for her, claiming her brilliance as a caring and wonderful mother, certain that it could never have been her. Not in a million years. We'll see about that.

'I've no idea,' I reply, biting back the finger pointing. The boxed presents point at someone who either has it in for Queenie and Travis, or perhaps someone who hates children. Then again it must surely cross his mind that someone has it in for me. I told him over supper about the dead badger saga. Although he didn't say much at the time, he must surely be putting put two and two together that I might indeed have a vicious vengeful stalker playing some weird game of tit for tat.

'That sword could have sliced my head off. Or Emily's.' He doesn't mention that my head could have ended up on a platter, perhaps because I wasn't home at the time and therefore he doesn't think I was ever in any danger. But I don't think that's the reason.

Travis' tone is chilly and accusatory and he's looking at me strangely, inching his way along the wall. I'm reminded of Scott who was cold and censorious when he wanted to pass the buck, like my father.

'But it didn't, did it? There's no harm done. Look. They're playing happily. That's Mercy, the neighbour's cat.'

Freddie and Emily are chasing a fat ginger tom through the garden, the lethal weapon forgotten, buried at the bottom of the refuse bin in swathes of newspaper and cardboard.

'Glass of wine? Go on. It'll be okay.'

'Go on then,' he says. Scott would have refused,

kept the blame going and my father would have pummelled my mother in the face if there'd even been a smidgeon of doubt that she was in the wrong.

But Travis is weak and apathetic with nowhere else to go. He'll not dare to try to walk out on me, not yet.

'Cheers.' I come back and hand him a long cold glass of Sauvignon.

'Whatever,' he replies and knocks it back in one.

38

Scott's eyes bored into Colgate as the detective read through the entries. Incidents, times and dates were clearly marked and Scott had also attached email and photographic evidence.

'Quite a whizz with a spreadsheet. It's all very clear, Mr Barry. Well done.' Full marks young man but 'I wish you'd stop wasting my time' was shot through Colgate's tone.

Scott needed him to understand that this wasn't simple amorous revenge. He leant forward in his chair, pushed his face closer. 'Listen, I've had twenty-four silent phone calls, sixteen rogue emails and fourteen anonymous photographs sent to me and Cosette.' Scott stubbed his finger hard onto the spreadsheet, making Colgate recoil. The detective's lips puffed out.

'Look. This has all been since the dead badger incident.' Scott carried on, pointed his finger at the date column and ran it down through the entries. 'There's been no let up.' Christ. The detective was treating him like the mad person. Scott stared across the table, his eyes pleading with Colgate to understand.

'I see.' But Colgate didn't see. 'Mr Barry. Old and young are winding people up all the time on social media, texting, posting unflattering photographs and suchlike. Also, I have to tell you that Miss Digby has made similar accusations against you. It's looking a lot like tit for tat from where I'm sitting.'

Colgate picked up the photographs and casually flicked back and forth through the pile.

'That's me with my ex-girlfriend, Danielle. Remember she had the nasty accident and lost our baby? You were the SIO on the case.'

'I remember. Why have you put this photograph in the pile?'

'Because it was sent to Cosette, my new girlfriend, addressed to her personally. It's a deliberate attempt to cause us problems. You see, I met Danielle for a drink after she rang me; I didn't think it would do any harm. I thought it best to tell her, face to face, that I was with someone else and hoped there'd be no hard feelings. It was a chance to draw a line under the past.'

* * *

Colgate was finding it hard to take the guy seriously. Mr Barry had real ego issues and seemed to be under the impression that all three women hankered after him. The detective couldn't see the attraction, especially now that Mr Barry was on part-time stress leave from work, citing depression and panic attacks. His hair wasn't so slickly styled and his eyes were red and puffy; blotchy cheeks hinted at too much alcohol. Far too much time on his hands.

'Do you think Cosette might have followed you, taken the picture herself? Perhaps she was trying to catch you out?' Colgate knew it was a ridiculous suggestion but it was too tempting not to wind Barry up for being such an arrogant prick.

'She wouldn't. I know it's from Beverley.'

'How can you be so sure? Have you any proof?'

Scott let out a dry cough and sipped from a water bottle. 'I just know. She's still angry and jealous.'

Scott's voice was ragged as if a saw had hacked through his voice box.

'Okay, Mr Barry. I hear you. But according to Miss Digby, she has a new boyfriend, who's living with her. She seems to have moved on.' Colgate hesitated, cleared his own throat and teased out the punchline. 'Is it possible you've got another enemy? Another woman perhaps who's got it in for you?'

* * *

Colgate was on a roll and Scott could feel the tables turning back on him.

'Beverley told me that herself, but she still won't let up.'

'Do you think she's hoping you'll get back together? Seems a bit extreme to have another man move in to make someone else jealous.' A sarcastic chuckle popped out from the back of Colgate's throat, and a questioning eyebrow shot up.

'No. It's nothing like that. I'm afraid of what she'll do next.'

Colgate stacked the evidence neatly together and thanked Scott for taking the time in collating such a succinct report. The detective offered polite platitudes, and assured Mr Barry they would look into the case but Scott knew he was being panned off. Unless Beverley arrived at his home with a handgun and a shitload of pellets, he was on his own.

As Scott slipped on his jacket, Colgate sat forward and peered more closely at the last couple of photographs in the pile. The detective's tongue ran over his lips and his eyes moved rapidly from one picture to the other.

* * *

The Grim Reaper, black-cloaked and wielding a scythe, Colgate knew was the personification of death. The scythe was for reaping the dead. Yet these photographs were no caricatures, or cartoon drawings of the imagined monster that had first surfaced in the Middle Ages. Someone had dressed up in a costume. A hard theatrical skull had been placed over their head and long skeletal hands protruded from the cuffs of the cape. It was the attention to detail that caught the detective's eye.

He knew these last two pictures were no wind-up holiday snaps or photographic evidence taken by a private detective. These were death threats, plain and simple. Maybe Mr Barry wasn't such a timewaster after all.

'When did you get these?'

'Yesterday. I thought it best to bring them along. Why? Do you think there's a problem? Should I be worried?' Scott gripped the edge of the table.

'Not necessarily but someone's gone to a lot of trouble here. I'd just say to be vigilant. Same goes for your girlfriend. We'll follow up with Miss Digby and let you know of any progress. I'd like to keep hold of these pictures if you don't mind.'

'Yes, of course. Keep the whole log.'

'I will if that's okay.'

Scott hovered but Colgate managed to convince him that they were taking his claims seriously and would be investigating.

* * *

Back outside, Scott turned the collar up on his jacket and shivered. The sun was high overhead, the sky cloudless, but cold sweat bathed his body and the tremor was back in his hands. Why had the Grim Reaper photographs caught Colgate's attention? Christ, what was he dealing with?

* * *

Colgate returned to his office and shut himself away, pouring out a neat malt and wiping a clean handkerchief across his forehead. The pictures of the Grim Reaper had churned up memories.

He'd been on the force, in the area, for only a few months when he'd had his first taste of a real case which brought him face to face with murder. It was the sort of incident that feeds a true detective's appetite. As rookie sidekick to DCI Quinn, Colgate learnt that sometimes there was no escape from the gore. Cops had to swallow back the bile, take deep breaths and force themselves to look.

The murder scene had been a small back-garden shed of a semi-detached house a few streets away from Southgate Police Station. It had involved a 160mm miniature garden sickle with a curved blade and finely serrated edge. One tiny slash had been enough to sever the victim's carotid artery. The weapon had lain abandoned on the victim's chest without trace of a fingerprint or drop of blood, other than the victim's.

The murderer had never been caught. But when Chuck 'Chuckles' Curry, the fat bastard who died, was posthumously convicted as a serial paedophile, no one really cared. Six boys and girls, aged between eight and thirteen inched their way forward. The newspapers were mainly concerned with the grue-some details of the death and the horrors of abuse, but Colgate always wondered what happened to the perpetrator. They'd been no nearer to making a conviction at the end of the case than at the beginning.

Call it instinct, a detective's best weapon, but the photographs in front of him were bringing it all back. It was a nagging suspicion, but Colgate thought it might be possible that he was looking at pictures sent by the paedophile's executioner.

The more he thought about all the weird stalking reports on his desk, combined with this latest montage, the more uneasy he felt. Stalking might be the outward manifestation of obsessive, unhinged behaviour, but the roots were often deep-seated, planted by more than amorous rejection. Stalkers with serious issues, those who needed to regain control, could be extremely dangerous, even murderous. He thought of John Lennon, gunned down outside his apartment, and JFK shot in broad daylight, both incidences carried out by psychopathic stalkers.

Colgate sat back and let the malt sting his throat. Maybe he was overtired, stressed or overreacting but there was definitely something sinister afoot and, if his hunch was right, something he shouldn't ignore.

39

The rain is a relief. I turn my face heavenwards as I amble towards the hospital and let it wash over me. No doubt Ms Evans will try to look for some deep-seated psychological reason why I've decided not to bring an umbrella. Perhaps I have masochistic tendencies or it's down to a dearth of sexual activity that makes me crave wetness. Truth is, I don't own one.

I've left early today, desperate to escape from what was meant to be marital bliss but has instead turned into a nightmare. Travis can't go home as Queenie won't have him back and he's nowhere else to go. The kids are inconsolable, caught between the warring factions and banned from seeing us again since the sword incident. I'm not denying involvement in the incident too vehemently, as it's giving Travis a strong motive to leave. He won't give up seeing the kids and on his own, he knows he stands a much better chance that Queenie will capitulate, although I'm not so sure.

Travis doesn't yet know that I'm in therapy, seeing his wife for so-called stalking addiction. While I've never told him, I'm amazed that his darling Queenie hasn't imparted this rather colossal piece of information to her cheating spouse. After the sword incident there was no doubt that she realised I was the other woman, but I'm not sure how long she has really known. I suspect it could have been all along and she's been masterful at hiding the knowledge.

But it looks as if we might continue the pretence for my remaining two therapy sessions. Ms Evans is the consummate professional, able to completely separate her work and private lives. Yet it's starting to feel that she's glad to be shot of Travis and I'm the one to have opened the door.

Targeting her husband was meant to be fun, especially as he was such a suitable substitute for Scott and with a ready-made family in tow. I wanted Ms Evans to condone my ability to move on, be pleased that I'd found what I was looking for. Only when she discovered I'd stolen her husband from under her nose would her mask slip. With the jigsaw pieced together, she was meant to lash out; lose her cool and then she might understand my own actions. This now doesn't look likely as she is one weirdly controlled piece of work.

As I approach the hospital entrance she's standing by her window, watching me. She's dressed in yellow, a strange choice for someone who normally courts duty in dark colours. I think of a canary in a cage and wave back. The bright, happy attire might be to play me at my own game, no dull shades of defeat in sight.

In the foyer I shake myself down, dripping large water globules onto the smart marbled Italian tiles, and tiptoe gently towards her door. A distinct trail of brown muddy spots, like drips of freshly spilt paint, follows me.

'Come in!' she calls out, before I knock, and then opens the door wide.

'Hi. Sorry about the mess.' I look behind me.

'Don't worry. It'll be easily cleaned off. Come on in but maybe leave your shoes at the door.'

Her sunny outfit is accessorised with matching yellow shoes and white shiny pearls; an over-the-top reflection of an upbeat mood. Although we're both playing a dangerous game, I suspect she now can't wait to see the back of me.

'Well, Beverley. We're nearly at the end of our sessions. Take a seat.' She indicates the armchair rather than the couch. Perhaps she thinks I'm already well on the mend, lying down no longer necessary to help me relax and encourage conversation. Or perhaps it's her way of punishing me by keeping me upright, unable to close my eyes and soul to her beady stare. It crosses my mind that she might be preparing to confront me about Travis and wants to do it face to face.

'Okay. Let's start off by you telling me how you are. What's your week been like?'

Where to start? I have a lot to offload and although she'll have guessed at most of it, she'll listen for the money.

'Not great. You see my new boyfriend, Terence, has moved in. Left his wife and kids but it's not as I imagined.' I stick my chin out, expression deadpan. My thespian skills are every bit as good as hers. Let the farce begin.

'Oh. In what way? What did you imagine, Beverley? And isn't his name Travis? Come on. You can be honest with me now, surely.' She grins, all perfect teeth.

I ignore the fact that the gameplaying regarding my theft of her husband is up, and carry on.

'I thought we'd be happy. I'd been planning it for so long. Our living together, building a relationship but it's not working out.'

'Why not?' Ms Evans is blinking hard. The pollen count must be high but at least it's wiped the smirk from her face.

'He's not very well and I'm not a very good nurse. I'd been looking forward to the fun things. Also his wife won't let the kids visit, she's overly protective.' Ha. Take that.

I don't mention the sword incident which led her to ban further visits to my house. In her shoes I'd probably do the same. She guesses Travis still doesn't know who sent the weapon and he seems to have labelled both me and Queenie as likely perpetrators. He's not sure which way to lean. He isn't blaming either of us for evil intent but rather stupidity and carelessness where his kids were involved.

Knowing Travis, he's most likely to blame the person who won't provide him with a roof over his head. Also when he learns his wife has known all along about our affair, he might consider it a possibility that she sent the sword with the intention that the outside world, the unbiased eye, would be likely to point the finger my way. After all, I am certified clinically unbalanced.

'Tell me more.' Her forefinger has lodged in her eye, stuck in situ but she doesn't rub at it.

'Also Terence, oops. Sorry, I meant Travis, doesn't know that I'm in therapy for stalking. I'd hoped to come clean, tell him everything once he moved in but now I can't; well, not so much can't as can't be bothered. I no longer see the point.'

'Why's that, Beverley?'

Her manner is starting to rankle, like the first time I came. Short, pithy questions are loaded with sarcastic innuendo and she's playing the 'let's pretend' game with increasing aplomb. She's emphasising that all I am to her is a patient, not the mistress of her errant husband. Ms Evans knows that Travis and I have no future together, that I'm already bored in my new role but I'm sensing that she doesn't really care. If I'd hoped to rattle her, I've failed. She's no interest in her husband, probably hasn't done in a long time and she's definitely coming across as the star of our two-man show.

'I think he's got too much baggage. Also he doesn't trust me.'

I recap on how we met, the sexual attraction and my hopes of a happy ever after. I think it only fair she knows the truth, it's what she advocates after all. She listens carefully and tosses out a few random questions as if she's been rehearsing how to approach the session.

I came prepared for anger and even a measure of vitriol should she decide to bring the subject out into the open but it's a relief that she wants to carry on with the charade. For now it's easier. It's what we've being doing for weeks anyway, pretending, so why open up now?

'Should he? Trust you, Beverley?' Her eyes have shrunk to slits and she peers at me like a stuffed un-purring Siamese cat.

'He doesn't believe I have a stalker. He thinks I'm making it up to cover tracks of things I've done that make him uncomfortable.'

'Do you really have a stalker?' She cocks her head to one side with a mildly patronising look.

'Yes.'

40

Ms Evans has been waiting for me to talk about my own stalker. So far we've only touched on it, yet it would seem central to my case considering we've spent the last few months trying to unravel my inclination to stalk and torment my lovers. She's never really got to the bottom of my behaviour so how could she understand? The only thing I felt might make things right, give my life meaning and bury the past was children, but Scott killed that chance. I don't really expect Ms Evans to get it, although taking her husband out from under her nose was meant to give her a better handle on emotional abandonment.

I want to lie down and run through the possibilities and talk about my fears. I'm still finding it hard to pinpoint who hates me sufficiently to keep me awake at night with all manner of silent phone calls and online threats, not to mention the red paint sprayed across my car.

It's most likely to be Scott, after payback for my collusion with Cosette. He's still convinced I'd something to do with Danielle's accident and the loss of their baby, so certainly he's got motive.

Then there's Ms Evans herself. She must be furious that I spent so long enticing her playboy husband into my bed and then into my home. On the outside, she seems a caring hands-on sort of mother. But I wonder what she's like behind closed doors and what she might be capable of; especially with two small children to protect. She's plenty of reason to send threats, get up at night and torment me with nasty emails and phone calls. The problem is that, face to face, my instinct tells me she's little feeling left for her husband. Why waste her energy on someone who seems to have done her a favour?

Danielle's a possibility. Maybe I've been too introverted, too distraught over my own inability to have children, that I haven't given her enough attention. Now Scott is playing happy families with Cosette, I've kept my distance from Danielle. But perhaps she still blames me for the death of her baby and might not be so motherly towards children in my care.

Then there is Cosette who is as obsessed with Scott as I was, determined to keep him at all costs. She could be looking out for him, keeping his fear of me alive, to feather her own nest, but I can't see it. She's too nice.

Lastly, I want to ask Ms Evans about Bob Pratchett. I know he's a paranoid schizophrenic, believing in a world conspiracy that is out to kill him. He follows people around, attaches himself to the most unlikely candidates. A lover of pretty women, he fantasises about sexual conquests. The whole of the Abbott Hospital has heard of the famous movie stars that he's bedded, but it's not his boasts of impossible exploits that bothers me. It was seeing him with Queenie that day at the hospital and the red paint along the side of my car. Could it be possible he is my stalker? Or is he working hand in glove with Queenie; Ms Evans? It's not impossible they could be having an affair.

* * *

'Beverley?' Her voice jolts me back. I've been so deep in thought it's as if I've been hypnotised again.

'May I have a glass of water? Sorry, I'm really parched.' My throat is scratchy, stress threatening a summer bug. Ms Evans hands me a filled glass from the chilled plastic water dispenser by her desk.

'It's nothing concrete, but sometimes I think someone is watching me. Got it in for me. A bit like I had it in for Scott.' The past tense here is good, confirming it was the old me who trailed my ex-lover. I need to be signed off.

On the spur of the moment I decide it wisest not to say any more. An inkling of relapse, of a greater unbalanced state of mind, and I'll be enrolled for another six weeks. It crosses my mind that Ms Evans is enjoying the session and might be consciously using the time to make me squirm. She might never let me off the hook and might even use her authority to have me sectioned.

'Go on. I'm listening.' She's nudging me towards the landmine.

'Oh it's nothing. Just my imagination.'

Ms Evans sighs and sets her pen down. 'Okay. But if you change your mind, I'm here.' She pauses. 'Anyway, we've nearly reached the end of the road. I think it's our last session next week. Then we'll be out of each other's hair. Why don't you tell me how you think the therapy has gone?'

She's disappointed that I've clammed up but she's letting it go. She's got that fed-up look of a mother, unable to stifle the leaden sigh of disappointment in her child. For now the caring façade has been replaced by a look of resignation. My first impression that she's plain nosey hasn't been dispelled. She'll be wondering why I targeted Travis, especially after I knew they were a couple, and won't be certain if it was deliberate or coincidental. She might even be wondering if she was my choice of therapist after I met her husband or before.

'I think it's been really helpful.' This is what needs to go in her professional report.

'I need to let Mr Hoarden, and the police, know that you have your stalking habits under control and won't be bothering Mr Barry any more. Can I assure them of this, Beverley?'

'Definitely.' I smile. Bright and breezy. La-di-da-di-da.

I don't voice my opinion that it's all been a colossal waste of time and taxpayers' money, as Ms Evans has probably come to the same conclusion. But I can't back off from Scott, especially if he's my tit-for-tat stalker and sharing this information would likely put me back to square one. I'll only leave Scott alone when the punishment fits the crime.

'Well, it looks as if next week will be our last meeting. I hope it all works out well with Terence-slash-Travis. Whatever his name is.' She gives a wry smile but keeps her head buried in her notes and scribbles furiously.

'Thanks. It feels good to be moving on.'

We stand up at the same time, like a couple of business colleagues who have concluded a satisfactory, if relatively unproductive, meeting. Ms Evans extends her hand, clasping mine in a conclusive gesture of solidarity, but then she tightens her grip until my bones rebel with a faint crunching noise.

'Well done, Beverley. I think we've covered a lot of ground. Till next week.'

'Thank you. Maybe we'll open a bottle of champagne and toast my progress and the end of the road. Bye for now.'

With that I am gone.

41

When I get back from my therapy session, an empty, desolate feeling engulfs the house. As soon as I step into the hall I know he's gone.

'Travis?'

There's no reply and no pungent smell of coffee which was his calling card and the lingering smell of rank roll-up tobacco has faded.

'Travis?' I check the rooms on the ground floor, one by one. He'd been up and about when I left, so I don't bother going upstairs. Once Travis came down in the mornings he didn't venture back up until bedtime as the steep stairs made him breathless. By the time I reach the kitchen I know I'm on my own again and relief mingles with anticlimax.

A white envelope is propped up against the scented candle in the middle of the table. I rip it open and one of Travis' business cards falls out, a message scribbled on the back.

Sorry, Beverley. I can't stay as I need to see the children. Leaving is my only chance that Queenie will mellow. I've booked into a B&B for the time being but will be in touch.
 Thanks again. Travis x

I drift towards the kettle, wondering at the illusion of it all. So much effort and planning and what for? Perhaps playing happy families is not the answer, and Ms Evans has a point, that it's time to move on, face the demons on my own.

The sight of the dead plants through the back window makes me shiver. *Project Travis* was never meant to end so suddenly and the scattered wilted flowers and decaying greenery mirrors the shallowness of our relationship. The roots had been weak, nothing to bind them together. My relationships all seem to skim the surface. The new plants are still sitting by the back door in their plastic containers.

I turn on the radio, inviting the noise of upbeat melodies to smother the sadness. I think Ms Evans would prefer to hear about misery, let down and neuroses following on from her husband's departure so it's hard not to laugh. What a wicked web we weave.

I carry my coffee through to the store room and pick out a new tin of green paint from the rack, holding it up to contemplate the colour. My eyes scan the array of shades lined up in both gloss and matt.

* * *

With my tin of choice, I trundle up the stairs with the small ladders, winding my way up three flights of steep rickety stairs and past three landings towards the attic. As a child I was a mountaineer, each step inching towards the summit, careering backwards more than once.

The attic needs a complete revamp. It sits on top of the world, my world. It was a good hiding place, a place to be alone where the noise couldn't reach. Farther away from my warring parents than the cellar, distance drowning out the toxic decibels.

With the long window pole I push open the skylight, blinking away a dust shower that cascades over me. Cleansing away the memories of the past will be the way forward and I'll tell Ms Evans next week; she'll be proud of me.

I trundle back down the stairs again, having forgotten the brush and paint tray, and, as I walk past, can't resist the temptation to open my laptop. I'm not expecting any new messages but it's a habit.

I'm soon staring at the computer screen and wonder what's going on. There are three new emails from someone purporting to be from a website called *thejokesonus.com*. The website is like YouTube for the illusionist. Impossible magic tricks are paraded on the home page. Passing coins through glass. Walking on water. Climbing skyscrapers side on and levitating rogue pieces of paper into the air. I'm mesmerised by each clip even though I've seen them all before. The site is trying to convince the watcher of magic powers, rather than sleight of hand. *Seeing is Believing* is their motto which is printed large, in bold red, as a strap line which moves continuously across the top of the home page.

The first email is inviting me to join up. It's not clear at first what I'd be signing up to other than having the chance to watch online videos of weird and whacky illusions free of charge. But it seems to be some sort of a club. Become a magician, become an illusionist. They'll show you how.

Hi Beverley

Now is your chance to join our very exclusive club, thejokesonus.com. This is a once-in-a-lifetime opportunity not to be missed. Learn the tricks of the trade; perform in public and line your pockets. This is a personal invitation extended by one of our team of Master Tricksters.
Reply today or lose the chance.

The email is signed from JY at Master Tricksters. I'm not sure why the email didn't hit my spam box but I click delete and move on to the second message.

Hi Beverley
I wonder if you've worked out who I am. I know your love of tricks and illusions, and as we're recruiting, you were obviously my first port of call. Go on… join us. What fun it'll be.
Master Trickster

At this point I'm feeling uneasy at having been addressed by name in both messages. The personal touch encourages me to read the blurb.

It's the third email though that really grabs my attention, and as I stare at the content I wonder, for a second, if it could be genuine. My stomach does a somersault.

Hi You

Don't you recognise who it is? Come on, it's not been that long, surely? I just couldn't resist getting in touch. You see, I'm back in England. Yes, I am a Master Trickster but have decided to continue my trade back home.

If you've forgiven me (????) then I'd love to meet up. Have a few drinks and grab a bite to eat? Let me know. Send me your number and I'll know I'm in with a chance. Where are you living these days? Back at the family home? Anyway, hope to see you soon.

Lots of love

Jeremy x

I delete the email and snap shut the laptop. My hands are shaking, my neck flushed. A sudden cramp shoots up my left calf, the pain drawing tears from my eyes.

I pull up the cuff of my sweatshirt and look at the deep red angry welts across my left wrist. With the passing of time they're more, not less, pronounced. I wear long sleeves as camouflage when I visit Ms Evans.

The Stanley knife cut sweetly, seamlessly and the first cut was the deepest. That was Jeremy; my first lover, the man I dared to trust after my father let me down. I opened up, bared my soul and let him in and tried to draw a flimsy curtain across the past. It didn't keep the darkness out but softened the edges. When he disappeared, raised his anchor and set sail, I was adrift and death seemed the best option.

I go to the fridge, lift out the white wine and release the cork from last night's half empty bottle. I fill a large glass until liquid drizzles over the top, the tremor in my hands like the precursor to a major earthquake. With eyes closed, I tilt my head and gulp, wiping my lips with the back of my hand before choking the final mouthful into the sink.

* * *

The barren stalks outside remind me of death. The wilting stems, dead men walking, remind me of how I felt when Jeremy left. After the failed suicide attempt, despair turned to fury; then fury to action. Finding an outlet took time but I learnt not to give up, not to let go. The solution that afforded the greatest satisfaction, if not peace, was meting out punishment.

The clock ticking interrupts my thoughts. It's like the crocodile in *Peter Pan*, *tick-tocking* its way to eat me up. I refill my glass and wonder at the timing. Jeremy's emails have hit my inbox the moment Travis has left. I'm not sure what is making me so uneasy. Surely I should be pleased that he has returned, eager to inveigle his way back in? Yet it crosses my mind that someone could be playing tricks on me; someone who knows about Jeremy's and my past together and about that particular Achilles heel.

I became a so-called *stalker* as a way to regain control after Jeremy left and the failed suicide attempt. A determination never again to be treated badly gave me a goal, a way to deal with things. Stalking just sort of happened and the word became linked to my behaviour. 'An eye for an eye' became my mantra. It's taken up all my time and energy ever since, giving me a reason to get up in the mornings.

Perhaps Jeremy really is back. He won't know about my abortive trips to America to track him down. Only Ms Evans is privy to that information. What does he want? Why now?

A bird is pecking at something on the patio, his beak persistent against the sandstone. There's a small piece of stale bread stuck between the slabs and he's determined not to fly away without it. The persistence and intent reminds me of Jeremy when he wanted something, his beak every bit as sharp.

If he is back, it looks as if he's brought a whole

new bag of tricks with him. He was a master illusionist who tried to wow me with magic and sleight of hand. It was lucky he wasn't around when Danielle fell down the stairs as he would have guessed what had happened. He would have been proud, as he used to think I wasn't listening, wasn't interested. Little did he know.

'Not a real profession? That's what you think. Isn't it?'

Yes. That was what I thought. His tutorials bored me to distraction but turned out to have their uses.

I certainly won't be meeting up with Jeremy, if he really is back. It wouldn't take him long to piece together the puzzle of Danielle's accident. He was the person who taught me how to make people fall down stairs without leaving a trace, a clever stunt but one that might yet put me in prison.

I finish the bottle and bang hard at the window. The bird flies off, shocked into dropping the morsel from its beak. Persistence needs to be accompanied by awareness, otherwise all can be lost.

42

Queenie's emotions were bottled up like a sealed jar of pickles, the acidic bite locked inside. It was time to take the lid off, talk to someone.

She finally plucked up the courage and went to the police station, but DCI Colgate didn't seem particularly interested. When she mentioned the name Beverley Digby, he clapped both hands over his face.

'Okay. How can we help, Mrs Lowther?'

'I hope I'm not wasting your time but I'd like my concerns noted.' Queenie took a deep breath and gently whisked her fringe away from her eyes. 'I've already talked to the head teacher at my son's school but I'm not sure they're taking me seriously.'

'Go on. I'm listening.' Colgate rubbed his chin, sat

back and swizzled the end of a pen round in his mouth. PC Lindsay, with a fresh notebook in front of her, proceeded to date the page neatly across the top.

Queenie spoke quietly, her voice shaky. 'Miss Digby is a teacher at my son Freddie's school. She's only there a couple of afternoons a week, so I haven't met her properly in the school surroundings. I work daytimes and a neighbour picks up the children. It's just that...' Queenie cleared her throat, a dry nervous sound, and took a sip of water from a plastic cup. 'It's just that, Miss Digby has been seeing my husband, Travis, behind my back and he's moved in with her.'

'I see.' Colgate's fingers reached down his back and scratched, as if trying to ease a nagging itch.

'Oh, that's not what I care about. That's not why I'm here,' Queenie continued, reading his thoughts. 'The kids are my concern. They went round for tea last weekend and something very unsettling happened. I wanted to report it. You see, Miss Digby bought our son, Freddie, a present, which according to my husband was an innocent mistake. But the present was a samurai sword. It wasn't a plastic make-believe toy, but it had a sharp steel blade, like the real thing.' Queenie lifted her phone off the table and scrolled through some photographs, her fingers damp as she tried to wipe off smudge marks with a tissue.

'Look. Freddie took this picture himself after he had deadheaded flowers in the back garden with a single flick of the blade.'

Colgate took the phone, checked the screenshot and turned it towards Lindsay.

'You see my problem? What normal person would give a boy of ten a sword that could chop someone's head off?' Queenie took another sip of water, uncomfortable doing the talking but if the detective had kids of his own, he'd understand.

'Yes, I do. It seems a very strange gift indeed. Do you think she realised how sharp it was? Perhaps she bought it online and thought it was just a toy?'

'She's passing the buck. She says she didn't buy the sword, that it had nothing to do with her and that it was in a parcel which arrived for the children. She maintains she knew nothing about it until Freddie had ruined her precious garden. My worry is, whether she knew about it or not, she's not the sort of person who should be teaching my children. Or any children for that matter.'

* * *

Colgate listened to Mrs Lowther's calm precise delivery but was hit by the intensity in her words. This was no rantings of a spurned wife, rather the fury of a mother whose children had been put in danger and the outcome could have been very different.

'Thank you, Mrs Lowther. Have you got all this down, Lindsay?'

'Yes, boss.'

'We've logged your concerns and the school will be notified. While we've no jurisdiction over their staffing policies, we can at least make sure they're aware of the incident.'

Queenie stood up, straightened her skirt, and smoothed it down with both hands. 'Thank you. That's all I want. If she steps out of line again, they'll have to take action.'

'I'm sorry about your husband, by the way. That must have been upsetting.'

Queenie's cheeks flushed, a wry smile on her lips. 'Not really. He's already moved back home.'

* * *

Once Mrs Lowther had gone, Colgate turned to his colleague.

'Lindsay. Can you hang around? I've got something I need to run through with you.'

Colgate disappeared, and returned a few minutes later holding a pile of box files balanced precariously one on top of the other.

'I need you to go through these case reports with a fine toothcomb, and do some serious digging.' Colgate pushed the hefty boxes towards Lindsay.

'Yes, sir. What's it about?'

'I want you to look into an old case from some twenty-five years ago. A guy got murdered in a garden shed in Holdenhurst Avenue not far from here. Off Southgate High Street near the Tube station, and no one ever got charged. It was a strange case because as a serial paedophile, the guy who got murdered warranted little sympathy. No one seemed to care at the time. "Just deserts" and all that. The thing that bothers me is that the victim was garrotted with a garden scythe. It might be nothing but I'm putting two and two together with recent events and coming to ten.'

'What recent events? Sorry, I'm not quite with you.'

'Firstly, Mr Barry receives pictures of the Grim Reaper holding aloft a deadly weapon, as a sinister threat. Then Mrs Lowther tells us of how her son received a random but deadly samurai sword in the post around the same time. The one thing that links the two events is Miss Digby. Get my point, so to speak?' Colgate laughed at his own joke. 'Also, I don't believe in coincidences. Two sharp-bladed instruments have caused alarm bells with several people in a very short space of time. Do you see what I'm getting at?'

'Sort of. You think there's a connection between these two incidents and the Garden Shed murder? Seems a bit of a long shot.'

'I haven't had many murder cases over the years to deal with but I can smell a rat at fifty paces. Call it gut instinct, but I think whoever sliced Mr Chuck Curry's throat open could be back to haunt us.'

'You don't think his murder could have anything to do with Miss Digby, do you?'

'Perhaps. Maybe in some roundabout way. She would have been only about twelve or thirteen when the murder took place. I want you to check out the names of all the children who came forward at the time; victims of Curry. Check out where they are today and if any of them still live in the area. You know the drill. See if Digby's name comes up.' Colgate paused, pursed his lips and chewed the inside of his gum.

'Also it might be a good idea, if you've got any spare time, to check out the names of other kids around then who were taken into care.'

'Why? You don't think it was a kid who killed Curry?'

'Yes, I do actually. It's always been my suspicion. I think it was one very strong, determined child who severed the bastard's carotid artery.'

* * *

Queenie felt light-headed as she strolled home in the warm afternoon sunshine, letting the fine summer breeze tickle her skin. She knew so much about Beverley Digby, it would have been good to share more but patient confidentiality meant the only concerns she'd been able to raise with the police were those relating to her children's safety.

Queenie had never been a talker, always a listener. She'd bottled up so much, so many secrets over the years, but today she'd inched the memory door ajar. It wasn't much, but it was a start.

43

U

Uncle Chuck had a small back garden, which he nurtured with meticulous care. He also had an allotment on the other side of the tall spiky hedge but although he talked about it, I was never allowed to visit. I was kept hidden inside the shed.

'I don't want to share my special friend, now do I?' he would say. I realised shortly after I killed him that he was scared people would see me; know that I was there. That was why he never let me wander.

He talked to the plants, coaxing and cajoling them to full bloom. The first time I heard him outside the shed whispering, I thought he had a sick child wrapped up *tightly between the stalks; or perhaps he was minding a bird with a broken wing.*

'Come on, my beauty. Drink the water. Take in the rays and you'll grow to be big and strong.' He sprayed rain from a watering can over the mysterious object, looking skywards when he talked about the rays, spouting forth about the beneficial effects of the sun. Of course he was just a weirdo who talked to plants.

I would peer through the muddied windowpanes, tugging back the stiffened netting which smelled of damp cardboard. At the same time I crunched madly on biscuit crumbs trying to bury the taste of semen and vomit. It was this caring, nurturing façade that made me question where the blame lay for what was going on. If Uncle Chuck was so kind and considerate of plants and sick beings, then perhaps I was the one who deserved punishment.

That's when I took an interest in gardening. Perhaps if I was kinder and more nurturing, I would no longer deserve the punishment.

'This is a spade. You use this for digging holes for the larger plants and this smaller tool is a trowel. It's what I use for the bedding plants and for the colourful pots. You can have this one. Here.' He handed over the tool, his kindness confusing. It was as if the last half hour hadn't happened.

But it was the implements hanging inside along the length of the shed wall that grabbed my interest the most. Some had long handles; some short. But they had one thing in common; they all had sharp edges.

'Can I hold one?'

'They're much too heavy for little hands. When you're older.' He shouldn't have said that. The older bit. It made me think that I'd be coming here for ever.

'What about the little one on the end? What's that? Perhaps I could hold that.'

'My, you are a pest. That's a scythe. It's for dead-heading the really tough weeds. The allotment grows wild in the spring and summer and that's when the scythe comes out. I can clear the weeds in ten minutes, it's that sharp.'

'Can I try?'

'Not yet. Perhaps one day. You can finger the handle but you mustn't lift it down. It's very dangerous.' He patted me on the head, like he cared.

The handle was solid oak, smooth and fine. My hand fitted round it perfectly. I felt it wriggle in the metal slot and knew if I could stand on something, like a crate or a box, I could push it up over the top and get it down.

'How dangerous? Does it kill the plants?' I widened my eyes in childish innocence. Uncle Chuck didn't realise he'd stolen it long ago. I feigned excitement in being allowed access to adult danger. Uncle Chuck would have likened my glee to when he let me sit in his Ford Escort and turn the wheel without a key in the ignition.

His chins wobbled when he laughed. Jelly on a plate. Jelly on a plate.

'It doesn't kill the plants exactly but takes their heads off. It stops them growing and coming back. I only use it on the bad weeds, the ones that suffocate the goodness.'

My final question, and his answer, made up my mind. I knew I was strong enough to manage the scythe.

'So you only need to take the heads off and that makes everything else die and makes the soil good again? The weeds are bad then.'

'That's right, my little friend. Slice the tops off and the rest wilts and dies. No one misses them when they're gone. That's what the scythe is for.'

'Show me how you use it? Go on. Please?'

'Like this. Keep clear. You swish the blade along with a quick flick, turning your wrist as you go and everything drops in its path.'

'Like this? Is this right?' I had to make sure. I swished left and right and back again with the imaginary tool in my hand. I laughed and Uncle Chuck seemed mesmerised by my mood, my sudden hysteria.

'Come here, my poppet. Come to Uncle Chuck.'

He put the scythe carefully back in its slot and lifted me gently onto the sofa.

I no longer had to count spiders. I closed my eyes and practised swishing. Left and right; right then left. I could deadhead with one slick movement.

I also knew where the carotid artery was. It was a random fact I'd picked up at school; during a talk on parts of the body. Everyone giggled at the words penis and vagina but the jugular vein drew my attention. This titbit of information was my 'get out of jail' card. It was all I needed to know.

I was only twelve and gruesome, macabre stories had become my bedtime reading of choice. Under the warm damp duvet I concocted sinister plots, but unlike the Brothers Grimm's fairy stories, my tales had no happy endings.

44

A summer thunderstorm finally breaks through the early dawn. Dark, threatening clouds burst and release their laden contents, like a dam bursting its banks and lightning streaks herald in the deafening thunderclaps. Slumped in the driver's seat, the noise is comforting and I'm glad to have escaped the quiet confines of the house where the silence has become amplified by menaces.

Last night the phone calls started at one; then two, then every hour on the dot until sunrise. It's a nightly ritual. The ringing tone tells me I'm not mad, that it's not in my imagination. Heavy breathing follows long eerie silences and each time the caller disconnects I find the handset stuck fast to my ear, disbelieving that they've gone. I know they'll be back so don't see the need to hang up.

I keep an eye on the entrance to the police station, waiting for the first signs of life. It's still only 6am. I don't want to speak to the night officer, I need to see Colgate, my old nemesis. With what I'm bringing him, I think he'll listen. I'm banking on it.

My mind races, digging around the detritus of my brain for clues. I'll need to keep my statement clear, or I'll be palmed off, but it's not going to be easy as there are so many possibilities for who my stalker is.

The emails from Jeremy have doubled my anxiety. There was a time when contact from him would have made me euphoric, victorious that he might want me back. Now all I feel is dread and I'm worried the emails might not be genuine, but from someone playing with my mind. Scott knew about Jeremy. I'd told him often enough when we first got together. But it wasn't long before I made snide little asides about the differences in their characters, in a negative way as far as Scott was concerned, when he started to pull back and treat me badly. Jeremy wouldn't have done that. Jeremy wouldn't have said that. 'Then where the hell is this fucking precious Jeremy?' Scott would yell. I didn't know, of course. I hadn't been able to track him down. I wanted to find him, punish him and wrest back control but he'd been too slippery.

Travis also knew about Jeremy. He asked me why someone like me would be interested in an old married fogey like himself. Wasn't I interested in single guys? But Travis was cocky and stupid enough to assume his charms were ample compensation for his marital status. I couldn't tell him it was the full package, with the inclusion of two children that had fed my determination to pin him down. And of course, I was driven to wipe the smug smile off Ms Evans' face. Stealing her husband and children had been a coup d'état as far as my plan was concerned.

Ms Evans herself, of course, knows about Jeremy. Perhaps she's had a fiery argument at some point with Travis about my relationship history. She might not be as chilled as Travis lets on about our affair or as she acts in our therapy sessions. She's doubtless still trying to pin the sword incident on me as well as the crime of stealing her husband.

I start to sweat as the possibilities and permutations run through my mind. I can't halt the flow. Danielle springs to mind. She lost her baby. That would be a strong motive for hatred and revenge if she had any proof that I was involved. Perhaps Scott and she are in cahoots.

Also, Bob Pratchett makes me uneasy. I've spotted him more than once wandering around outside my house. He has the excuse that he's coming to and from the hospital but the hours don't always coincide with his appointment times and he seems to loiter.

I turn off the engine and close my eyes.

* * *

A violent rap at the window shocks me back to life and Colgate's lined weather-beaten face stares down at me. Shit. It's nine. I've been asleep for three hours. The rain has stopped and the strengthening sun has turned the car into an oven.

My eyes open and close like a camera shutter trying to focus. I slide down the window but Colgate walks on and pauses to speak to an officer loitering by the entrance before disappearing inside. The young man, crisp and fresh, nods at his superior and heads my way. He knocks more gently than Colgate but I ignore him, pull my collar up and apply a thin coat of lip gloss. When I do step out of the car, I beam at him.

'Good morning. I'm here to see DCI Colgate.' I swing my bag over my shoulder and sidestep his hovering form.

'I'm afraid he's busy this morning. Perhaps I can help you?'

'No. You're all right. It's a matter of life and death. I have something I think he'll want to see.' I stick out my chin, throw my shoulders back and stride forward. If Colgate thinks he can fob me off with one of his juniors, after having wasted so much of my time in the past, he's another think coming.

45

'Well, Miss Digby. How can we help?'

Colgate sits on the edge of his seat as if he's waiting to make a dash for it. He's fiddling with a pen but the absence of paper lets me know that he's not going to be taking notes.

I detail the late-night calls, sightings of ghostly shapes in the blackness but Colgate's face is deadpan, his mouth hanging open. He reminds me of a dog waiting for a walk, alert but immobile. When I produce my coup d'état, his bottom lip reels in and his ears prick up as if I've taken the lead off the peg, ready to go.

'What's this?' Colgate peers at the grainy photograph. It's a picture of me with Jeremy, Photoshopped in, standing alongside. A ghostly outline hovers over us. Colgate's liver-spotted hands turn the picture over and back again.

'Where did you get this? Is it recent?' He carries on squinting.

'Yes. Yesterday. It was pushed through my letter box.'

'Do you mind if I hang on to it? We'll look into your complaints and get back to you.'

'Is that it?' I knew I wouldn't get star billing with a random list of threats, but the picture of the Grim Reaper wielding a scythe over my head has hit the mark.

Colgate stands. 'That's all for now but you've got my attention.' His gritted smile presents crooked little teeth like an uncultured string of off-white pearls.

* * *

'Have a look at this.' Colgate held out the photograph with one hand and gripped a plastic coffee cup in the other, taking regular little sips. His nose curled with the bitterness.

'What is it?' Lindsay asked, studiously eyeing the snap.

'It's another Grim Reaper picture.'

'I can see that, but who are the people in the foreground?'

'It's Miss Digby with another ex-boyfriend, a Mr Jeremy Yates. She says she hasn't seen the guy for years but the picture appeared through her letter box a couple of days ago. She's convinced it's been sent to wind her up and she's freaking out. That's the Grim Reaper in the background. Notice the scythe in his hand?'

Colgate opened up one of a pile of files sitting in front of him and took out a much older, even more grainy, photograph.

'Take a look at this. Dated 13 July, twenty-five years ago. This is a murder scene with the offending weapon lying across the victim's chest.'

Lindsay swallowed. Unlike Colgate she hadn't yet experienced death in the field. There'd been a few near misses, police chases that had ended with badly smashed-up vehicles, but as yet no corpses.

The picture showed a huge, fat, white male probably in his early to mid-forties lying prostrate across a small sofa. His unclad legs hung off the side, his flaccid penis shrivelled like a dried prune perched atop his left thigh. His eyes stared in the direction of the window with fear and pleading etched large on his rigid features.

'Christ. Is this Chuck Curry? The Garden Shed Murder guy?'

'The very one. Take your eyes off his body for a minute and check out the weapon. It's a garden scythe. Not very big but lethal. One swipe was all it took.'

'They should have lopped his prick off in the process. Shit.'

Lindsay set the picture alongside the one of Miss Digby and her ex-boyfriend and looked from one to the other.

'What do you notice?' Colgate asked.

'The scythe is the same in both pictures. It's about the same length and the same shape. It could almost be the same weapon.'

'If you look very closely, you can see in the latest picture a small maker's mark at the bottom of the handle. It's a *Boysen and Horton* scythe. It's a newer model of the one used twenty-five years ago on the 13 July. I believe they're still in production.'

'Same make? How do you know?'

'It's in the file. All details of the murder weapon were logged. It had been one of a set of garden tools that the guy used to look after his allotment and if you look here, you can see the rest hanging behind the sofa, a bit to the right. The weight was also logged at the time and there was a theory that it might have been light enough for a youngster to handle, but no proof was ever found that's what happened.'

'But you think so?'

'Yes. I think some sad, molested, traumatised child took the tool and made one almighty slash across the pervert's throat. They were clever enough to wear gardening gloves, as no prints were left at the scene and gloves were never found. The child would have been smart and probably planned the whole thing in advance, as their only way out. They committed the perfect premeditated murder.'

'What's your thinking in relation to Miss Digby's and Mrs Lowther's claims? Do you think they're in danger?'

Colgate's lips were tight as he thrust the latest picture back under his colleague's nose.

'It's the date. 13 July. That's next Friday. It's not just the date that's got me worried. It's the fact that a time has been recently pencilled in alongside. 4pm.'

'You don't think...'

'You're sharp, Lindsay,' he snorted. 'Yes, I do think. Whoever murdered Chuck Curry all those years ago is warning us all that they're back on the

scene and if my hunch is right, they're planning another scythe attack next Friday at four.'

* * *

I have a list of things to do and it's getting longer by
the day. Keeping on top of life is challenging but
catching Colgate's attention has filled me with renewed energy, not to mention the heavy three-hour
slumber in my car. Two more simple tasks have been
added to my regular schedule, both pencilled in for
before lunch.

I'm back in front of my computer screen by
eleven, an edgy determination fuelled by a double
espresso. Crystal-cut plans can't be side-tracked by
random events, hard-earned control squandered in
the blink of a few emails. Loose ends need to be tied
up, wrapped and sealed away like leftover stew in a
deep freeze.

Jeremy
Thank you for your interesting emails. Glad you're still
alive, ha ha. Hope your career plans, in how to trick
the world, will work out and make you your millions.
I'm in a committed relationship now, so can't meet up.
Anyway, have a good life.

Best
Beverley.

I fiddle with the wording, directing sarcasm like a poison dart, not sure I'm glad he's still alive, but he'll get the gist. Ms Evans would be proud that I'm walking away from dangled carrots.

The second task involves a bit of googling. But it doesn't take me long to find a good local painter and decorator. Vince Vickers lives in Cockfosters and an email bounces back straightaway, telling me he'd be delighted to pop round and give me a quote. Concern about the speed of reply is brushed aside when he assures me he's free to start anytime.

46

It's like a leaving party but I suppose in some ways it is. I've brought cake, a Victoria sponge, hoping to tease Tamsin with a sliver. Perhaps the icing will melt in the mouth rather than choke her.

Today is my last group therapy session and Ms Evans is encouraging us to bare our souls. As I'm not planning on keeping in touch with the motley crew, I'll make the most of my one last time on the soapbox.

* * *

In front of me, I've jotted down the list of possible stalkers who are hounding me and, as I wait for the others to arrive, my thoughts once more skitter around the possibilities. I'm not certain how much to share when it's my turn to speak.

Scott, Danielle and Cosette are likely suspects, either working in a group or singly. Perhaps Scott and Danielle are in cahoots; having some fun at my expense.

Cosette might be tracking me, warning me off her new boyfriend to get rid of the competition but she doesn't strike me as the type. Her youthful confidence hasn't taken sufficient battering to make her desperate, and it's unlikely she would have the time.

Travis and Queenie certainly wouldn't be working together. Travis may have tried to turn the tables my way after I sent the photograph of him and Gigi to his wife, as he rightly assumed that was down to me but I remind myself that the stalking against me continued after I let him move in when he wouldn't have needed to carry on.

I've had plenty of time and access to browse Travis' laptop and there was no evidence of damning content pointing in my direction, although his regular browsing of porn sites came as a bit of a shock. My obsession to win him over certainly blinded me to his seedier side.

Then there's Queenie. She's got motive as she's

probably known for quite some time about my affair with her husband and wants to get her own back. She's still harping on about the sword incident, won't let it drop, and it's fuelling an obvious dislike. Travis doesn't know what to think as he's caught between the proverbial devil and deep blue sea.

Then there's Bob Pratchett, who's definitely got more than a screw loose. Although he suffers from hallucinations and paranoia, all part of his schizophrenia, I think of him as mad rather than bad. Stark raving loopy.

The sighting of Bob and Queenie together at the hospital, that day when they were visiting Travis, still bothers me. The red sprayed 'Bitch' on the side of my car points squarely in their direction. Perhaps they're working in tandem and Queenie, in her professional role as Ms Evans, has led Bob down new paths; encouraging him to bond with 'normal' people. Yet the double-edged personality of 'Queenie-cum-Ms Evans' appears to me anything but normal. As a wife and mother her actions seem responsible, predictable, but then there's a lot I don't know about her.

Jeremy's a possibility, a dark shadow lurking in the background, fogging my head up even further. I feel as if I'm sitting on an unexploded time bomb, dreading sightings of the postman. It used to be because I couldn't pay the bills but now his cheery smile brings with it terror. I watch out the window to make sure he's not walking up the path with a ticking package and breathe more easily when thin envelopes and pizza flyers drop onto the mat.

* * *

Bob has brought the ginger wine. Tamsin chocolate eclairs, pretending these are what she eats, day in, day out. We all know the six raisins will stay in her pocket until we've gone and then she'll try to force them down.

We are all telling lies. Perhaps that's what humans do. It's not the lies we tell others, lies they won't believe, the truth blatantly obvious, but the lies we tell ourselves. It's these whoppers that let us carry on with the robotic dysfunctional behaviour. Problem is, while we're patients of Ms Evans, we're encouraged to dig deep and own up. I'm not sure she has succeeded with any one of us but then again she's the biggest liar of the lot. She keeps her secrets well hidden.

Today there's a distinct lack of eye contact from our therapist. I reckon it's the party atmosphere as she's definitely more at ease on the opposite side of a sturdy desk. Perhaps it's my imagination, but her professionalism hasn't seemed so pronounced of late, the school ma'am efficiency not so slick. Maybe she's not coping as well as she lets on with the errant husband issue and having to face his mistress across a busy room.

Ms Evans has baked cupcakes, neatly displayed on a three-tiered plate stand. The cracked yellow glaze is overlaid with sickly pink flowers, a charity shop 'steal' apparently. Cupcakes are her speciality and Freddie helped with the adornments by sticking small treats in the centre of the buttery icing; a silver star here, a jelly baby there. A tinge of colour surfaces on her cheeks when she speaks.

'He ate more of the sprinkles than he put on the cakes.' She laughs, flicking away stray coloured dots that have fallen onto the table. She's laid out a vinyl tablecloth, green and white striped, as if we're at a children's tea party, expecting us to make spillages which she'll carefully wipe away. Today Ms Evans is like our mother.

'No more treats for you today,' she'll say, waggling a finger, when the cordial is spilt.

There are helium balloons stuck in the corners of the room and an old CD player pumps out songs from the eighties. Jeez, Ms Evans has been busy. I wonder if it's part of her training to finish on a high, make her patients feel as if they've achieved some hidden goal; like a birthday milestone, but it all seems rather ridiculous.

We sit in a circle as we have some talking to do before we eat.

'Are we playing pass the parcel?' Dave. Deadpan. We laugh and chip away at the ice.

'No, Dave. We're not playing pass the parcel.' Ms Evans smiles and I half expect her to pat Dave on the head and tell him to be patient. 'Okay. Welcome to our last session together. Let's begin by telling the others how we've been.'

Manuel hasn't learnt any more English, or so he indicates with a mute hand gesture. He's allowed, as usual, to sit and watch, his smirk suggesting that he understands much more than he's letting on and I still suspect he's bilingual.

'Dave? Do you want to go first?'

'Not really. I'd rather play pass the parcel.' No one laughs this time.

We listen to his tales of misery and self-loathing as he sidesteps mention of the drug and alcohol addictions which we know he uses to mask the hell. We also know that he's been charged with possession of class-A drugs but no one bothers to mention it. His folded arms hide the syringe marks on the insides. Ten minutes of self-denial seem to make him feel better as he lets out an extended sigh.

'Tamsin. What about your week? I hear you've put on two pounds. You should be very pleased.'

Tamsin looks horrified. The last thing she wants is for us to know that she's put on weight. She sucks air in, checking her concave chest for unwelcome signs of non-existent shape but her tight T-shirt does its job, accentuates the bones.

It's finally Bob's turn. He's cleverer than the others, too clever, and likes to lead us all a merry dance.

'Everything is good. I've started work again. Two new commissions on portraits, although I can't let on who they're for. All very hush-hush.'

'Are they for agents at MI5?' Dave asks, voice thick with sarcasm.

'Dave, let Bob continue, please.' We all turn towards Ms Evans and I wonder how she can listen to this shit, day in, day out. The pay must be really good. Or perhaps her relationship with Bob really does run deeper than they both let on.

I wonder why she decided to be a therapist, what led her down such a career path. Bob says she is fighting demons of her own, trying to find answers through all the probing interrogations.

'My neighbour hasn't been giving me any problems recently but, although you might laugh, Dave, I am having threats from the government. And yes, it is very hush-hush.'

Bob omits a strange hyena squeal which we've all heard before, but it's still alarming.

'Okay. Thank you, Bob. We'll be finishing early today so that we can enjoy the tea and cakes and it'll give you a chance to talk more intimately to each other. Less pressure.' Ms Evans is right there.

'Beverley. How are you getting on? Perhaps you'd like to tell the group how you've been coping.' It's my cue and I'm quickly out of the blocks.

'I've received threats; by post, email and text. I've had my new car defaced with bright-red painted obscenities and received a dead bloodied animal in the post and am up all night long taking phone calls from an unknown madman. Or woman. I haven't slept since I was last in therapy.' It sounds very dramatic, especially as I don't pause for breath but it gets everyone's attention.

There's a long silence as the circle members simultaneously look down at their feet, apart from Bob and Ms Evans. They weren't expecting such a blunt melodramatic tirade as I'm usually the reluctant in-control storyteller.

'Jeez. Perhaps the sad git who has been trying to murder me has moved on to you!' Bob throws his head back and roars like a lion.

'That's enough, Bob. Carry on, Beverley.'

'It's just that...' I look directly at Bob at this point. 'It was when I was visiting a friend at the hospital that my car got red paint sprayed along the side. Perhaps you saw something, Bob, because you were coming out of the hospital as I was going in?'

The laughing stops as if a big game hunter's dart has found its mark. Tamsin is jolted out of her self-obsession and peels her eyes off the floor. I stare at Bob and he takes forever to answer.

'When was this? Jesus, that's dreadful. I was at the hospital; a couple of weeks ago. I was with a friend visiting her sick husband.' Bob blushes, as if he's been caught out.

'That's right. A couple of weeks ago. Let me see. I think it was a Thursday? Late afternoon. The car park wasn't that busy. Maybe you saw my car? The blue Mini with the white stripes? It's hard to miss.'

'Sorry. I didn't see it. I got the bus back.'

'You didn't go home with your friend?'

'No. She wasn't going my way.'

He could have waited until Queenie left, turned round and gone back to my car. There's still the possibility that Queenie went back after he left and sprayed my car herself. The one thing that does ring true is that they weren't in it together. If one of them is my stalker, they were working alone. If neither of them did the damage, then someone else must have followed me to the hospital separately.

It's also possible that the red paint incident has nothing whatsoever to do with my stalker but a one-off payback, from either Queenie or Bob, for having an affair with Travis.

'It sounds as if you have indeed got your own stalker, Beverley,' Ms Evans continues, diverting the conversation away from my veiled accusations. 'That must be very unsettling.' She's biting the inside of her cheek, chewing on a smile.

'Do you think that this person who's on your tail, might in any way have been affected by your own stalking behaviour? You have admitted to following quite a few people in the past. Perhaps someone is getting their own back? Being stalked is a very upsetting and disturbing form of persecution. Maybe you never realised how harmful and distressing being spied on can be.' It's a long speech for Ms Evans but she's trying to ram the point home, no sign of subtlety.

'Be careful, Beverley. Predatory stalkers can be

very dangerous. They have intent. Often can be deadly intent.' Manuel speaks in pidgin English and the group members all turn his way, having taken a second to work out who has spoken.

His Spanish accent is thick, his voice deep but the delivery is perfect. Manuel has been the best deceiver of us all. He *has* understood everything we've been saying and yet chosen not to join in, until now, keeping his secrets close to his chest.

But that's not what has caught my attention. Manuel is telling me he has worked things out and his narrowed eyes alert me to suspicions which he won't, perhaps can't, voice in front of the rest of the group.

47

'Dead Head. Head Dead. Dead Heading. Head Deading.'

Chanting was cathartic. The words were gritty, purposeful and reinforced my determination. I composed a tune which I hummed in accompaniment as I practised my moves. Deadheading plants was a skilled art, origami without the neatly folded lines, and it left the carved-up flora bedraggled and contorted.

My classmates had started laughing at me; pointing and whispering behind filthy little hands. They tried to muffle their giggles when I walked past but I egged them on, babbling out loud to myself. But they soon sidestepped when I approached and stared unwaveringly back. It was the deadly intent that made them back off and their fear spurred me on.

Friday 13 July finally came around. It was the day earmarked for Dead Heading. The teacher on duty, Miss Forshaw, smiled as I hurried outside when the bell rang. She must have wondered why I wasn't hiding in the cloakroom but today, she didn't need to coax.

'Have a good weekend. Enjoy the sunshine.' She mustn't have read the forecast because thunderstorms and heavy rain were on their way. The next couple of days would be a washout and I couldn't wait.

'You too, Miss Forshaw.'

It was 3.45 before I realised something was up. Uncle Chuck was nowhere to be seen. I sat jittering on the bench as the minutes ticked by. How many times had I prayed that he wouldn't turn up? In two years he'd never missed a Friday.

I decided not to wait. As Miss Forshaw headed in my direction, I hurtled out the gates and veered left towards Uncle Chuck's house. I ran so fast I thought my lungs would burst. Uncle Chuck would have had no need to chivvy me that day nor pull me reluctantly along behind. I had wanted him to be excited by my eagerness and speed.

'You promised we were going to be deadheading to-day. I've been looking forward to it.' He would have believed me. Today he said I could have one go with the

scythe. 'Just one, mind.' He'd shown me what to do. I was growing up after all. 'Ready for some adult tasks.'

When I reached his house, the small pebble-dashed semi on the corner of Holdenhurst Avenue, I peered in through the window. The panes were caked in greasy green slime but I was able to make out the slumped shape on top of a dirty maroon sofa. Uncle Chuck looked like a beached whale, grey rolls of blubber splaying out over his trouser tops. He was asleep.

It was then that I remembered he hadn't been feeling well the week before. 'A summer cold. No worries. I'll be right as rain in no time.'

I counted to ten then banged hard at the window. It had to be today. I couldn't wait any longer. I banged again, this time with both fists. There was no movement and for a few seconds I wondered if he might already be dead.

But his eyelids peeled back and he looked out the window.

'Snippet? Is that you?' His voice was weak, crackling like a foggy radio transmission and a hacking cough rattled the glass.

'Let me in. Let me in. I've been waiting.' I waved frantically and then went and banged even harder on the front door. I closed my eyes and looked heavenwards. That was the first and last time I prayed.

'Please, God. Let him be well enough to open the door. Let me have my chance today. Please, God.' An eternity passed before he appeared.

'Come in. What a nice surprise. I thought you'd have gone straight home or waited at school. Come in. Come in.' He sounded like a croaking frog.

I followed him across the rough flooring, stepping gingerly over beer cans and empty McDonald's cartons. In the kitchen, he took my hand. His had the icy feel of death.

'We'll give the shed a miss today, Snippet. I've not been too well.'

'You promised. I've been practising my deadheading. You promised.'

I managed to cry, a large blubbery deluge. I'm not sure how I was so skilled in the art of stagecraft but it was as if the water had been stored in a reservoir and someone had unlocked the dam. I pleaded, eyes wide, appealing to his perverted sense of caring.

'You can't let me down. You promised. You promised.' I didn't stop. Dirty dribbling snot mingled with wet rivulets and he handed me some kitchen roll. When he reached across and took the key from the rack, I knew it was going to work out.

'Okay. Just one go then.'

I walked along the length of the garden, behind the

monster, counting my steps. Twenty-two paces to the door. I almost turned back and ran but remembered that there would be another Friday; and then another. Fridays had defined my life. Today would be the last.

Uncle Chuck was wearing baggy striped pyjamas and dirty black slippers. The white cord which held up the trousers dangled down, fighting a losing battle to stay closed around the mountains of flesh. He kept wiping his brow, wet with fever, and his thinning hair was stuck fast and damp to the top of his head.

God had listened. He had made Uncle Chuck sick and weakened to make my task easier. I told him to sit on the sofa while I practised with the tool. I wouldn't be long; just a few plants. I'd be careful, that was a promise.

'Okay. I'll stay here, if you don't mind. Help yourself to biscuits. I'll sit a while.' His breathing was laboured, heavy as he slumped down into the sofa. I managed to extricate the tool by standing on a wooden crate and gripped it firmly in both hands. My sunny delight drew a watery smile.

'It's okay. After I've had a go, I'll put it back. See, I can squeeze in behind you and reach up. Look? I've grown.' I stood up on tiptoes. Up and down. Up and down. It was hard to keep his attention as he drifted in and out of sleep.

'Good. I'll close my eyes awhile.'

I didn't want him to close his eyes. But he'd open them

wide, I was certain, when I sneaked back round behind him.

'Dead Head. Head Dead. Dead Heading. Head Deading.'

He heard me, a slight spasm of his lips gave confirmation, but no words came.

Not until I screeched into his gaping eardrums.

'Boo. Boo. Boo.' From one ear to the other and back again. 'Boo. Boo. Boo.'

'Shit. What the fuck?'

He was sluggish, slumped too low to react. I held the scythe aloft behind him with both hands and teased him to look.

'This Dead Head is for you, Uncle Chuck. It just takes one clean slash, right? You've taught me well.'

One deft splice was all it took, like cutting the top off a boiled egg. I flicked my right wrist twice before releasing my left hand and with an almighty sweep sliced through the carotid artery. The runny egg yolk turned red.

He tried to talk through the bubbling seeping spurts of blood as I revelled in his lingering realisation of what I'd done, my glee bursting out like exploding fizzing champagne.

'What's that? Sorry, I can't hear you. I'll get going once I've tidied up. I know you don't like a mess.'

I stuffed a couple of biscuits in my mouth as I cleaned

up. His eyes didn't leave me as I wiped the scythe down with a cloth. The gardening gloves had kept my prints clear from the tool and with my school shoes neatly placed outside, I was certain there would be no telltale traces of me inside the shed. The weekend rain would wash away lingering clues. I had made notes, one to ten, in black ink in my school jotter as I planned the perfect murder.

'Who says children are stupid?'

I talked out loud, relief washing over me like a tsunami. I hovered for a minute to make sure he couldn't get up but I knew he was dying. The life was literally pouring out of him. I averted my eyes from his penis which was on display, the flimsy cord no longer holding his trousers up. It looked like a shrivelled raisin from one of the boxes of dried fruit I ate at break times.

I locked the door behind me, and buried the key under the cabbages. I wondered how long it would be till anyone came looking for Uncle Chuck. It could be a long time because he didn't have any friends and never spoke to his neighbours and the other garden shed children certainly wouldn't come looking. I was their saviour.

I took one last glance through the window at the wet and fading eyes. I waved, with a little trill of my fingers, and mouthed, 'Bye, Uncle Chuck. You fat bastard.'

I skipped away; not yet done with skipping.

48

She strode down Hampstead High Street, checking her watch every couple of minutes. Time was tight, in five minutes she'd be late and Olga was a stickler for punctuality.

Queenie's tardiness had been the cause of many spats over the years, but after today there'd be no more clandestine meetings; no more cloak and dagger skulduggery. She was going to give Olga the good news, news that her lover had been waiting years to hear.

When Travis had come into Queenie's life, his ardour spurred on by her apparent apathy, she realised that he might provide answers to her dilemmas and offer a cloak of respectability. Standing out from the crowd, announcing her deviances to the world wasn't an option. Success and survival depended on the façade of normality.

But things had changed. Now Travis was back home, physically weakened and contrite, she realised that throwing him out after his sad tawdry dalliances would give her more respectability in the eyes of the outside world rather than letting him stay. To be a cuckold in the eyes of her colleagues wasn't the way forward.

She pushed open the door of the café, chock-a-block with boisterous customers but she didn't need to sift through the faces, Olga was always early and Queenie knew she'd be sitting in the same seat she had done every Monday for the last ten years. There would be a spare chair pulled up alongside, reserved with an old canvas rucksack on top.

'Hi, hon. You're late.' Olga feigned a scowl, patted the seat as her girlfriend approached and then threw her bag under the table.

Queenie leant in and kissed Olga full on the lips, lingering longer than usual.

'My. You're pleased to see me then?'

'You could say that.' Queenie sat down and took Olga's hands between her own.

'Go on. What's up?' Olga motioned for the waitress. 'Let's order our coffees before you drop it on me.'

As the waitress set down their drinks Queenie began.

'I'm throwing Travis out. I want you to move in.' She took a sip of coffee and waited. 'What do you say?'

'Shit. Where's this come from?' Olga set her mug down, fell back heavily into the faux leather seat and let out a deep breath. A film of tears rimmed her eyes and Queenie handed her a tissue.

'It's a long story. Please say you will.' Queenie tensed, for a second fearing rejection. She had kept her girlfriend waiting, dangling on a string for so long but Olga pursed her lips, raised her eyebrows and burst out laughing.

'Try stopping me.' She leant across and pulled Queenie close, kissing her passionately and pushed a stray strand of hair back behind her ears. 'I love you, you silly mare. Just say when and I'll pack my case.'

'There's a few loose ends to tie up, the kids to deal with, but this weekend I'll start the ball rolling. You see, Travis was having another affair. This time with a girl named Beverley. She's a complete *psycho* and he soon crawled back home when he realised she was deranged. She's been coming to me for therapy as well, if you can believe it.'

'I always told you he was a loser. I'll not let you down. I promise. Good for this Beverley then. Even if she is mad she's done me a few favours.'

'Egg and soldiers? My treat?'

'Yes. Why not?'

'And a glass of champagne? This calls for a celebration.'

* * *

It was around 11.30 when they said their goodbyes. Olga promised to wait for the nod to pack her bags and Queenie was already planning how to decorate the bedroom once Travis had gone. She and Olga would do it together. Also, the kids loved Olga who was like a grown-up best friend although, as yet, they had no idea she was their mother's lover. All in good time.

Queenie strolled towards the Tube station, light-headed with the enormity of her decision. For the first time in so long, it felt good to take back control.

At the top of the High Street she paused outside a kitchen shop tucked neatly between NatWest bank and a delicatessen. She would pack up the old china of Travis' mother and the sad collection of mugs and glasses jammed higgledy-piggledy in the cupboards and make sure Travis took it all with him. She and Olga would start afresh; a whole new beginning.

Suddenly she froze. The outline reflection in the shop window was ill-defined but sharp enough to make out the jogger on the other side of the road, heading towards the Tube, headphone cables dangling. It was Beverley, dressed in bright sports gear and it was the third time that week that Queenie had spotted her.

Queenie put a hand out to steady herself and pulled off her jacket. The sun scorched her head and as she glanced down a drop of sweat landed at her feet.

In her imagination she heard the relentless beat of music that Beverley was listening to. Bruce Springsteen. Queenie knew Beverley's playlist by heart. She also knew far too much about her patient's unbalanced state of mind. Stalking ex-lovers was one thing, but letting Freddie play with a lethal weapon had been something else entirely.

The silent late-night phone calls, threatening email messages and weird random packages arriving at both Queenie's home and office had been logged as actions of an unhinged patient. She'd treated many over the years, male and female, and had mostly managed to ignore threats, knowing they would eventually abate. It was one of the downsides to the job.

Yet the recent barrage of menaces was escalating, the content increasingly personal and sinister, and Queenie didn't know which way to turn. She didn't want to confide in Olga and scare her off but the recent sightings of Beverley weren't random, they were more than coincidence.

When she dared to look back across the road, Beverley had disappeared. Queenie looked up and down the High Street, but she'd vanished. Or had she? Perhaps she was hiding in a doorway or had started her descent into the bowels of the underground.

As a migraine intensified, Queenie staggered to find shade from the relentless heat under the cool of an office doorway, where she slumped against the cold concrete. As her guts churned, the egg and soldiers lost their battle and she threw up.

It took all her energy to reach the Tube entrance and once inside, she leant against a newspaper kiosk and wiped her forehead with the back of her hand. Caged behind the wired billboard she caught the evening headlines.

The Garden Shed Murder

Case to be reopened after Twenty-five Years

Queenie lifted a copy, folded it under her arm and walked slowly downwards towards the platform. The rumble of an approaching train enticed her closer and closer to the edge until she stepped over the yellow line. One more step and she could slip away, under the approaching train, out of sight, and away from view.

49

Ms Evans likes to compare our personalities to giant jigsaws; complex, many-faceted and each individual piece totally unique. Apparently, we should strive to complete our own picture. People with pieces missing visit her to find out where they might look, under a sofa perhaps or in a dark corner. She's smug with her jigsaw analogy but even smugger in her attempts to prove what a great detective she is, ferreting around and poking about in the recesses of people's minds.

Personally, I prefer to blame the manufacturer. When I can't find the corner piece I'm more inclined to point the finger and apportion blame elsewhere, starting with my father. Ms Evans has helped me though to question my mother's role in the whole miserable affair that was my childhood. After all, my mother let my father get away with his monstrous behaviour. I have agreed with my therapist, more than once I might add, that if my mother and father were still around today I would certainly confront them both with the evidence.

However, this week I've been feeling quite gleeful since I discovered a large missing piece of my therapist's own jigsaw. Olga is her name. Ha. Ha. I must say I hadn't seen it at all. Ms Evans has kept her sexual preferences and her long-term lover well under wraps. I wonder if Travis knows and this is why he wanders so freely from the fold, and I can only imagine how he'll feel when his wife finally throws him out and moves her lover in.

As I walk down King's Road towards Sloane Square, purposeful in my step, I'm increasingly agitated to think that Ms Evans might come out on top. The smugness at having solved her puzzle has quickly faded. Whereas Travis got his *just deserts*, his wife is like the *cat that got the cream*. I paved the way which wasn't part of my plan.

As I head for my destination, I can hear her admonitions. '*You need to move on. Leave the past behind.*' She's hinted more than once that my tiredness, lack of sleep and lack of appetite might be down to bitterness and inability to let go.

'Let sleeping dogs lie. Do you know what that means, Beverley?'

Bitch. Who doesn't? But sometimes it's good to give the dog a good kick, pick up its lead and drag it off to the park; especially when Rottweilers are out to play. Why let them lie?

I force thoughts of Ms Evans to the back of my mind for now because my stride today has meaning. You see, I've also found the missing piece for my Scott Barry puzzle. Although I have quite a few puzzles to solve, today I need to keep my mind focused on the one in hand. Ms Evans can wait. My plan for her is complicated, but all in good time.

Each click of my new sharply filed kitten heels lends rhythm to my journey. Today I have found a resolution for all the hours invested in following, watching and waiting for Scott Barry over the years. Doing him physical harm was never an option; for someone my size it would have been well-nigh impossible. Hiring a hitman is not my style and far too extreme.

So I've wracked my brains, day and night, for an alternative course of action that might help put my mind at rest and let me move on. Vigilance and patience have finally earned the prize.

Cosette has never been to Sloane Square. She's rather a home bird, despite being a French student in a foreign country; she doesn't seem that interested in sightseeing or nightclubbing. To date, she's only travelled as far as Oxford Street and once to Harrods. Scott sent her, shortly after they started dating, to browse the food halls in search of truffles. This would have been part of his attempt to mould her into the perfect partner; accomplished in the kitchen, hot in the bedroom, and in thrall to his manhood at all times. He wouldn't want her visiting too many London hotspots; certainly not without him. I remember the MO, the modus operandi.

Cosette is in the early stages of infatuation where Scott's actions and behaviour all equate to caring and commitment. The apron and toaster were fun birthday gifts but what girl wouldn't prefer diamonds and pearls?

I'm whistling as I cross into the square. Cosette has texted to ask the whereabouts of the café. Is it the one beside the Italian deli or the one next to the champagne bar? I see her some feet away, texting furiously on her new iPhone.

'Yoo-hoo. Cosette. Over here.' My voice is sing-song, screechy, but the buzz around the plaza dulls the scale of my excitement. Cosette won't notice. She's far off the age where doubt and cynicism have taken hold. I like her and think we'll become good friends. She'll help me to loosen up once she's shot of her much-too-old boyfriend.

'Hi. It's really busy. Is it always like this?' Cosette puts her hand up to her forehead and scans the square. She's like a frightened rabbit in the glare of oncoming headlights. Her family home is in the heart of the Auvergne, in a small village in the middle of nowhere. The only buildings of note are a town hall and a patisserie. She doesn't speak the language of big cities yet.

'It's London. It's never quiet. Also the weather pulls out the punters, especially as it's Friday lunchtime. It's always busy at the end of the working week.'

I lean across and kiss her three times in greeting. Right cheek, left cheek and back again. It's meant to confirm our friendship, using the French three-cheek custom to gain her trust. She needs to trust me, believe me, when I tell her later I had no idea of what is about to unfold.

'It's across the road. Over there. Can you see it?

Café Pierre. It's always packed but I've booked a table. My treat.'

She doesn't protest. Her evening bar job pays peanuts and I certainly don't mind footing the bill; today it will be money well spent.

'I love your shoes,' she says as we stroll towards the café; side by side like a couple of besties. She eyes my expensive Christian Louboutin kitten heels, black and shiny. I stop and turn up the sole.

'Look. Do you like the red sole? They weren't cheap.' I laugh and take her arm.

By the time we reach the entrance to the café she is relaxed and I notice her glance in the spotless glass window at her reflection. She smooths down her hair and pushes the curly fringe back from her forehead. She's underdressed for the occasion but she wasn't to know.

'You look fine,' I say. 'They're not stuffy about dress code.' It's another lie but I don't want her suggesting we go somewhere less formal, more relaxed.

'If you're sure,' she says.

A waiter pulls the door wide as we approach and asks if we have a reservation.

'Miss Digby. Two people at 12.45.'

'Perfect. Come this way. You've requested number 24 at the back. That is correct?'

He leads us through the jam-packed room. Diners chat loudly and everyone seems to be drinking champagne. It's that sort of place; in-your-face ostentatious. It's too late for Cosette to change her mind and I bolster her confidence by suggesting she might like to do the ordering as the menus are in French.

'*Bien sûr!*'

We settle down, order a bottle of Chablis and wait for the waiter to return. It's exactly 12.45. Not long to go.

50

Cosette and I chat about our college courses, plans for the summer. Scott is taking her to Germany; a river cruise on the Rhine. Well, that's the current plan but in about fifteen minutes time I suspect he'll be hoping the travel agents offer full refunds.

Table number 24 is in the back corner. It has a great view of everyone coming in and going out of the restaurant. The lighting is poor though; soft and romantic was how I found it the first few times Scott and I came, but now it seems very dull and the corner spot rather dingy.

I see Scott long before Cosette does. I nearly jump up and whoop in delight when I see Danielle is with him and they are holding hands. This is better than I could have hoped for. He can't squirm out of this one with excuses of a last-minute casual catch-up. You definitely don't hold hands for those sorts of meetings.

His other hand is on the small of her back and he's gently propelling her towards the bar. He'll have booked table number 22, as this was the fallback option if someone beat him to number 24. Not quite as romantic and definitely second best. Today is Danielle's birthday, a special occasion.

Cosette has her head buried in the menu.

'There's rabbit. And quail. The menu's super.'

I seal my lips and will her to look up.

'What's up? Are you okay?' she asks.

I turn my head round to the right and nod, indicating something not far away.

'What?' she repeats. I wait, not sure what she'll do; what her reaction will be when she sees what I'm looking at but I'll let her take the lead.

'Are you ready to order, mademoiselles?' The waiter appears like a white rabbit out of a hat.

'Just give us another minute, please,' I say.

I'm not really prepared for what Cosette does next but I think I have definitely underestimated her feistiness. She gets up, gently sets the menu back on the table.

'*Excusez-moi*, Beverley. I'll only be a minute.'

She threads her way carefully past the tightly packed tables, weaving this way and that until she reaches the bar. Scott has his back to her but Danielle has seen the slight young woman. She doesn't know Cosette, of course, and thinks she's a random customer ordering a drink.

I take out my phone. The moment screams to be captured. I hold the screen up and prime my finger in preparation to start videoing.

Cosette pokes Scott in the back. He doesn't feel it at first, no doubt suspecting some impatient customer pushing their way through. She tries again, this time with the tips of all four fingers, making a hard and brutal stab.

'Shit. What the hell?'

I can lip-read from where I'm sitting. I press record. Wow. Cosette lifts her right hand and smacks it hard across his cheek; not once but twice, before Scott manages to grab her wrist. She then kicks him in the shins with the toe of her sturdy boot.

Danielle's face is a picture of horror. Did he really not tell her he was co-habiting, or is it the covert nature of relationships that gets her hot? I can't hear what they're all saying but an officious-looking gentleman, who has been studying table bookings to the right of the bar, gets up and approaches the fractious party.

Then something makes me sit back. I've caught it on video. While Scott is fending off his petite attacker, Danielle places the flat of her palm across her stomach. It's an instinctive gesture but enough to make me sit up. I wonder if Scott knows she might be pregnant. Perhaps she was intending to tell him today.

Scott throws his hands down by his sides in an insincere gesture of capitulation as the maître d' arrives but keeps talking, trying to convince Cosette of his innocence.

It takes a few minutes before his eyes skate across the restaurant towards table number 24. I take my right hand momentarily off the camera and wave in his direction.

'Hi,' I mouth, my lips wide like a guppy fish as I beam from ear to ear.

'You fucking cunt,' he mouths back.

Cosette wends her way back, her eyes ablaze and tears streaming down her cheeks. 'Do you mind if we go, Beverley? I can't stay here.'

'Of course I don't mind. I'm so sorry.' If she wonders at my sincerity, she doesn't flinch. She lifts her bag off the chair and heads straight towards the front door before I've time to rustle my own things together.

I move as quickly as I can, avoiding the bar area, skirting round the far side of the restaurant but I'm aware of Scott heading in my direction. His aim is to block my exit but I'm too quick. I scurry under the arm of a waiter, who is holding up a loaded tray of drinks, and beetle outside. When I look back I see the tray upended and, as if in slow motion, I see the glasses crash to the floor. Scott's face is crimson and his mortification is complete.

I see him glower through the window before I take Cosette's arm and propel her as fast as I can back the way we came.

'Shit. I thought he was going to kill me. I'm not sure what I'm supposed to have done wrong,' I say as we jog away.

We collapse breathless onto a small wall, once well out of sight of the restaurant.

'He's the one I'm going to kill. Thank you, Beverley. What a complete shit. You knew, didn't you?' She doesn't ask how I knew but I seem to have come out on top when my plan could so easily have backfired.

Her eyes are wet, cheeks pale, and her hands are shaking. Yet, I must say, Cosette has proven that she is no pussycat; no doormat. I can see why Scott likes her.

'I guessed. Leopards and their spots and all that. I didn't know he would be there today though,' I lie. Cosette doesn't know it is Danielle's birthday and for such a noteworthy celebration this was always going to be Scott's first choice of venue.

'It doesn't really matter. The fact he was is enough. He told me he was up in Peterborough today on a conference and wouldn't be home till late.'

'Oh. I'm so sorry. But perhaps it's for the best.'

'Thanks again,' she repeats.

'My pleasure.'

Yes, a real pleasure. I've managed to find the corner piece to my Scott Barry jigsaw puzzle. Ms Evans will be pleased, as I'm confident today's events will help me to move on where he's concerned. Meting out punishment was always going to help.

As we travel home on the Tube, Cosette lost in her own private thoughts and sobbing silently into her earphones, I bite my lip against the slight problem that Danielle being pregnant might cause me. I'm so hoping it won't set me back but then there are several possibilities that might help with the closure issue.

Firstly, the baby might not be Scott's. Secondly, he

might not know about it. These are significant trump cards for me to work with should I find out for definite that Scott is stalking me with tit-for-tat punishments. Although I'm not certain, at least I now have some leverage if he is and hopefully plenty enough to make him back off completely. Ms Evans is right. It is all about completing personal jigsaw puzzles.

At Southgate, Cosette and I alight and she hugs me with a tearful goodbye. I can't help the contented set to my lips and although I try to look sympathetic, I fear a random victory smile is evident. It helps that someone else now understands the pain that Scott Barry is capable of imparting and I'm not worried about Cosette; she's young enough to find another partner, preferably one not fifteen years her senior.

*   *   *

I amble home, feeling pleasantly contented; an *all is well with the world* feeling. As I approach the house, I stand back to admire the fresh coat of paint I've applied to the door and window frames. By the gate, I bend down and pick up a stray Coke can when something catches my eye on the front door.

A handwritten envelope is stuck to the wood and even from a distance I can see my name scrawled large in thick black ink. I step forward and rip it off, removing a sharp tack holding it in place.

The envelope tells me that Scott might not be my stalker. He's been in London all day. Someone else, closer to home, has been here and is reminding me they're watching; waiting. I scramble for my door key, hands wet and shaky, and check right and left before I duck inside, slamming the door hard behind me and setting the deadbolts.

I put the envelope down on the kitchen table, unable to bring myself to open it. The house is drowning in an eerie silence, the bare walls closing in. I'm sure I can hear a creak upstairs in the attic and I glance at the ceiling, waiting for the noise to intensify. It could be the hot water system cranking up, or someone could have broken in.

As I stare at the envelope it hits me that I'm completely alone. I've no one left to talk to, discuss my worries with. The police aren't interested and I've no idea what to do next if the latest missive is a threat on my life.

51

Bob Pratchett lived on Southgate High Street, first-floor flat, over Kasbah Kebabs. Heat from the kitchens and a rank stench of greasy spit meat clung to the walls of his den. Opening the smeared window overlooking the street didn't help. He stuck his head out, wheezed as the hot polluted air filled his lungs and sneezed loudly to expel the toxins.

His head grazed the top of the frame as he dove back inside. Shit. There were two police officers down below, walking back and forth. He slammed the window shut, turned the music up and took up the Lotus position in the centre of the floor. Eyes closed, humming noises, like swarming hornets, zinged from his lips. Manufactured calm wasn't easy. Bob Pratchett guessed why the police were knocking.

* * *

DCI Colgate had got Lindsay to do some digging, deep archaeological spadework, to try to unearth hidden nuggets of information. The Garden Shed Murder was like a black hole, dark and cavernous, and was sucking him back in.

'Five children came forward after the Garden Shed Murder, sir. Three boys and two girls. Looks like the pervert didn't have a preference,' Lindsay began.

Colgate, shoulders hunched, scanned the open file on his desk. 'Have you managed to trace the kids? Do any of them still live around here?' His stomach felt the old familiar churn from the gruesome accusations in front of him and his heavy breakfast somersaulted. Child abuse was the worst.

'Yes, sir. Two of the victims committed suicide. Vicky Briers jumped in front of a train on her eighteenth birthday and Alan Stanton hung himself when he wasn't much older. His father found him dangling from a beam in their garage; only twenty-one. I managed to track down scant newspaper coverage of these two events. Pippa Nicholls, the third victim, emigrated to America, according to her neighbour, ten years ago and hasn't been seen or heard of since. Kevin Clements has dementia and lives in Finchley in a private nursing home. That only leaves one of the original five still alive and possibly capable of murder.'

'I see. Well done, Lindsay. Is this him?' Colgate pointed to the picture of a young boy, a tentative smile displaying a gap where a front tooth was missing.

'Yes, sir. Robert Pratchett. He still lives in Southgate. His address is listed as Selbourne Road but he seems to have moved out; marital problems. He's currently renting a room on the High Street above a kebab shop.'

'Good work, Lindsay. Listen, it's now Wednesday eleventh.' Colgate checked his watch to confirm not just the date, but the time. 'It's ten minutes past ten. We've got exactly two days and under six hours to follow my hunch and find out if Miss Digby's life really is in danger. Have we heard from her again?'

'She came in yesterday with more evidence of threatening emails, late-night phone calls and suspicious sightings of a hooded stranger wandering round her back garden in the dark. She's virtually barricaded herself in.'

'Okay. Let's get moving.' Colgate knocked back his plastic cup of coffee, wincing as the bitter dregs hit his throat. 'Christ this coffee's got worse. I didn't think it was possible.' He scrunched up the cup, threw it in the bin and lifted his jacket off the peg before striding out ahead of his young colleague. As an afterthought he went back and pocketed the photograph and statement of the young Robert Pratchett and folded them away in his top pocket.

* * *

Bob covered his ears against the drum roll of knocking. The rotting door frame shook on its hinges but the percussion beat wouldn't stop. Louder and louder. Surrender was nigh. Bob flicked off the music, ran a cursory hand across his thinning pate and tugged down the tatty T-shirt which covered his ribs. A rattle of empty beer cans drew a wry smile. One of the police officers must have tripped over the pile of crates stacked on the landing.

Bob unfastened the chain, puffed out deep regular breaths, remembering Ms Evans' advice. Her calmness infiltrated the darkness. 'It'll help against hyperventilating.'

'Yes. How can I help?' Bob's fingers beat on the door frame. 'I'm rather busy,' he continued, peering through a reluctant gap.

'Mr Pratchett? Mr Robert Pratchett? I wonder if we could come in and have a chat. DCI Colgate and PC Lindsay.' The detective flicked open and closed an identification wallet.

Bob inched the door back and the detective raised an eyebrow as the unoiled hinges creaked. 'Come in. Excuse the mess.'

Bob led the way across a corridor strewn with clothes, papers, shoes and all sorts of random paraphernalia. Two tennis rackets and a can of balls leant against one wall and tucked behind the door was a rickety bicycle and a large pile of unopened letters and junk mail atop a rotting wooden crate. Bob's barefooted tread was light, his thin wiry legs, encased in voluminous shorts, picking their way carefully through the debris.

A black cat tore past, a meaty tail wriggling in its mouth. PC Lindsay's scream pierced the air while Bob's laugh kept sync with Colgate's disapproving stare.

'Mr Pratchett, we're looking into an old murder

case from some years back and were hoping that you might be able to help us.'

'Oh. What case would that be?'

'The Garden Shed Murder. Do you remember it?'

'Vaguely.' Bob scrabbled together a mess of papers, drawings, sketches and newspaper cuttings which lay strewn across a small table by the window and pushed them to one side.

'Coffee?' Bob rinsed through a couple of dirty mugs, banging the crockery carelessly as he went. With both hands he violently shook a large half empty jar of Nescafé before digging a spoon through the congealed granules.

'No, thank you. You're okay. This won't take long, but don't let us stop you.' Colgate's lips gusted out an aggravated blast of air while Bob filled the kettle.

* * *

'We've reopened the case of Mr Chuck Curry who was murdered twenty-five years ago in a garden shed a few roads from here. You were only a kid at the time but we know that you came forward, after the event, with accusations against the deceased.' Colgate paused as Pratchett digested what he'd said. 'However, recently there have been new leads in the case, which we've now reopened. I wonder if you could go over what happened all those years ago. I hope it won't be too upsetting, but we're really trying to get a grip on recent events. We have an original statement from you given after the murder and it would be really helpful to hear it from you again directly.'

Boiling water spilt over the work surface, as Bob's unsteady hands lost their grip. Colgate wasn't sure if the random whistling came from the kettle or from Mr Pratchett.

'Nothing new to tell. The fat bastard buggered me once a week for two years. That about sums it up. Biscuits?'

Several biscuits from a ripped packet fell on the wet floor and Bob trod on them, grinding the crumbs hard with his foot. He held out the remainder of the pack.

'No thanks. We're really sorry to be bringing this all up again but wonder if you might be able to tell us anything about the other children who came forward at the time. Or perhaps any children you might have seen or heard of but who didn't have the courage to speak out.' Colgate ran a hand under his collar, loosened his tie and undid the top button on his shirt, grimacing at the closed windows.

Bob ducked down and opened a cupboard below

the sink and took out a dustpan and brush. He swept the crumbs from side to side and pushed the soggy mess under the skirting board.

'Queenie. She's a good friend. We've kept in touch. She never talked about what happened but I know she was a regular visitor to Curry's. I often passed her going to and from the house but we never spoke. Not until it was all over. It helped to know that I wasn't the only one who'd grabbed his attention but it's not something we talk about much these days.'

Bob Pratchett scratched his skin, running his fingernails back and forth along his forearms. Bright red scabs had developed from the attention and Colgate suspected a skin complaint; psoriasis perhaps. He reckoned it was a nervous condition. Shit. He wasn't surprised.

'Queenie? Does she live locally? Perhaps you could let us have her full name.'

Bob turned his back, switched on the radio again and bobbed about on his toes. Lindsay glanced at her boss, eyes raised heavenwards. Colgate walked over to Pratchett, stood close, face to face, and spoke directly at him.

'Thank you, Mr Pratchett. We're very sorry to have bothered you but we may need to ask you to attend the station to help with further enquiries. If you could let us have the full name and address of your friend, Queenie, that would be really helpful.'

Bob danced round in a trance. Colgate considered that the guy might have taken some hallucinatory substance, magic mushrooms perhaps.

'Come on, Lindsay. Let's get going. Thanks again, we'll be in touch!' Colgate shouted back as they headed down the hall.

'Lowther. Queenie Lowther. She's my friend. She knows all about the Garden Shed.'

Colgate turned to Lindsay.

'Did you get that? I think that's Mrs Lowther, wife of Travis Lowther, the guy Miss Digby's been having the affair with. Thank you, Mr Pratchett. That's really useful. Goodbye for now,' Colgate said before they took the stairs.

* * *

Once they'd left, Bob ratcheted up the window again, leant out and dangled his head upside down through the gap. Below he watched the excited chatter of the exiting visitors. He guessed at the direction of their conversation. He could hear it in his head, bringing it all back.

* * *

In the car, Colgate didn't start the engine straight away.

'Travis Lowther is the link here. Pratchett and Mrs Lowther could be working together to put the shits up Miss Digby; perhaps retribution for stealing the husband. Although something doesn't feel quite right. Anyway, let's keep an eye on Mrs Lowther, put our minds at rest that she hasn't pencilled in a revenge attack for this Friday afternoon at four. Come on, let's go.'

Through the police car windows, the pair watched Bob Pratchett wheel his bicycle across the car park and out the other side.

'There must have been a back entrance to the kebab shop. Do you think he's headed for the Abbott Hospital? Looks like it to me.'

'Yes definitely, boss. He's heading in that direction.'

52

Hi Miss Digby

Was in the area, so thought I'd call round on the off-chance you were in. Just wanted to firm up the quote for painting and decorating.

Let me know when's a good time. You've got my number. Cheers

Vince Vickers

Painter and decorator

It took half an hour before I finally ripped open the envelope. I laugh out loud as my racing heart steadies and rub sweaty palms down my denim shorts.

Through the patio doors the new geraniums,

which I bought to brighten up the graveyard, are already in full bloom. Bright red. Mum used to plant geraniums to cheer her up; quash the misery for a brief period.

I wander out and pick up a few withered leaves, plucking wilted blooms as I go. 'Deadheading the plants,' Mum used to say, 'gives new buds a chance to flourish.' Her faint, half-hearted voice whispers in my ear.

I hold a small red petal to my nose and wonder at the lack of smell. The yellow roses against the wall reek with a heady aroma. No older than ten, I used to make perfume with their mushed-up leaves.

'Perhaps one day you'll be a perfumer.' Mum smiled as I ground the precious petals to a pulp. That's why I kept at it. Her smile. It was a rare sight. 'You have the gift.' But with a light kiss on the tip of my nose she'd be gone; back to her private prison where she'd throw away the key and ignore all who came calling; me included.

I sit on the small stone wall, wiggle my bare toes in the sunshine and close my eyes. Life has come full circle. I've travelled the long way round but I'm back, like the geraniums, where it all started. Back home.

Ms Evans is in my head. She's been trying to

deadhead me, get rid of the poisonous growth that I'm not quite willing to shed.

'Why do you think you stalk your lovers, Beverley?'

Ms Evans thinks I've been in denial all along. But I don't stalk them, I'm just keeping them close. It's become a way of life, gives me meaning and keeps my mind occupied; less time to mope.

A sharp little laugh gurgles out from the back of my throat. Ms Evans always uses the word stalking, never the word 'following'. Stalking seems to keep the guilt angle going, the sinister connotations that attach to the action and I think she needs to use the word 'stalking' to justify her part in my treatment. I wonder which bit of my behaviour is deemed to be a danger to the public; the bit which has already cost the government quite a chunk out of their mental health budget.

Taking pictures of Scott and Danielle wasn't in the least bit threatening. Perhaps slightly weird, and a bit obsessive, but I don't think I should have been threatened with prison and dragged off to therapy for taking a few blurry photographs. There was nothing linking me to Danielle's tumble down the concrete stairwell, so using the unfortunate aftermath as a means to get me 'under the couch' still seems completely unfair.

Travelling to America to try to find Jeremy, after he disappeared, was an attempt to get closure after the end of our all-consuming passion. I thought we had something special and I needed to understand what happened. I still don't get how people can walk away and start over. Shallow, unfeeling and rather fickle would be my summation.

'If someone doesn't want to be with you, what makes you want to be with them?' Ms Evans again. 'Wouldn't you prefer to be with someone who wants to be with you? Someone more loving?'

Ha. Of course. Who wouldn't? But I always feel there's work to be done; work to earn the love, the trust, the caring. It's a belief in the possibility of a normal stable relationship that keeps me going. If I can get the warm blanket cover of a perfect couple-dom, it will smother all the rest; the really bad bits.

'Why is that? Why do you have to work so hard? Try so hard? What started all this desperation to hold on?'

I blame my father. I need someone to blame; someone obvious to explain away my unbalanced behaviour to Ms Evans. My father took my mother from me and left me with no one. That was his sin and he had no idea of my torment.

I wander over to the roses and peek out through a hole in the trellis into my neighbour's garden. There's a rickety shed in the far right-hand corner and the doors are thrown wide open. Today I can see inside where a lawnmower, a wheelbarrow and a whole stack of tools are lined up along the back wall. Outside, in front of the cabin, is a small pebbled courtyard where Mr Tucker has placed a couple of rattan chairs and a small coffee table. He used to sit there in the summer evenings, drinking sangria from a pitcher, with his wife, Prue.

Funny what you remember. Prue died a few years ago and now he sits there in the evenings talking to himself. Beer is his tipple these days, not quite so celebratory. A tiny stereo system plays CDs until the light fades and the heat dies down. Frank Sinatra. Dean Martin. Engelbert Humperdinck and occasionally Elvis Presley croon until the moon appears.

My mobile suddenly rings through from the kitchen. I turn my head in the direction of the noise, but I don't move and instead look once more through the fence. I shiver as the sun slithers behind a cloud, darkening the sky and withdrawing its warmth. The smell of roses is overpowering, choking. Inside the flimsy wooden shed I eye the little row of neatly ar-rayed tools; spades, hoes, rakes and forks. But a small scythe holds my gaze. *A ghost walks over my grave.* It's a saying Mum used and I now know what she meant.

The Grim Reaper haunts me. I learnt his name when I was very young. He's only make-believe but underneath I know he's a real person. His thick layers of disguise are there to mask the evil. But I'm no fool. I know him well.

Then there are the newspaper reports. It's back in the headlines as if it were yesterday.

Garden Shed Murder – Case to be reopened after 25 Years

I remember my mother's horror at the headlines of the time.

Paedophile Monster slain with Half-moon Garden Scythe.
  The Grim Reaper takes Revenge

She didn't tell me what a paedophile was but she did tell me about the Grim Reaper.

There was whispered gossip over garden fences, my mother escaping her own misery for short periods while contemplating something far worse. I would put my hands over my ears until it quietened down. It took time, but Chuck Curry soon became a distant memory; a mythical evil monster. Life moved on as if it had all been a bad dream.

But now he's back, ready to wreak more havoc.

53

FRIDAY 13TH

Left down Burton Avenue, right into Salisbury Road and third left into Park Lane. I've done the route three times this morning. It feels good to be reliving the past; therapeutic. The well-worn pavement slabs lining the route are eerily familiar.

I count twenty-six concrete squares until the cracked one appears outside the post office which sits tucked neatly into the corner where Salisbury Road meets Park Lane. I jump over the zigzag line. I used to be superstitious. If I didn't step on it things would improve, a tale which offered false comfort.

Twenty-five years ago to the day, I gave up and jumped up and down on the crack. I was done with superstition, drawn instead to wobbly ladders and the number thirteen. Destiny was in my own hands, not some mystical power that had thrown me to the wolves.

I stop outside Uncle Chuck's old house. It's up for sale again. His ghost must linger. Twenty-five years has flown by but time hasn't dimmed the memories.

* * *

When I got back home from the shed late that afternoon my mother had the tea on.

'Fish and chips. Mushy peas. Your favourite.'

She was wearing a red scarf knotted round her frizzy bleached hair, a strange thing to remember on such a momentous occasion. She didn't take her eyes off the deep fat fryer which sizzled viciously in her hands. Each handful of diced potatoes sent scalding sprays of molten liquid up towards her face. But she was good at minding herself, always managing to sidestep the spits in time. The drips of blood on my hair, wet but rapidly congealing, didn't warrant a second thought. A cursory glance and I was instructed to tidy up my appearance.

'You cut yourself? Go and clean up before tea.' It was a casual command and she didn't ask why I was home earlier than usual.

Later, when questioned by the police, she seemed to recall that Uncle Chuck hadn't been well. That was why

I'd got home so promptly. My babysitter hadn't been up to entertaining so I must have wandered back from school alone. She suddenly remembered this fact and proceeded to tell the police what a terrible daydreamer I was, quick to deflect suspicion of neglectful parenting away from herself. I often wonder if she'd have cared if I hadn't come home at all.

I remember feeling a strong temptation to pick up the chip pan and empty the contents over her head. I didn't though. Childish logic told me that one murder a day was enough, two more difficult to get away with.

My mother was shrewd under questioning. I'll give her that.

'No. We haven't seen Uncle Chuck for a few days. He was off colour so he didn't babysit this week at all. The teachers will confirm that. He usually picks Snippet up from school on a Friday but yesterday you came straight home. That's right, isn't it?' Mum kept her eyes averted when she addressed me. She seemed to be covering for me, just in case.

It was in the way she spoke; the way she phrased her answers. I knew on that Saturday morning that she suspected more than she let on, yet her apathy played into my hands. She made short shrift of the Old Bill and when it came out that Uncle Chuck had been a sadistic pae-

dophile, she decided not to talk about it. Easiest that way, not wanting to be tarnished with the same brush.

When the constable directed the same questions to me, in a quieter more reverential tone, I stared down at my bare feet as they jiggled up and down, bony little appendages like myself. I knew when the police left, I'd got away with murder. Mum cried crocodile tears for Uncle Chuck. Her hysterics were firmly directed towards the loss of her step-brother although I still suspect that somewhere, deep down, some of the mania was driven by the realisation that she might have spawned a monster; a weird child killer.

'How dreadful. What a bloody awful thing to happen. Who could have done such a thing?' She cried for days, not once catching my eye as I laid my hands on her shoul-ders and hugged her tightly. I soon cared as little for my mother as for Uncle Chuck.

The newspapers couldn't get enough of the story. Local children, neighbours and parents all came forward, baying for blood. But it was too late. Someone had got there first. I never told, there was no need. Slicing through his neck had been therapy enough and no one bothered with me. It was enough that I hadn't seen him on that particular Friday afternoon.

Uncle Chuck was a stalker, a word I learnt much later. Uncle Chuck would pretend he was walking *through the park. I knew he'd seen me as he waited and wobbled. In the shops, he would be in the fridge aisle when I went to pick up a pint of milk. It got him hard, the fear that turned him on. Outside my bedroom window I'd see him in the black of night slouched against the lamp post with his hand down his trousers. He'd dare to wave up at me with the other hand as I tore the curtains closed. Several times I ripped them off the rails.*

When he wasn't there, or I couldn't see him, it was worse because then I held my breath in fearful anticipation. He had to be somewhere? Where? I tried to tease him out but, like a crocodile, he lolled low in murky waters, waiting until we were alone.

I learned the craft of stalking from Uncle Chuck. I knew how it felt to be hounded, day and night, by an unseen predator. But now it's time to show my face. The game is up. Today I'll finally blow my cover. The clock is ticking. Tick-tock. Tick-tock. Here I come.

I turn away and start the journey home. Left down The Broadway and I'm almost there. It's nearly lunchtime. I step on all the cracks and boldly dive under a workman's wobbly ladder.

'Mind out down there. That's unlucky, you know.'

The painter wiggles his paintbrush, dripping white dollops at my feet. 'Ooops.'

I laugh up at him, sidestepping with aplomb. I'm not the unlucky one today. Unlucky thirteen. Unlucky in love. Unlucky in life. She should have told.

Her luck has run out.

54

'Ms Evans. Come in. You're a bit early. But it's good to see you.'

It's really great to see her but only because it'll be the last time. I've been watching out for her and wondering why she didn't appear through the hospital gates as she's suddenly turned up at the front door. She probably left work early, leaving her car at the hospital and walked the scenic route through the park. Her cheeks are flushed. Today is the last time I'll have to face her and I've plenty to tell her, not to mention a few questions of my own to ask.

We're holding the last session in my house as Ms Evans thought it would be a nice way to round off the therapy, give her a chance to see me in my natural habitat, so to speak. She thinks it might help her make a final call on my state of mind.

She's not one hundred per cent confident, even after all the sessions, about signing me off; she's still got concerns which she's reported, in great detail, to Damian Hoarden. I can't for the life of me work out what is making her uneasy. I've played the game, answered all the probing questions carefully. But hey ho. There's more than one way to skin a cat. I certainly won't be agreeing to another two months of her stony stare and cross-examination. Today it's her turn to talk, to come clean.

'Beverley. What a fabulous house. I had no idea.' Her voice cuts through my thoughts; a knife through butter. I wonder why. She knows where I live as my home has been the backdrop to my unfolding story; it has been the corner piece of my therapy jigsaw. She must surely have been curious when she passed it every day on her way to work. I mention it in detail every time I'm lying on my back, when I try hard to paint as succinct a picture as possible for her; the picture that I want her to see.

'Hi. Thank you. Come in but be careful of the paint pots. It's still a work in progress.'

'Love the colour. It's nice and bright.' She smiles at the azure blue over which I've stencilled fluffy white clouds and grey floating seagulls. No Rorschach images of death and destruction in the hallway. My creative skills, sun, sand and seagulls, should help put her mind at rest.

'I've been painting over my childhood. I don't think my parents would recognise the place.' Moving on. That's what she'll see. Her professional eye should make positive summations and help her tick the right boxes.

'Do you fancy a coffee, or perhaps something stronger, before we get started? It's my last session, so thought we'd have a little celebration. Well, I'd like a little celebration and hope you'll keep me company. You've helped a lot, you know.'

I pretend that I don't know she's hesitant about signing me off.

'Why not? Perhaps we can chat like two old friends. Shall I leave my shoes by the door? The heels might cause damage to this fabulous wooden floor. Is it real oak?'

Ms Evans peels off her smart black patent heels and lays them neatly by the front door. She keeps her shoulder bag close though and doesn't take it off. It jangles against the floor and I wonder what's inside. Gaoler's keys more likely than hairspray.

'Yes. It's the real McCoy. This way. Follow me. I've

bought a few sandwiches and put the champagne on ice, ready to pop the cork. I feel really positive today.'

'Perhaps we should save it for after our session. One last clear head?'

'Fine by me. We can make tea upstairs. I keep a kettle and fridge there as it's a long way back down. The attic's been totally revamped, by the way, as a studio; somewhere I can study and paint. You'll love it. It's where I'll be working on my very own picture of Dorian Gray!'

Ms Evans gives a wry smile. I imagine she's seen many people like Dorian Gray, outwardly beautiful but with coal-black hearts. I wonder if she'll be impressed with my current work in progress, a small still-life garden scene. Red geraniums and orange-breasted robins have created a colourful canvas which perches on a rickety easel in the corner. It reflects a light-hearted hope for the future. Flora and fauna. What's not to like? If she's suspicious what lies behind the beauty, she'll keep it to herself.

But much more important, I'm wondering how quickly she'll recognise the layout. The tight walls hold a sofa neatly slotted between their confines. A drop-leaf table was a recent eBay purchase and the charity shop was brimming with chintzy china teacups. If Stockholm Syndrome (a weird, sad condition of becoming attached and dependent on one's evil captor) could relate to places, my attic should do the trick. It definitely has that homely familiar feel and the dimensions are spot on. I'm sure she'll recognise it, but I need to be certain.

I lead Ms Evans up the rickety stairwell. It's quite weird how I think of her as Ms Evans when we meet for therapy sessions and at all other times I think of her as Queenie Lowther, wife of Travis and mother to Freddie and Emily. She has definitely two personas. She's not unlike me in that respect. On a shallow level she's a rather average decent human being, the evil buried much deeper.

I wonder how many layers of personas she's scribbled in her notes that make up my character; certainly more than one. Any true professional would have picked up that my upper mantle is too vacuous to form the bedrock of my character. Ms Evans will know that but she's only bothered to peek underneath; too much effort digging for ruins in a built-up area. She should have got her hands dirty, shovelled away the grainy topsoil to reach the depths. Only then would she have got her answers.

The stairwell curves sharply round on both the first and second-floor landings until the final stretch which leads precipitously, like the final ascent of

Mount Everest, to a small door at the very top of the house, high up under the eaves.

This was always my space, long before it was cleared of clutter. It was my hiding place, far enough away to block out the noise, the nightmares. I didn't need to cover my ears when I was this far up. My frozen Charlottes were cold, present companions as I played, alone, on top of the world.

'Come in. Voila.' I proudly fling open the door and spread my arms wide. 'What do you think?'

Ms Evans is about to reply but her lips snap shut. She looks round the small cosy room with the bright skylight, sun streaming through, but doesn't speak. Her right eyelid develops a tic. Things are coming back. Bingo. I was right. She had been inside the garden shed. My efforts have been worth it and have confirmed my suspicions. She knew exactly what was going on, the pretence is finally over.

55

'Are you okay? Sorry, it's a bit of a climb. Here, have a seat and catch your breath.'

I extract a rickety wooden chair from under a table which is snugly aligned with the sloping roof. It's a perfect fit. She doesn't mention the stained wooden beams with their slick professional finish. They are thick and solid, holding the room together. It would have been impossible to replicate the leaking felt roof with corrugated iron surrounds and also, the beams help root me in reality.

I've become quite the dab hand with a paint-brush. I spot a cobweb in the corner and automatically reach for an extendable feather duster and perch on tiptoes to flick it away, the mesh sticking fast to the implement.

'Sorry. Spiders. They're everywhere.' My little furry friends. My lifeline. I'm careful not to kill them as they still keep me company.

Ms Evans scans the room as she does a full three-sixty, checking out the walls, the ceiling and the floor. There's a distinct tremor in her hands and she doesn't sit down, perhaps the chair's too wobbly.

'I'm okay, thanks. Sorry, I'm just not very fit. You're right. It is a long way up.' Her smile doesn't reach her glazed eyes. The turned-up lips are an attempt to maintain composure but she hasn't yet worked out what's going on, still doesn't remember me. Give it time. Give it time.

'Here. Let me put the kettle on. First I'll pull the blinds down on the skylight to block out the sunlight. Keep prying eyes at bay.' My hoot reverberates off the walls. There'll be no prying eyes this high up, yet closing the blinds is meant to mirror the stapling in place of the net curtains which blocked out the rest of the world.

'Less light should make it easier to put me under. What do you think? I've even bought an eye mask which I can heat up. Look.' I dangle my new purchase by the elastic and set it down when she doesn't respond. 'I can heat it up by plugging it into my computer. How cool is that?' La-di-da-di-da.

Ms Evans' sagging eyes are like those of a puppy coming face to face with a rabid Dobermann. She senses that I'm toying with her, detecting a madness in my actions and that must be why she looks so frightened. I'm surprised though, as she must be used to mad people by now.

'Why don't you sit here on the sofa? It's very cosy. I'll put the chair back. It fits perfectly, don't you think? You can interrogate me from here.' I nudge her towards the brown polyester-covered sofa.

Ms Evans is breathing slowly, in and out, trying to relax the way she suggests to patients who have anxiety issues; panic attacks and suchlike. I recognise the signs; shut eyes, a long slow intake of breath followed by gently measured exhalation. I'm fascinated. She's totally out of control.

'Thanks, Beverley. I'm fine. My heart seems to be beating very hard.'

She's such a liar. She recognises the interior of the garden shed which I've replicated in the finest detail. I've dug deep into my memory reserves, aided by the vivid nightmares, to get the layout exactly right. The sofa here. The table there with the two unstable wooden chairs slotted underneath. I have even laid out a gaudy tea set on top of a stained tin tray.

Yet in spite of all my efforts, Ms Evans is still going to try to pass off the scene in front of her as some weird coincidence, nothing at all to do with her. Over my dead body.

'Please. Sit. I'll put the kettle on. It's homely, isn't it?'

Ms Evans sits on the sofa, her body rigid. 'Beverley. What's going on?'

'What do you mean?' I walk round behind her as if to plug in the rusty kettle. I bend down, holding the lead attachment but with a quick sleight of hand I flick handcuffs round her wrist. It was a trick Jeremy and I used on each other all the time. The wooden slats running down from the armrest on the sofa provide the anchor.

'What the fuck's going on? Beverley, have you lost your mind?'

'Ha. That's a good one. There's nothing wrong with my mind. Milk, one sugar? I think that's how you like it. Recognise the custard creams? Uncle Chuck bought them in bulk. Those and Jaffa cakes. Remember?' I stick my face so close our noses skim.

The kettle comes to the boil, whistling like a

sailor. I pour boiling water into the mugs and mulch the teabags with the back of a spoon.

'Watch. It's very hot. It's awkward with only one hand free. Maybe wait till it cools down a bit.'

Uncle Chuck made me tea; warm and milky. 'Full-fat milk. It'll fatten you up, Snippet,' he said.

It's strangely silent. Ms Evans doesn't move and doesn't touch her tea.

'I remember the first time I saw you. It was the very first Friday. Uncle Chuck told me he'd something to show me, a rare and special treat. He opened the dirty white PVC front door and the first thing he did was call out your name. "Queenie, are you there? Yoo-hoo. It's Uncle Chuck."'

I thought he was having some sort of a party. Other girls and boys. What fun. He poked me from behind to move me further down the hallway. The linoleum floor was engrained with dark brown skid marks and a rank smell of urine, wet dog fur and bad breath hung in the air. My stomach churned from the smell but battled with the excitement. I grip the table edge, knuckles white.

'You know that I didn't get out much, don't you, Queenie? I've told you what it was like at home. Anywhere seemed better than being around my parents. Uncle Chuck appeared as my saviour. He was my mother's stepbrother. Did you know that? No of course you didn't because you weren't interested. You turned a blind eye. Didn't you?' I'm hissing like a disconnected hose, spurting vitriol.

'That first Friday we stopped by an open door to the lounge. Chuck's bulk blocked the doorway and I couldn't get a proper view inside. But I saw you. Sitting like you're doing now, on the end of a sofa. The remote control you clutched told me you were having fun. Fun. Fun. Fun. Your eyes never left the telly. That was the easiest thing to do, wasn't it? Pretend not to see. But I caught you. Out of the corner of my eye as we walked away, you turned your head.' I pause for breath before I spit it out. 'You ignored us all, and turned a blind eye.'

56

I'm hopping like a rabbit, in and out between memories, unsure which way to turn and although I'm talking out loud there's no response from the sofa, only a deathly hush, a prickly fear.

'You recognised me as Hannah from the year below at school. Beverley is my middle name, by the way. It's a nicer name don't you think than Hannah? My mother was a fan of the Beverley sisters. He called you Queenie, didn't he? The nickname stuck. You were his special little queen. He called me Snippet. It sounded like something small and crunchy that could be shoved away in a trouser pocket.'

I spin round, pirouette on one foot and momentarily lose my balance.

'Oops.' I move in close again. 'But there was one glaring difference between us, wasn't there? You weren't his type. "Not my cup of tea," he said. "She's a cold, funny little uptight lass that one. Not like you, Snippet. Come on. Let's go and see what I've got in the garden shed." But he couldn't let you leave, you knew too much. You might tell all and he couldn't take that chance. Instead you became his lookout. He blackmailed your silence with all manner of treats, didn't he?'

'Beverley, I had no idea. I'm really sorry. I didn't realise it was you.'

'You're sorry? Sorry because you didn't realise who I was or because you didn't tell?'

Ms Evans is propped against the armrest at a weird angle and jangles the handcuff as if trying to shake free a plague-infested rat. I lean down, pretend I'm going to help, maybe even take the cuff off but instead pull her free hand down and clip it next to the other one.

'Better safe than sorry. Now where were we?'

'Beverley. There's no need for the handcuffs. I'll not run away.'

There it is again. The use of my name to suck me in, the one word, over and over. She's still trying to control our session but she's only making it easier for me to carry on.

'What are you going to do?' Her distorted torso slumps to the side as she gives up twisting.

'That's the thing, Ms Evans. Or should I call you Justine? The thing is, Justine, I'm not certain. All I know is that I have to do something. This has been a long time coming, you can see that.

'There are two possibilities. I could frame you now for the murder of Uncle Chuck and destroy your life for ever. Imagine that. You would be in therapy yourself. I wonder how you'd cope with all the probing, especially when your sexual proclivities become public knowledge. How cool would that be? *The lesbian therapist goes down for murder.* I can see the headline. Can't you? DCI Colgate has been following the trail I've left for him. The finger points firmly your way.'

'What the hell are you talking about? What trail?'

'Where should I start? There was the samurai sword for Freddie. You'd been googling for such a present for ages. I'm good at hacking. It's a stalker's skill. So when a sharper more lifelike weapon arrived at my house, it looked as if it was from a rather careless, unbalanced mother. Also a sharp blade? A big clue combined with Freddie's masterful skill at deadheading the plants. As if he had been taught by a master.'

'Christ. That's all bullshit. You'd never convict me with that. Is that it?'

'Then there were the pictures of the Grim Reaper. Scott Barry took these to the police station, as I knew he would, and they warned Colgate that something was awry. I also took one of Jeremy and myself for Colgate to mull over, in case Scott didn't behave true to form. As planned, Colgate put two and two together and reopened the Garden Shed murder. Today's date, by the way, was put on the pictures. 4pm.'

Ms Evans frantically tries to wriggle her watch face round to see what the time is.

'It's 3.45. Look, there's a clock on the wall. Bakelite frame. Familiar? Anyway I'm certain Colgate will have dug out the files. He's pretty astute, even if he is a pain in the ass. He'll have studied the trail of evidence left at the time, and you see, I'm not in there anywhere. There's no trace of me. My mother would never have suspected that her devoted stepbrother would ever have touched me. You know. You've heard it often enough. My mother never really noticed me. Not much time in her sad life for a skinny little daughter. I slipped through the net. But you... that's a different matter.'

I'm starting to enjoy myself. I have all the time in the world. I swivel the chaise longue round so that Ms Evans doesn't have to strain her neck to look at me. She's like a scraggy old chicken with her white scrawny flesh.

'I didn't come forward either. You're wrong there. There's no trace of me either in any of their files.' Ms Evans is panicking.

'Ah, but Bob Pratchett did. You're good friends. He did me a favour by spraying that red paint all over my car at the hospital. He thought he was doing you a favour. Getting revenge for how I'd stolen your husband. Bob doesn't know you're a lesbian, does he? He's a big mouth and he'll have told the police that you were a regular at Uncle Chuck's house. That's when you two linked up.'

'Go on.' I've got her full attention and she's desperate to find out what I know.

'You're looking after him though, aren't you? Giving him free therapy; for life I suspect. He'll never get over what happened to him. Chuck didn't have a preference. Boys and girls, he wasn't fussy. You're trying to make amends for what happened and Bob doesn't blame you but rather leans on you for support. He thinks you understand. That's a joke!'

I suddenly pick up my mug and fling it across the

room, narrowly missing her head. Brown viscous liquid slithers down the freshly painted walls and the shards of china scatter across the floor, a couple of pieces landing on the sofa.

'Jesus Christ. Calm down.'

'Calm down. Calm down. Relax. Deep breaths. You think that'll make it all go away? You're fucking mental. Next time I'll not miss.' I hiss like a ready-to-explode hand grenade. If I was Ms Evans, I'd think carefully before speaking.

'Anyway, Colgate will work out that you were at the scene. I've told him of all the rogue threatening emails, late-night phone calls which have come my way. He'll probably put two and two together.'

'Those weren't from me. I haven't sent you any-thing. I don't stalk my patients. It's the other way round. You're the stalker, Beverley, not me.'

'I know that, but Colgate is looking for someone to pin the murder on. Scott has done me a favour with his tit-for-tat revenge, but he'll never own up. I'll suggest that the threats came from you all along and my hunch is they'll buy my story. There's too much evidence pointing your way. Anyway, it's a murder they need to solve, not domestic stalking issues.'

I get up and walk round behind the chaise to face the back wall. It's hung over with a large sheet which looks as if it's covering wet paint; perhaps a still-damp mural to liven up the space. Like a magician uncovering a white rabbit, I pull the sheet away.

'Voila. What do you think? Recognise the rusty display rail? It took me a long time to find an exact match.' I stretch my arm wide in front of the recent acquisition.

'You see, I had to look at it every Friday, week after week. Do you remember it? Probably not. You weren't interested, were you? You got all your treats indoors. Did you even dare a peek into the garden shed or did you hibernate in the warmth of the television room?' I rear back like a dragon breathing red-hot fire.

'You turned a blind eye. Didn't you? It was easiest. You knew what was going on. Even after Chuck was killed you stayed quiet. You know exactly what you turned your back on. Do you really think I chose you to talk about my ex-boyfriends and my stalking issues? I'd have much preferred a man. You're a real nosey bitch when it comes to digging.

'I chose you from a whole list of possible psychotherapists. I've waited and plotted for years on how to make you pay for what you did and I had to get close. Travis was the icing on the cake, although it would have been more effective if you hadn't been a dyke.'

I turn back towards the hanging rack. The structure is identical to the one Uncle Chuck kept in the garden shed, hung with bespoke gardening tools.

'On the right. Look here. This is what spliced his carotid artery. A small handheld scythe. After I've got your fingerprints on it, I'll decide which way to go. I've a couple of choices. I can put you in the frame for murder and ruin your life that way. It'll be your word against mine and my history of stalking lovers and boyfriends is a great smokescreen against anything more sinister. That's just become my way of life. Or, perhaps the other possibility is more exciting.'

I lift the scythe down and swish it round in the air. Left and right. High and low, flicking my wrist with agile movements. I'm still a dab hand at the actions.

'I could come over there now and deadhead one last thing. I could say you brought the weapon with you and waited until I was in a deep hypnotic state before lunging forward to take me down. Your motive would be hatred because of how I stole your husband, spurred on by your sick unbalanced mind which has always threatened to explode following on from the trauma over your murder of Chuck Curry.

I'll plead self-defence after I've killed you, finished you off. Mine would be the only voice left to speak and I'd claim that you were seething from hatred and had finally had enough.'

Ms Evans has gone white as her eyes skitter from side to side.

'What about this room? It's a replica of the garden shed. Don't you think Colgate will recognise it? It's not a normal room. It's a cell; a prison of your mind.'

'Oh I'm well ahead of you on that one. Why do you think I've got a whole decorating ensemble of paints and papers up here? Look.' I fling open the doors of a small cupboard built into the wall. 'I'll have completely changed the layout before the police twig. Don't forget, I'm an expert with the paintbrush. I'll have a coat on it no time. Anyway, it's unlikely to be the first thing the police will notice and by the time they've worked it out, it'll be much too late. The proof will be long gone.' I throw the large white sheet back over the tool rail, push the cupboard doors shut and wander back towards the sofa carrying the scythe.

'Here. Let's get those fingerprints on the handle. Gently does it. That's right. Grip firmly. No, your right hand. I'm not that stupid. We all know you're right-handed. Well done. Give it back. That's a good girl,

Queenie.' I take the lethal weapon, lay it on the tabletop before removing my gardening gloves.

At this point it's pretty much fifty-fifty which route I'll go down, but the way I'm feeling, I think I'm slowly starting to prefer deadheading the bitch.

57

'I think it's time for me to lie down so that we can get on with the session. You're being well paid so no point in wasting taxpayers' hard-earned money. Agree?'

I keep the chaise longue facing Ms Evans and then plump a cushion up, easing it in under my neck. I close my eyes, let out a deep breath and don't move for a couple of minutes. Then I peek back at the prisoner.

She's still frantically jiggling the handcuffs in the vain hope that the action will free her from the metal vice. The soft cushioned coating on the inside of the cuffs isn't hurting and won't leave any marks on her wrists; bare metal on her skin would be a lot more painful and I don't want to leave evidence of her bondage.

'It's no good. They're on tightly. Go on. First question. I'm ready.'

Without her notes the quizzing doesn't roll so slickly off the tongue and I'm thrown by her opening gambit.

'Did you kill Danielle's baby? Or have any part in it? That was the reason you were forced to seek counselling, wasn't it?'

'That's three questions. Come on, one at a time.' She doesn't have a quick answer to that one. 'What do you think? I wasn't even there so what makes you think I could have been involved?'

'You were in the area. The police have CCTV footage.'

'No comment.' I laugh at this point. No comment. No comment. No comment. Colgate nearly put his fist through the wall with my chirruped chorus.

'If your aim all along has been to get revenge on me, why bother persecuting your ex-boyfriend? Why follow everyone you're involved with? Including their partners.'

Ms Evans is trying to sit up so that I'll take her

more seriously, but it's difficult as she's hunched awkwardly. It's a good set of questions though.

'It keeps me busy and it's second nature, a way of life. You see, Uncle Chuck taught me the damage that stalking can do to the mind; the fear and nightmares that don't go away. It feels good to punish Scott. Oops. Felt good. Past tense. You still need to sign me off. Remember?'

'What do you want to achieve? You've followed Travis and me; not to mention Danielle, Cosette, Scott, and God knows how many others. Couldn't you find a better way to occupy your time?'

I jiggle my foot up and down. She's starting to really get under my skin with all the digging, but she should be careful as she's in no position to wind me up. She's the one who needs me to hold it together.

'Children would have made my life better. Scott took away that chance. Don't you think he should be punished? Go on. Doesn't he?' I put my hands on my thighs to stop a sudden spasm.

'You could have talked to me about Uncle Chuck. That's the root of it all, isn't it? You need help, Beverley. Not punishment. I can help you.'

'You could have helped me. But you didn't. Did you? You turned a blind eye. I know how different my life could have been. My father never abused me and my mother just didn't care but I'd have survived the family shit if it hadn't been for Uncle Chuck. That's the blackness. How the fuck can you help? I've no intention of going down for murder or being locked away in a unit for the criminally insane.'

Ms Evans is crying, wet torrents rolling down her cheeks. I'd like to think she's sorry, but suspect they're tears of self-pity.

'Did you know that our personalities are like layers of rock formation? Starting with childhood we deposit little seams of rich experience, right the way through to adulthood and onwards to old age. Most people have little nuggets of gold sprinkled here and there. Freddie and Emily, they're your little gold nuggets, aren't they? I don't have those. Travis must have been like a black viscous oil slick though. Not quite so precious.

'Then there's your girlfriend, Olga. She'll leave something else entirely. Probably a good solid coating of shiny marble. You see, I think of these strata like strands of personality DNA. Rich and complex. But you see, Ms Evans, Justine, Queenie... whatever. I don't have layers. On the surface I've worked hard at creating a pristine lawn of manicured perfection. But underneath there's nothing. Just a hard black immovable boulder which is Uncle Chuck.

'You were meant to dig and find some answers but you never did. You fiddled around on the topsoil. You thought my issue was one of stalking lovers who rejected me. Ha. That's a joke. You saw nothing. Maybe I should ask for a refund for the cost of my treatment. Call yourself a psychotherapist? I could have done a better job.'

The sodden tears on her ashen face have turned to large snotty blobs and her breathing is patchy, rasping.

'A paper bag? It helps with panic attacks. I have some in the kitchen.'

'If you let me go, we can sort this together. I'll tell the police everything. They'll listen to me. I can help you get through it all. Please, Beverley. Don't make it worse.'

'Why didn't you tell at the time? You didn't even come forward after the murder. You scuttled back into your shitty little hole, and pretended none of it ever happened. You pretended to yourself that you'd never been a part of it all. Is that why you became a therapist? To work through the guilt?

'Therapists all have dark filthy little secrets which they try to exorcise and understand. You had to find a way to work through yours; to deal with the shame. The one thing you never did was come clean; tell the truth. I bet it feels good listening to Bob Pratchett. He gets his treatment free. Lucky Bob!'

I stand up, lift the scythe and swish it around until the sight of her pleading face nudges me to a third option, an option other than framing her for Curry's murder or killing her myself.

'Perhaps I could let you go. But what guarantee do I have that you'll tell them everything? You might tell them I'm totally insane and get me locked away.'

'You have my word, Beverley.' She's using my name over and over. Christ she must think I'm totally naïve. It's as if I'm a potential suicide victim she's trying to stop from jumping off a road bridge.

'I'll think about it. But first I need to pop to the bathroom. It's all the liquid, but relax, I'll be back.'

With that I move to the door, open it and check over my shoulder at the Quasimodo form before gently closing it behind me. The third option is looking like it might be the way to go. Not quite so messy. But before I unlock the handcuffs I have a couple of little jobs to do.

I check my watch. It's now 4.15pm. The police will be here any minute. Colgate is so predictable and he won't delay when he realises that Ms Evans isn't at work. Any minute now he'll be banging on the door. I'm surprised, but relieved, he isn't here already. He thinks Ms Evans is here to kill me, slice my head off with the garden scythe. No one, apart from Ms Evans, knows about my visits to the garden shed. If she can't tell then Colgate will always put two and two together and get six.

* * *

I need to get the staging spot on before Colgate arrives. He needs to be certain that Ms Evans was the Garden Shed murderer who has hidden behind her profession and life of respectability all these years in an effort to cover her heinous crimes. Good old Bob Pratchett. He never did know when to keep his mouth shut. He'll have told Colgate about his friendship with Ms Evans and how they became best friends after it was over and how she's still helping him to deal with the abuse.

As I set to work, I wonder if my therapist ever owned up to Bob Pratchett that no one ever laid a finger on her. It's much more likely that they share horror stories and she lies by telling him how awful it was and about how she totally understands. I can't help wondering how he would feel if he knew she'd been the lookout facilitating the sordid string of events. She kept the very people out who could have saved us all. She turned a blind eye, to save her own hide.

I tug the wire hard, yanking it in place and draw blood as it cuts through my fingers. I lick away the redness, stand up and survey my handiwork. Showtime!

58

Colgate's eyelids flickered open and shut and his temples throbbed as he tried to stay awake. The clock on the dashboard showed 3.40. Lindsay's head bobbed up and down, like a buoy in the water, to a music beat and her pink AirPods reminded Colgate of Percy Pig sweets. He put a strong mint in his mouth and hoisted himself up. Only another twenty minutes to wait.

His mind played over and over what he thought they were up against. It was Friday 13 and exactly twenty-five years ago to the day that the Garden Shed Murder had taken place. His inability to solve the case back then still rankled, an irksome itch that wouldn't go away. The recent Grim Reaper photos, coming on top of all the random stalking and harassment claims, churned up the memories. An unmovable hunch had taken root, the unyielding tentacles choking his thoughts.

Colgate coughed as the mint slithered down whole and for a second blocked his airways. Lindsay's head continued to bob. Suddenly, the hardwhite globule shot back up like a bullet. He picked it off the floor, chucked it out the window and wiped his sticky fingers on his trousers before he checked the time again. A quarter of an hour and Ms Evans would be finished with her patient. The receptionist said they'd have to wait until four to talk to the therapist but keeping Ms Evans close, until four came and went, was Colgate's priority. The time and date, inked boldly on the Grim Reaper photographs, had convinced him that Ms Evans had earmarked today's date for revenge.

Colgate nudged his colleague, opened the car door and stepped outside.

'I'm going to walk round the grounds. Back in ten,' he mouthed.

He stretched out his arms and shoulders, raised his face to the sun before sauntering past Ms Evans' bright-red Audi sports car. A loud crunch of gravel behind made him turn. Bob Pratchett, astride his bicycle, dragged his feet across the loose stones.

'Good afternoon, officer.'

'Mr Pratchett.'

'Hope you haven't come to make an arrest?' Pratchett's spindly white legs swung over his bike which he leant up against the wall.

'No, you can rest easy. We're only here to ask a few more questions.'

'Garden Shed Murder stuff? I see it's back in all the papers.' Pratchett bent down and fiddled with wires on a back wheel.

'Do you have an appointment?' Colgate asked.

'No, not today. I pop by most afternoons, chat to friends. Helps keep me sane.' A high-pitched laugh cackled through the air.

'We're here to see your friend, Justine Evans.'

'Oh. She's not in this afternoon. She's on a house call.'

Colgate took an unsteady step nearer to Pratchett and pointed. 'That's her car over there, isn't it? We've been told she's in with a patient.' Sweat rippled across Colgate's brow as pins and needles shot up his left arm and his right palm sought contact with the brickwork.

'Oh, she leaves her car here sometimes and walks home. She doesn't live far away.'

'Who's she gone to see? Perhaps she's taken the day off,' Colgate croaked, a frog stuck in his throat.

'No, I saw her last night. We're good friends, you know. She's helping me to come to terms with all the shit.' Pratchett's ribs stuck out like a rack of lamb as he straightened up. 'She likes to visit patients at home. It helps her understand them better when she meets them in their natural habitats. Like studying gorillas in the wild. Know what I mean?' Pratchett's fingertips on both hands poked up under his armpits like a chimpanzee.

'Shit, shit, shit.' Colgate slid over the gravel as he lost his footing and raced back to the car. He banged on the window. 'Get out, Lindsay! She's not bloody here. We've been wasting our fucking time and it's already four o'clock. Hurry the fuck up. It'll be as quick by foot.'

'I think Ms Evans is seeing Beverley Digby, across the road, big detached house opposite the entrance.' Bob's voice screeched after Colgate and his outstretched arm flailed in the air, like a bothered windsock, in the direction of the winding driveway.

But Colgate was already forging ahead towards the main road with Lindsay close behind. As he ran, he glanced heavenwards, saying a silent prayer that they wouldn't be too late.

59

'Boo. I'm back. Sorry, didn't mean to scare you.' Although my blood's pumping, I'm enjoying myself. The stairs are quite a challenge, even for a seriously fit person but it's been a long time since anything gave me this much pleasure. Up the ladders and down the snakes and Ms Evans is definitely on a viper.

Her body is motionless and I wonder for a moment if she's having a petit mal fit. She's like an alabaster statue; white, powdery and deathly. I pull out a chair and sit astride, as if riding a horse, and turn it towards her. She's probably in shock.

'Are you okay? You don't look so good. Not long to go. Bet you're keen to know what I've decided? Which option is coming out tops?' Her lips don't move, so I lean across and prod.

'Well?' I ask.

'Beverley.' There it is again. One word. La-di-da-di-da.

'Justine.' Two can play.

'Let me go and I'll put it right. I promise.' The words escape like furballs from a cat. Hoarse and choking. Her choice of words isn't good though. *Put it right*. That's a joke.

I get up and lift the scythe which is lying bereft on the sofa. I hold it up as if I'm deciding what to do with it and the action makes her cry. I do it again, for fun. Up and down. Up and down. Cry baby.

'Justine. I think it could be your lucky day. But I'm relying on you to follow through on your promises. If you don't I'll be behind you, every step of the way. Okay? You know how it works.'

'Yes. I promise. I promise. I'll tell them everything. From the start.' Her eyes light up as if she's won the lottery, all six numbers plus the bonus ball and she can't believe her good fortune.

'Okay. I'm going to unlock your hands and you'll be free to go. I'll be waiting for the police to come calling when you've been to the station. I'm not guilty of anything today except for my role as a mad patient at the end of a hard week. Understand?'

I wonder if Ms Evans is surprised by my sudden calm. She probably thinks I should be looking for more assurances, but I don't need them. I'm pretty certain her first intention will be to go directly to the police station and tell them what's happened. Exactly what's happened. She's a slippery fish and I can't be certain she'll own up to her part in events, but for now I'll give her the benefit of the doubt. Anyway, I'm confident she won't get that far.

When I unlock the handcuffs she shakes down her wrists, like chicken bones, sinewy and meatless. She continues to cry and wobbles as she stands up, her legs threatening collapse.

'Go on. Off you go. Mind your way. I'll tidy up here but remember though, if you don't play along, I'll be back. And by the way, don't forget to sign me off. Bye for now.'

She ignores my outstretched hand and quietly picks up her shoulder bag and heads for the door. 'Goodbye, Beverley.'

She moves slowly while I stand and listen. I take the zapper out of my pocket and hold it up. I count her steps. One, two, three, four, five. Then I click.

The screams are piercing. I move to the door and

watch the spectacle. Unlike Danielle, she's not such a tumbling cheese but the hard wooden risers provide an unforgiving landing pad. Side to side, boom, boom, boom. Her arms flail out wildly in a futile attempt to find some purchase. She's all arms and legs. Danielle was one round fat ball but Ms Evans is much more edgy; sharp and defined, but it's not helping her.

Then there is one almighty crack, followed by silence. I think of the film, *Silence of the Lambs*. After all the screeching of the mothers when their lambs are led to slaughter, there is silence; piercing and shrill. It is the silence of death, but I'm not sure I've been that lucky.

I hover at the top of the stairs and wait a few seconds to make sure there's no movement; no open eyes, pleading for mercy. I haven't got long. Firstly, I click the zapper again to turn the piercing light beam off and move to unwind the clear taut fishing line from across the top step. Easy to reel in. Fluorocarbon. Thin, lightweight and strong. A fisherman's favourite for catching the most slippery eel with its invisible thread.

I then unclip the fasteners which hold it in place, one both side of the top step, and shove them in my pocket along with the line. Once the police have gone

I'll get rid of the evidence. Perhaps I'll drop it in a bin when I take the train back up to Covent Garden. I wonder how Scott is getting on. I'm still curious. My mind wanders, agitated by the thought that Danielle might be pregnant again.

A sudden loud bang on the front door jolts me back from my reverie. It's my cue; the green light. Centre stage, here I come.

I let out the most blood-curdling scream as I wend my way down the stairs, carefully stepping across Ms Evans' inert body. I look down at her, continuing to scream as I check for signs of movement but there aren't any. I then dishevel my hair, using both hands, to give me the look of someone who's been in battle and narrowly escaped the enemy, and begin a cautious descent.

As I reach the bottom stair into the hall, the front door implodes in on itself and DCI Colgate appears in front of me like Doctor Who coming out of the Tardis in a cloud of mist. He's gripping his shoulder, grimacing in pain from the force of entry. Over his shoulder, Lindsay hobbles heavily forward on one foot. I suppress the urge to laugh at the duo; the cavalry who have arrived to save me from certain slaughter at the hands of a deranged killer. *The*

Garden Shed Murderer takes their Revenge. I can see tomorrow's headline.

'It's okay. You're safe now, Miss Digby. Tell me what happened. Slowly does it.' Colgate approaches me gingerly, much the way you would a sick lion. He glances at Lindsay to make sure she's alongside.

'I think she's dead. She tried to kill me.' I collapse on the bottom stair, amazed once again at my ability to cry on cue. My shoulders heave up and down.

'Where? Where is she?'

I point skyward, back up the stairs. Less said and all that.

'Lindsay. Call an ambulance and hurry.'

Colgate pushes past me, taking the risers two at a time. He should be more careful but if he tumbles he'll know the stairs are dangerous. I don't warn him as it might help if he experiences their threat first-hand.

Once Lindsay has put her phone down, she drapes her coat round my shoulders. I must be in shock. Maybe she'll offer to make me some sweet tea.

'You're safe now,' she repeats. The wording seems to have come from some police manual. Yet the content makes me think my plan has worked. They're already treating me as the victim, having come here convinced that Ms Evans was going to kill me. They've no idea that it was the other way round.

'Thanks,' I mumble.

'Perhaps we could go into the kitchen and I could make you some tea?'

Yes, I was right. Lindsay's studied the manual carefully. Sweet tea must be pointer number two on what to offer in an emergency. I could offer her a glass of champagne but think I'll keep that for myself and enjoy a silent toast when they've gone.

The future's looking bright. Some peace at last. *Saluti!*

Cheers!

60

London Echo – Isaac Gatward

Suspected Garden Shed Murderer in a Coma

After 25 years, revenge attack backfires.

Justine Lowther, known professionally as Justine Evans, has been left in a coma after an aborted revenge attack aimed at Miss Beverley Digby. Miss Digby had been having an affair with Ms Evans' husband, Travis Lowther.

Twenty-five years ago, Justine Evans was a child victim of the Garden Shed Murderer, Mr Chuck Curry, but she never came forward after his death to tell her story. It has only recently come to light that she was in fact a victim of his heinous crimes against children.

It would appear that Justine Evans had been planning revenge on Miss Digby for some time, sending threatening messages and stalking her at all hours of the day and night. The police were alerted when photographs of the Grim Reaper turned up, all dated Friday 13, 4.00pm. DCI Colgate, who is heading up the investigation, followed a lead that took him to the house of Miss Digby where Ms Evans appeared to have planned to cut off the victim's head with a garden scythe, identical to the one used to behead Chuck Curry. The scythe had Ms Evans' fingerprints all over it.

However, Miss Digby managed to escape from her attic room where she was being held hostage. In the ensuing pursuit, Ms Evans missed her footing and fell heavily down the steep flight of hard wooden stairs, cracking her skull as her body came to rest at the bottom.

The police are waiting to speak to her should she wake up from her coma. At the present time the signs are not looking good and they may have a long wait.

Miss Digby is in shock and refusing to discuss what happened with the press. She has asked that her privacy be respected at this difficult time.

Paper clippings, heroic headlines, lay strewn across Colgate's desk. It was exactly one week since the event and there was still no let up. The story was front-page news and he was man of the moment; the hero of hunches. Yet he felt like a fraud. He'd got lucky, pure and simple.

To escape the claustrophobic atmosphere of the police station, as well as the hungry hacks camped out front, Colgate sneaked out through the back door. He headed towards the Abbott Hospital grounds, his lungs craving fresh air. His mouth was furred, a metallic taste glued to his tastebuds and he didn't feel so good. Sunlight seared through his pupils and starry zigzag lines played havoc with his peripheral vision as the migraine got worse.

Outside the hospital building, a small group of patients lolled on the grass and sipped water from plastic bottles. Christ, he could do with a proper drink. He veered to the right but was too late.

Bob Pratchett stood up, his arms criss-crossing in

the air as if guiding a plane to land. 'Yoo-hoo. Over here. Come and join us.'

Colgate wandered over. 'Hi. Sorry, guys, but I can't stop. Just taking a short break. Lovely day,' he offered, squinting and using his hand as a visor to shield his eyes.

Bob Pratchett scratched furiously at his bare arms. The psoriasis had turned them into a minefield of erupting scabs. He was overly agitated. Colgate should feel sorry for the guy, but Pratchett got under his skin, made him uneasy. Following on from the incident at Miss Digby's house, Colgate had heard Pratchett's account of his relationship with Ms Evans and what had happened when they were kids. Apparently, they'd formed a close bond after Curry's murder and Bob had promised not to tell anyone that Ms Evans had been there at the time. He told the police that she'd been too traumatised to come forward and wanted to suppress all memories of what had happened.

Yet Colgate wasn't convinced. Ms Evans didn't seem like a victim of abuse. He'd seen enough cases over the years. She was too controlled, professional, and lacked the psychotic symptoms and cycles of heavy depression shown by other child victims. But Pratchett was confident in his storytelling.

Colgate raised a hand and wandered on past, but Pratchett's grating tones followed him.

'The attic. Check out the layout. Ever heard of Stockholm Syndrome? Well, Beverley's attic is a mirror image of the garden shed. Down to the chintzy teacups. It's like a comfort blanket to the past.'

The sun slipped behind a cloud and Colgate shivered.

'Sorry. What's that?' A chill, like an arctic blast, attacked his bones. He turned round to face Pratchett.

'We were given a guided tour when we went for a session at Beverley's house,' Pratchett continued. 'She showed us the attic, but it was only later I realised there was something odd. At first, I couldn't put my finger on it. You see I'd been in the shed enough times to remember every nook and cranny. How come Beverley, who claims never to have been there, has just decorated her attic in an exact replica of the garden shed?' Pratchett's head nodded as if on a spring.

Colgate swallowed hard and tossed a reply back. 'Thank you, Mr Pratchett. I'll definitely look into it.' His legs moved like unoiled pistons, eager to work but creaking under the effort. He moved as fast as he could, his head thumping as the blood pumped and thoughts scrambled round his brain.

When he saw the station up ahead, he checked his watch. He'd done the return journey in little under ten minutes.

* * *

How the hell could he have missed it? Colgate swilled the whisky round the tumbler, threw back his head and swallowed. Fire burned his throat and made his eyes water. It had been right in front of his face and now the archive evidence spread across his desk, confirmed Pratchett's observations.

Colgate looked at the faded colour print of the inside of the garden shed. Memories of the green flaky paint, the chintzy china tea set and brown poly-ester-covered sofa, which seemed to hold the shed in place, flooded back. The sofa had acted as a buttress to save the building from collapse. He was now certain Digby's attic layout was identical, except for the flaky paint; although the colour was the same. The Bakelite radio, as well as the wall clock in the picture were, without doubt, replicas to the ones he'd noticed in the attic.

He shook the whisky bottle, held it up to the light

and emptied the contents into his glass. His shoulders slumped as the alcohol took hold and his thoughts unravelled. On the other side of the locked door the muffled sounds of the night-time station activity was distant.

There was no such thing as repeat coincidence in murder cases. Two bodies falling down hard unforgiving flights of stairs were both linked to Miss Digby. He banged his fists hard on the desk. Christ. How the hell had he started to believe in all that coincidence shit?

The blurry picture in front of him, when compared with Miss Digby's current attic layout, might give him enough to prove that he'd been right all along to harbour doubts about the woman's innocence. The evidence could help prove that she intentionally tried to cause serious harm to both Danielle, Scott Barry's girlfriend, and to Ms Evans. If the latter never came out of a coma, Miss Digby could be looking at a murder charge.

Colgate dragged himself up and neatened the pile of papers. He needed stronger evidence to show that the two ladies' tumbles were no freak accidents. He had to get back to Miss Digby's house as soon as possible, and photographing her attic was top priority.

61

I smile to myself, realising that Ms Evans would be very disapproving. I can hear the sharp intake of breath and feel her stony admonishing stare. But I've no intention of stopping what I do best, what has become a way of life and gives me good reason to get up in the mornings.

As I stroll through Regent's Park it's as if the weight of the world has been lifted off my shoulders. I'm not sure how long the levity will last but today, Friday 20 July, I feel as if I've finally been let out of prison; on parole pending further investigations. Time will tell.

I pass the tennis courts and listen to the pit-pat of balls ricochet back and forth across the nets. 'Good shot.' 'My advantage.' 'Well played.' 'Hard luck, old chap.' The green painted playing surface is smooth, hard and unforgiving. The balls bounce so high, mini kangaroos, that one pops over the fence and I catch it in my left hand.

'Well held,' whoops a sweaty player with a paunch. His hand shoots up, indicating that he's waiting for me to send it back. Suspicious idiot. I toy with pocketing it but decide against. Not today. Today he's in luck and I toss it back.

I used to think of my outward appearance as that of a pristine Wimbledon lawn but today I consider that I have become much more like the courts I wander past. Not a blade of soft grass in sight. My surface is still green but with a sturdier, tougher, all-weather coating and the lines are much more defined than the threadbare chalk markings of Centre Court. My barrier against weeds and dormant threats is more robust.

I wave at her. She's on the court farthest away and as I draw close, I watch her bounce up and down eagerly between points. A whippet of a thing. Still all curls and giggles but some of the excitement has definitely gone; dissipated through disillusionment that has stolen some innocence and the belief that love conquers all. All down to Scott.

Cosette waves back and uses her fingers to beckon me over. It feels good to know that I was successful in ruining their relationship. Scott definitely doesn't deserve her.

'Hi, Beverley!' she shouts through the fencing. 'I'm nearly done. Just a few more serves.' The tennis coach is standing in close, pulling back her arms, like a ventriloquist controlling its dummy, to demonstrate the right action, and his groin is rubbing up against her thigh. I smile. She's already moving on. Perhaps I'll take up the game.

I sit down on a bench and wait for her. She heads over once she's finished.

'Hi,' she says.

'Hi. Good to see you. Shall we grab a cold drink? It looks too much like hard work out there.'

'Sounds good. Yes I'm, as you say in English, knackered.' She wipes her brow with a small hand towel and flicks her hair loose from a hair band. 'Claudio works me hard. Money well spent.'

She waves back at her coach and I can see what she means. I suspect Claudio is the gigolo of Regent's Park.

'Same time next week?' he yells. Money for old rope springs to mind; a bit like therapy. Although I'm not sure he's what she needs at present, much too smarmy for my taste but I need to remember that Cosette is no longer my problem. It's Scott I have to keep abreast of.

Cosette sits down while I buy a couple of Diet Cokes from a vendor whose van is parked alongside the courts.

'Well, how are you?' I hand her a can and we open them at the same time, giggling as foam spews out over the tops.

'I should be asking you. I read about what happened. It's dreadful. I can't believe your therapist tried to kill you. Are you okay?' Her eyes are doleful, soft and trusting, like a puppy's. I think fluffy bichon frise with its powder-puff coating. Cosette is incredibly nice, too nice perhaps, but then I'm a cynic.

'Getting over it. At least she's not likely to recover and shouldn't be coming back to try to finish me off. Thanks for asking. It's not been easy,' I lie. There was nothing to get over, my planning couldn't have gone better. 'Tell me how you're getting on. Any news of Scott? I think you had a lucky escape.'

She slurps her Coke, throwing her head back, greedy to rehydrate until a sharp explosive hiccup escapes.

'He's back with Danielle. I went to pick up a few things from the flat after I'd stormed out and she was there. Sitting in the kitchen as if she'd never left. She even apologised to me. Can you believe it? Scott didn't apologise though. He doesn't think he's anything to answer for.'

The story tells me what I suspected, but I needed to know for certain and my young friend has confirmed the details. I wonder if she knows about a possible impending pregnancy. Perhaps she'd be able to let it go, move on and forget but that's where we're completely different.

I've bought a new oversized desk diary which sits proudly next to my computer, a dated wall chart and yesterday I installed a calendar planning app on my phone. It's a very trendy weekly organiser. My future will be as a well-programmed vigilante, punishing those who abuse, mistreat and toy with other people. I've special skills and there's plenty of work to be done. No more classroom assistant jobs or Spanish lessons for me as wiping out evil is a full-time job.

'I'm sorry. Perhaps it was a good thing that we went to that restaurant in Sloane Square. Otherwise you might never have found out. He's a bastard and you've had a lucky escape.' I pat her on the shoulder. I won't push her on the Danielle thing; she doesn't deserve it, and I can find out for certain on my own.

'He's moving away. He's already packed up and

they're emigrating. He wouldn't tell me where but I don't think I really want to know.'

He'll be off to Italy; the Amalfi Coast, or Rome perhaps. But more likely it will be to the tumbledown farmhouse in the depths of Umbria which caught his eye. He always was a dreamer.

I consider how nice it might be to move away myself and leave recent events behind. Forget about Ms Evans and Uncle Chuck. Italy might be the very ticket. I smile, doubting the Italians will be too concerned about stalking issues between English ex-lovers.

'From what I see, I think you've already moved on.' I tilt my head in the direction of the tennis courts.

Claudio is watching us, in between giving scant instruction to a middle-aged woman while he scrolls up and down on his mobile phone. Cosette blushes.

'Listen, I'd better make a move. I've left a man painting and decorating the house. I need to get back and check on progress. He's been clearing out the attic, painting the walls a different colour and throwing out the tatty furniture. I don't want any reminders of the visit from Ms Evans and I couldn't face the task myself.'

'Well, good luck. Keep in touch.' With that,

Cosette picks up her racket and rucksack. 'I must get going too as I've got an exam tomorrow. I'll be glad when the term's over.'

I stand up, lean in and hug her close. She's like the daughter I'd have liked; the one I'll never have. But we'll keep in touch. I'll let her know when Scott and Danielle's move to Italy doesn't work out and we'll share a good laugh.

We walk off in opposite directions, I go backwards and she goes forwards.

'Bye, Cosette.'

'Bye, Beverley. *Adieu.*' And she is gone.

62

Standing across the main road, directly opposite the entrance to Beverley Digby's house, Colgate squinted against the sun. The upstairs windows were flung open, unusually wide. The attic dormer stuck out at a ninety-degree angle to the roof.

Colgate quickened his pace as he and Lindsay weaved between the rush-hour traffic. He strode up the front path and stubbed furiously at the doorbell, wiping his damp brow with the back of his left hand. 'Shit, shit, shit. Answer the bloody door.' He peered through the frosted panel and unglued his finger from the button as someone approached.

'Hi. Can I help you?' A young man appeared,

straggling hair scooped back in a ponytail. The baggy tattered jeans, underpants visible over the top of a waistband and the paint splatters on a threadbare T-shirt confirmed Colgate's worst suspicions.

Colgate screeched over the din of background rock music. 'We're here to see Miss Digby. Is she at home?' He waved his identification badge and, without preamble, pushed across the porch into the hall.

The man wiped down his hands on his jeans and whipped back a stray flop of hair. He apologised for the noise and went back to close the kitchen door. 'Sorry. She's gone out for the day. Can I help?'

'I hope so. May we come in, Mr...?'

'Vickers. Vince Vickers. I don't live here, by the way. I'm just doing some odd jobs. Is this about what happened last week? Dreadful business. Miss Digby doesn't like to stay in much as she's still really upset. Could you blame her?'

Colgate sneezed, the fresh paint fumes riding up his nostrils. 'We'd like a look around, if that's okay.' Without a search warrant, Colgate knew he was going against the law, but he had to act fast. 'Starting in the attic.' He moved towards the stairs without waiting for approval and climbed.

By the time he reached the last flight, Colgate was gripping the handrail and his breathing was laboured, heavy in his chest. The rickety risers challenged each footstep and he could see how easy it would have been for Ms Evans to lose her footing.

At the top, Lindsay and Vickers passed him, entering through the already-open door. The brightly coated walls screamed with a blinding red gloss. The garishness was a taunt, teasing at his tardiness, and Colgate knew he was too late.

'It's a bit bright, isn't it?' Vickers said. 'Miss Digby wanted to remove all traces of the room as it was before Ms Evans tried to kill her. She was determined to use red but it's a nightmare to work with.' Vickers blinked rapidly.

'I bet. Where's all the furniture? There was a sofa here, a table there, and where's the kettle?' Colgate wandered round, opening and closing empty cupboards. The only signs of recent activity were half empty paint pots and brushes.

'I took almost everything to the dump. She wants a fresh start, a complete makeover.'

Colgate stood in the middle of the room, surrounded by red flames of hell. Conniving bitch. The whole thing had been planned, always one step ahead of him. Beverley Digby, the piece of shit, had put Ms Evans in the frame for murder and attempted murder.

The policeman turned to Vickers. 'Can you remember what you took to the dump?' Colgate was grasping at straws, knowing full well that verbal confirmation of what had been in the room before the makeover was never going to put Beverley in the frame. Even concise descriptions of all the furniture items would be flimsy at best.

'Yes. A sofa. A table with four chairs. A Bakelite radio and matching clock, of all things. I took *them* to the charity shop. Worth a few bob.'

Vickers' hand scrabbled in the tight back pocket of his jeans. 'Here. Have a look. I'm taking progress pictures, before and after shots. Beverley keeps texting to see how I'm getting on.' He turned the mobile screen towards the detective and scrolled through a series of pictures. 'This is the room before I started work. You can see all the items and layout.' Vickers' chest puffed out.

Colgate snatched the phone. 'These are brilliant. Can you send them through to me?'

Colgate jotted down his number and as Vickers forwarded the shots, the detective went back out onto the landing. His head swivelled through the full 360 degrees, his eyes working up and down the walls and across the ceiling.

'What's that on the wall up there? Halfway up.'

'Where?' Vickers appeared alongside, his phone stuffed back into his jeans.

'Between the beam joists. Look.' Colgate pointed to a small round silver unit jammed between the wooden slats.

'Oh, that's a light. Very bright. It's normally pitch black up here and it comes on automatically with movement. There's a switch here on the outside of the door. You need to have it set to "on" and then, when you come in and out, it lights up. It's bloody bright though.'

Vickers flicked the switch and jiggled his arm around in front of the sensor. 'There's also a remote control here which can be used as a zapper.'

Colgate and Lindsay automatically put their hands up as the searing light from a fluorescent white strobe hit them between the eyes.

'I keep it turned off when I'm working otherwise it blinds me every time I go up and down the stairs.'

'Lindsay. Walk from the attic door to the top of the stairs. I want to see exactly when the light clicks on.' As an afterthought he added, 'Be careful though.'

As Lindsay approached the stairs, the light

clicked on the moment she went to take her first step down.

'Christ, boss. I can't see a bloody thing.'

'Don't move. I'll turn it off. What height are you, Lindsay?'

'Five feet six. Why?'

'So, I suspect, is Ms Evans. I think the light was strategically placed to hit right between her eyes.'

* * *

Colgate was now convinced that Beverley Digby had caused both tumbles, using invisible trip wires and in the case of Ms Evans, the addition of a blinding strobe light. Yet, the detective still hadn't enough to make an arrest; he needed facts, hard evidence.

'Lindsay, we need to dig around and find out who Beverley Digby really is. I suspect she's changed her name. We need to know who she was back then, at the time of the Garden Shed Murder.' Colgate strode ahead. 'She seems to have staged the whole bloody incident in her attic.'

The traffic on Southgate High Street muffled the DCI's words but when they reached the station, he stopped, leant on the railings and faced Lindsay.

'You see, I think Miss Digby knew Ms Evans at

the time of the Garden Shed Murder and any revenge has probably nothing at all to do with the errant husband. That's just been a red herring. I think she's got a much greater axe to grind and that's what we need to find out; her motive for putting Ms Evans in the frame for Chuck Curry's murder and for wanting her out of the way. Come on. The clock's ticking.'

63

I

Italy, here I come. I pull along a small hard-shelled cabin bag which I've just picked up; 'cheap as chips', as my mother would say. It's like a pink tortoise on wheels. I'm toying with adding a couple of pink streaks through my hair to accessorise the sassy style, as life is all about co-ordinating.

I jiggle the suitcase over the threshold of 'Cutting Edge'. It's little more than a kiosk on the end of the row of shops but a sign boasts an after-hours locksmith. Once I'm gone, no one will be able to gain access to my house. Vince Vickers won't be getting paid, that's for sure, and the spare key he's got to finish the work won't be any use. When it sticks in the lock, he'll get the message. The 'before and after' snaps have sealed his financial failure and I'll be long gone before the painter or my nosey keyholding neighbours are any the wiser.

Colgate will no doubt have displayed his little rat-like teeth, gritted together, in a smarmy victory smile when Vickers produced the photographs. The detective is one snooping, nosey, sneaky bastard. It's not that I think he's got it in for me per se, but he's an arrogant prick who can't take defeat. He failed to nail the Garden Shed killer and he failed to convict me of Danielle's accident and now he's like a dog with a bone, desperate to convict me of Ms Evans' tumble. He'll be working on the premise 'third time lucky'.

Once I've arranged for the locksmith to come round in the morning and change the locks, I decide to take a detour home. I have a definite masochistic streak of which Ms Evans tried so hard to make me own up to.

'Why do you keep going back for more punishment? For more rejection, Beverley?' I can hear her. Dig, dig, dig. She had more shit below the surface than I ever did and probably more than most of her patients.

As my pet tortoise and I trundle along, I realise that masochism has become part of who I am. Like bulimia, it provides a comfort blanket of familiarity even though it's covered in vomit. It's the friendlier neighbour of sadism as I'm only tormenting myself, no one else.

This invitational punishment leads me to retravel the old familiar route one last time. I count the paving slabs, tripping over the old well-worn cracks, amazed as always that they're still here after twenty-five years. Down Burton Avenue, past the post office, into Salisbury Road where Uncle Chuck enticed me into the sweetie shop for treats. Finally, on past Holdenhurst Avenue where I pull my case faster and faster until I break a sweat, hearing the stealthy tread behind.

Once I reach the safety of my front gate I slot the handle neatly back into the case, preparing my tortoise for hibernation. I'll hide it in the hall cupboard before I yell out to Vickers. He's upstairs and I can see the brush strokes flowing back and forth from where I'm standing. Ha. Little does he know he's working pro bono.

I open the front door and yell up.

'Hi. I'm home. It's only me. Hannah.'

Hannah McGregor. That's my real name. Dad was Willie McGregor, a renowned Glaswegian drunkard whose claim to fame was the successful smashing of my mother's jaw in several places. But I'll let bygones be bygones. I'm going back to my real name now. It's been a while but I need to get used to it because it's emblazoned across my passport. Hannah Beverley Digby-McGregor. My mother liked the double-barrelled pretension; it made her feel special like nothing else did.

'Who?' Vickers appears above me, sliding to earth along the last stretch of banister.

'Hannah. Hannah McGregor. Don't look so surprised. You don't really think I look like a Beverley, do you?' I laugh. 'Fancy a drink before you go? I need a drink and company would be nice.'

Vickers checks his watch. 'Yes, go on then. Why not.'

He thinks he's coming back later in the week to finish the job and get paid, a nice hefty wad of cash, but hey ho. Serves him right.

'I'll explain over a drink, about my name change. Come on, let's go into the kitchen and I'll get out the wine.'

He follows me through and takes a seat on one of my newly acquired bar stools. I uncork a bottle and hand him a glass, raising mine towards him. 'Thanks for all the painting. You've done a brilliant job. Not much more and you'll be finished.' Vickers blushes like a five-year-old.

We clink our glasses and Vickers knocks his back in one.

'Top up?' I offer.

'Go on then.' He holds out his glass, sits back and I tell him why I changed my name. I lie, tell him it was a teenage rebellion thing and chuckle. As he begins to tell me about his family and kids, I stifle a yawn and let his voice waft in one ear and out the other.

This time tomorrow I'll be on the last flight out from

Stansted airport to Perugia in Italy. The plan is to mosey around Tuscany and Umbria for a while, get my bearings and find a nice little place to lay my hat until I find a permanent base. It'll be near to Scott and Danielle, but not too close as I'll need some space.

In Italy, I'll not have to worry about accusations that my choices are anything more than coincidence. The Italian carabinieri is much more laid back than the British police force and will most likely ignore approaches by Scott when he points accusing fingers. He'll need to learn to hold his tongue because he'll be no match for the machismo of the Italian men. Fluttering my eyelashes is a backup plan.

I close my eyes as the Merlot washes over my lips and the soft waves of nectar ripple down my throat. Vickers stands up, pushes his stool back and my eyes pop open. He looks at me strangely but at least he's stopped rambling.

'Sorry, hope I didn't bore you. Thanks for the drink, but I'd better make tracks. I'll see you Thursday.'

'Not at all, thanks for stopping, and sorry, but I was miles away.'

I walk him down the hall, open the front door and wave him off.

'Bye, Vince. Great job, by the way,' I say in hushed tones. 'Cin Cin! Alla Salute! Cheers!'

64

As Colgate drained a second full tumbler of whisky, with only a faint streak of light from a desk lamp for company, a sharp burning sensation hit the back of his throat. His eyes were bloodshot, dried like shrivelled prunes from scouring old files, looking for evidence to link Miss Digby to Chuck Curry and put her at his house on the day of the murder, along with proof that she'd met Justine Evans at the same address.

Googling into the small hours had finally thrown up some important information. As Colgate suspected, Miss Digby and Hannah McGregor were one and the same person. Passport identification showed her full name as Hannah Beverley Digby-McGregor, and Hannah McGregor was mentioned in the Garden Shed files. She was the daughter of the bastard's stepsister, and Mr Curry had been her regular childminder; babysitter.

Beverley's mother had eventually committed suicide following a history of violent abuse from her husband. There was little in the files relating to the girl herself, other than her name and nothing untoward relating to a relationship with her uncle had been flagged up. There was no evidence that she'd ever been abused. Her parents obviously suspected nothing, probably too wrapped up in their own domestic war and the girl herself had kept quiet.

Colgate, hunched over, felt the old familiar creak in his back. He still hadn't enough evidence to make an arrest. Digby had framed Ms Evans for the Garden Shed Murder by making it look as if Ms Evans had it in for her instead. The therapist appeared to be getting revenge for Miss Digby's affair with her husband. Colgate knew Ms Evans had been at Chuck Curry's house often enough; Bob Pratchett had confirmed the details. Yet for some reason, Miss Digby had drawn Ms Evans into a web of intrigue, having some sort of axe to grind against her therapist, but Colgate had no idea what it was. But he knew for certain now that this was not some sordid *crime de passion*. Mr

Lowther had nothing to do with events, rather the Garden Shed Murder held the answers. The two women must have met there and for some reason Miss Digby sought revenge. Revenge for what? There were no obvious pointers.

Colgate winced as he reached for the bottle, his body sore and stiff. Even with new evidence, what did it prove? He still had nothing concrete as far as the murder was concerned and he couldn't prove Miss Digby culpable of anything. The facts swirled round in his head.

There was the attic, kitted out exactly like the garden shed had been twenty-five years before. A strobe light inserted at such an angle that it most likely blinded Ms Evans in her haste to descend the steep rickety stairs leading away from the attic. He suspected that, most probably, a trip wire, something like invisible fluorocarbon fishing wire, had been used to trip up both Danielle, Scott Barry's girlfriend, and then Ms Evans.

Perhaps Miss Digby got lucky in the stairwell with Danielle as Colgate was certain a strobe light hadn't been used but he was convinced a trip wire had been. Probably the pregnant woman didn't have a clear view of the ground under her bump. Yet it was all conjecture. A wire would have been easy to reel in and dispose of, but there was no CCTV footage and nothing to place Miss Digby in the stairwell on the day Danielle lost the baby.

With Ms Evans in a coma, it was Miss Digby's accusations that held sway. Even if Colgate could prove the two ladies had been victims of Chuck Curry around the same time, he only had Miss Digby's statements to go on. She would doubtless offer up a reason why Ms Evans had it in for her after all this time, even if it wasn't solely to do with the errant husband.

Colgate downed the whisky and switched off the lamp. At fifty-eight he ought to be considering early retirement. He could hand in his badge, take to the golf course and enjoy holidays in the sun with his wife, enjoy some well-earned quality time together.

Yet, as he reached for his jacket, he knew he wasn't ready. He'd worked too long and hard on this particular case to walk away with nothing to show for it. There'd be no happy retirement until he had Miss Digby banged up behind bars; either in a top security prison or a remote mental institution. He didn't care which but he couldn't live with the failure for the rest of his life.

65

Justine didn't want to open her eyes. Safe behind shuttered eyelids, not ready to tell her story, she feigned sleep as her mind wandered.

* * *

Uncle Chuck had been her first customer. It was only a Saturday morning job in a sweet shop but it was a start. He'd winked, told her to keep the change. Fifty pence was a lot for an eleven-year-old, but she didn't tell about the tips which soon became regular. She pocketed the coins and waited until her empty growling stomach sucked them from her grasp.

It had all been about the money. Uncle Chuck

picked up on her plight and used the insight to feather his nest. It worked; for both of them. She started earning good money and, in return, she turned a blind eye to the depravity. It began when she followed him, one Saturday afternoon, to his house. He led her down a side alley into the back garden which was awash with flowers and colour. The sight and smells were intoxicating.

'Help yourself to the strawberries. There's loads. And look here. Take some tomatoes with you too.' He proudly stroked the plants, treating them like fragile precious babies' heads. His fat fingers, weirdly gentle, feathered the surface of the delicate leaves.

Then he opened up the garden shed and showed her inside. 'What do you think?'

She didn't know what he wanted her to say. It stunk. Dirty tools lined the walls, the neatness of the display at odds with the rusting implements. She pretended to be impressed. She needed the money. When he produced the biscuits and made her a creamy mug of hot chocolate, she overdid the enthusiasm, telling him it was a palace.

Only after her stomach was full did she start to feel uneasy.

'Here, pet. Sit on the sofa. It's really comfy. I might get a television set in here. What do you think?

Put it up in the corner and you could watch your favourite programmes.'

He pointed with his arm and his dirty tight shirt reared up to display a bare hairy midriff pitted with angry pockmarks.

'It's hot. Why don't you take your jumper off and we can get comfy?' With that he slipped his own shirt over his head. If she hadn't been freaking out it would have been funny. His fat head got stuck and he couldn't shake the shirt off.

'Fuck,' was all he said.

At that point she stood up and looked at the door.

'Not so fast. You've had your treats. What about mine? Come on. Fair's fair.'

The biscuits and hot chocolate exploded in a sudden projectile missile of vomit, spewing a deep yellow concoction onto his bare sandalled feet. The slime congealed over his black nailed toes.

'For fuck's sake. What's up with you?'

It seemed to do the trick, because his hand moved away from his trouser belt and he stepped outside, inhaling greedily at the fresh air.

'Sorry. I feel sick and want to go home.' Queenie didn't cry. It didn't seem right considering the mess she'd made. He stared at her as if she was a scrawny horse at an animal auction and he was weighing up whether to put his hand in his wallet or turn around and go home.

His next words stuck in her mind, sealed her fate and explained what happened next. He patted her on the head, handed back her jumper and said, 'Don't worry. You're not really my type.'

With that he locked up the shed and they walked back towards the house in silence. She didn't dare pick any fruit on the way and he didn't encourage her.

It was only when they were inside that she started to panic that he mightn't give her any more tips. She'd become dependent on the ever in-creasing amounts as the money put food on the table.

Yet Uncle Chuck made a serious miscalculation. He underestimated her cunning. Kids were gullible, trusting and needy but not stupid.

'Go along then. See you around. Sorry about your upset tummy.'

'Bye, Uncle Chuck. I'll be able to tell my friend, Bob, that I've now seen the inside of the shed as well. He's been desperate to tell me about what goes on but he's been sworn to secrecy. He'll not need to worry now because we can share all.'

Chuck pushed in front of her and blocked the

exit, slamming the door so that the noise cracked through her ribs.

'Bob? Bob who?' Chuck's jowls wobbled, and his breath laboured. At one point, he put his hand to his chest and closed his eyes.

'Pratchett. Bob Pratchett. You know him. He comes into the sweetie shop all the time. He's my best friend.' She hardly knew Bob at that point but had seen him follow Uncle Chuck, more than once, back to the house.

'Listen, Queenie. I'm going to call you Queenie, if that's okay? You're one special little lady. I bet you're a good friend to Bob. But let's keep it among ourselves. If you fancy you can come back and watch telly here any time you like. Look.' With that he flung open the door to his living room where a massive flat-screen television sat atop a dark mahogany sideboard.

'Wow,' she said.

'Would you like that? Perhaps you could help me look after my dog, Ratty. Take him for walks? I'll pay well.' She might have only been eleven but she guessed what his game was. She knew she shouldn't, but she accepted and he was soon paying generously to buy her silence, even before the television was switched on and even when rain kept the dog's en-thusiasm for a walk at bay.

You see, Justine's mother was a gambler. A single mum who always thought the next punt would provide the big win; the solution to all their problems. But it never did and they lived hand to mouth. Social services had threatened more than once to take Justine into care.

If her mother thought the Saturday job was overly well paid, she didn't moan. She took the earnings and Justine pocketed the tips, the latter far outweighing the former.

It was only some time later that Hannah McGregor appeared on the scene, usually on Fridays. She was a year below Justine at school but they never spoke. When Hannah stopped outside the living room door on the way through the house to the garden shed, her eyes made silent pleas in Justine's direction. Yet Justine gripped the remote control and averted her eyes. It was her way of coping as she turned a blind eye.

Justine guessed it was Hannah who had sliced Chuck's head off. She hadn't been there that Friday but knew Hannah had. Uncle Chuck had been suffering with a high temperature and had sent Queenie packing before the younger girl arrived.

Hannah certainly had motive, opportunity and the weapon. When she didn't come forward after the murder and the police never found out who did it, life got back to a new type of normal for Justine. She never told anyone that she had become a lookout for Uncle Chuck and no one ever asked. The public were more than happy that someone had the guts to finish him off.

66

'Ms Evans? Ms Evans? Can you hear me? It's Detective Colgate. I need to ask you some questions. May I sit down?'

A chair was dragged closer, grating harshly on the hard floor, interrupting the steady hustle and bustle of the ward. Justine encouraged patients to be honest as the best way forward but she herself didn't feel strong enough to bare all. She needed answers, especially to questions concerning Beverley.

'Can you hear me?'

'Yes. I can hear you,' she whispered. Her lids peeled back and her eyes screwed up against the blinding light. Her throat felt as if a saw had hacked through her voice box, serrations ripping it apart.

'This is PC Lindsay. She'll be taking a few notes, if that's okay?' The detective nodded towards his associate.

Justine was a suspect. That's why they were here. It was all flooding back: the scene in the attic; the curved glistening scythe, the handcuffs and then the fall down the rickety stairs. Beverley had framed her for attempted murder, had set her up. Justine's thoughts scrambled for clarity.

She realised now that it had been Beverley toying with her for months, with all the threatening emails, late-night phone calls and sinister messages. The sword incident had been clever. It had appeared to be a present from Justine herself but what mother would have put their child's life in danger?

The police were here to get her version of events before applying the handcuffs. She closed her eyes again as the room spun. Where the hell was Beverley now? Could Justine convince the police, before it was too late, what the woman was capable of?

'Yes,' she said. 'Go ahead. I've nothing to hide.'

'We have reason to believe that Miss Digby tried to cause you serious injury and also that she might have been responsible for the murder of Mr Chuck Curry. We also think she was involved in the accident which caused Mr Scott Barry's girlfriend to lose her baby. Your testimony, we hope, will help us to convict her.'

Childhood trauma, neglect, and abuse explained the behaviour of the majority of her patients. Beverley was no different. Justine realised that the stalking habits kept Beverley occupied, helped her to maintain control of her life and of other people. But they were a front for the real darkness that lay beneath. As a professional psychologist, Justine had failed. She hadn't put two and two together and had no idea that Beverley Digby and Hannah McGregor were one and the same person. Not until the day in the attic.

'How did you first meet Miss Digby?' Colgate sat down.

And so it began. She told Colgate the whole undiluted truth. How Beverley had never forgiven her for not helping release her from the nightmare of the garden shed. She could have, but she did nothing. She had been young herself and relied on Mr Curry for money. Beginning the affair with Travis was only a small step towards revenge for Beverley. Breaking up the enemy's family would have given her little comfort and she would always have needed more.

'Why didn't you come forward when you received so many threatening emails, phone calls and sick messages? You only told us about a sword incident involving your son, if I remember rightly, but not about all the other threats.'

'I work with sick people all the time; delusional mental patients. I've spent many hours over the years dealing with such threats. It's one of the downsides of the job. I'd only take further action if I believed there was a threat to life. If I'd known who Beverley was, I'd have been much more vigilant and most likely gone to the police.'

The clock on the far wall clicked relentlessly forward. It was one hour later when the nurse approached and told the detective that time was up.

'Ms Evans needs rest.'

'Where is Beverley now? Is she in custody?' Justine's neck creaked as she turned to look at Colgate.

'Not yet. We're on our way now though. Thank you. You've confirmed what we suspected but we needed to hear it first-hand. Listen, we're really sorry for having put you through all of this but time is ticking. I hope you understand. Thank you, Ms Evans.' Colgate pushed his chair back, got up and marched towards the exit.

Justine's eyes followed him, a wry smile on her lips. Beverley would have probably left the country; she'd be long gone. Time spent in the company of

Chuck Curry had hardened her and kept her one step ahead of everyone else. Poor Colgate would be chasing his own tail.

As she drifted in and out of fitful sleep, Justine's mind wandered. Perhaps it was time to take retirement or change careers. She and Olga could move with the children to France; start afresh. They'd talked often enough of renovating a tumbledown chateau and Travis had slim chance of getting custody of Freddie and Emily. He had dug his own grave.

London and Southgate held too many bad memories, the past constantly hammering at the door of the present. Beverley had found a way and now Justine needed to as well.

67

My feet dangle through the balustrade and I let my toes, coated in a bright orange polish, wiggle back and forth. The midday sun is high in the sky, blanketing the terracotta piazza below in a shimmering heat haze.

The Umbrian countryside stretches out far and wide past Lago Trasimeno, which glistens like a large frosted pane of glass. My viewpoint is spectacular. I'm in Castiglione Del Lago, an ancient hilltop fortress once impenetrable to marauders. It's providing a heavenly sanctuary and I'm blending nicely into the surroundings, embracing all things Italian. The food, the wine, and even the men are delicious.

Today I've already moved on from cappuccino to

wine. It's a bit early, even for the Italians, but hey ho, I'm feeling very 'devil may care'. In front of me I've laid out, on a wooden platter, salamis, Parma hams and pungent cheeses which I picked up from the delicatessen two floors below. I wave down at Alessandro who is offering bite-sized tasters to passers-by and who loves to glance my way when Maria isn't looking. I pop an olive on my tongue and turn back to my scrapbook.

It tickles me to think that one day a film might be made of my story. Perhaps some savvy writer will pick up my likeness to Ted Bundy. Not because of my prolific, sadistic and vile murderous rampages but because of my rapt attention to all the newspaper articles, internet posts and television coverage of my case. I am quite the celebrity, albeit one that has disappeared; flown without trace. I wonder how long it will be before I am on the FBI's most wanted list. Colgate suspects I'm in Italy, but has no idea whereabouts.

Miss Justine Evans, now cleared of any involvement in the Garden Shed Murder, has told police and reporters though that she feels culpable by default. By not coming forward at the time and telling what she knew and what

she had seen, she deserved whatever punishment came her way. Children suffered because
she didn't speak out. Yet it must be remembered that, at the time, she was only a child
herself.

Bloody saint. Although I do agree with her that
she does deserve whatever comes her way. She's still
to blame in my book for not stopping Uncle Chuck
but she certainly deserves credit for not putting me
in any deeper shit. I suspect it is her way of atoning
but I do wonder if she realises how close I came to
finishing her off. I still feel the scythe twitching in my
hand.

Following a near-fatal fall down a steep flight
of stairs leading from the attic of Miss Beverley
Digby's home, Ms Evans declined to comment
other than to say she had lost her footing.
When told by police that the very same thing
had happened to a girlfriend of Miss Digby's
ex-boyfriend, she didn't react and replied, 'It's
most likely a coincidence.'
When asked if she might have been tripped
up deliberately, or blinded by a low eye-level
security beam directed into her line of vision,

she shrugged and repeated, 'I have no further comments.'

The cool heavenly nectar trickles down my throat. I have all the time in the world; no need to hurry. Colgate won't get this side of the Channel for months. By then I might have moved on but perhaps not. He'll maybe take a leaf out of Scott's and even Justine's book and take early retirement, except he's not a quitter, I'll give him that. He's the proverbial dog with a bone.

I cut neatly round the printed articles, labelling and dating each entry before sticking them down.

DCI Colgate of the North London crime squad is in charge of the investigation, and is working tirelessly to extradite Miss Digby from Italy for Mr Chuck Curry's murder. As yet the police are unable to pinpoint her exact location but are working tirelessly with the Italian carabinieri to find her.

It's amazing that they can't find me. They're not looking hard in this part of the world, if at all. The Italian police have much better things to be getting on with. Long lazy lunches with family and catching maniacal speeding drivers take up most of their time and I'm nowhere near the top of their agenda.

> When Colgate was asked what charges are to be brought against Miss Digby, he replied she would be charged with first-degree murder. When asked whether she deserved to be punished as she was such a young child at the time, he replied that 'all murderers must be held to account.'
>
> Yet the public support for Miss Digby is overwhelmingly in her favour. As a child of the most horrific abuse at the hands of Mr Curry, it appeared to be her only way out. She was just ten years of age when the abuse started. Local residents are saying she should be congratulated, lauded and not punished for getting rid of the monster the way she did.

I'm quite the heroine. The worst I'll get, no doubt, is some more lengthy therapy sessions but I'm a dab hand now where those are concerned. There's no proof that I came to Italy to evade capture and Colgate's useless at getting proof of anything. I'll play the victim to the end, whenever that might be, but for now I'll let the sunshine seep into my bones and help break down the cold layers around my heart.

It's only 1.30pm. I have a good half hour before they arrive and I've a little job to do first. I flip open my laptop, amazed at how little time I'm now spending on it. Sleeping through the night has meant I'm no longer drawn to the screen in the small hours and although the nightmares still break through the flimsy cracks, I'm working hard on sealing the gaps.

I read through, once more, the email from Cosette.

Dear Beverley
I just had to get in touch. I can't believe what I'm reading in the papers. They're saying that you killed a man, a paedophile (a new word for my vocabulary!) who tortured young children. I'm so sorry for all you went through and all the pain you must be in.
I know you've gone away and I won't dare ask where. After I told you Scott had moved to Umbria in Italy, I had my suspicions but I never said anything to the police. It's not up to me.
I wanted to say sorry about Scott's pathetic little games to get his own back. I knew he was sending you threatening notes and emails, and I even laughed at the pizza boxes. He didn't sleep too well and his

midnight trips round to your house to frighten you seemed to pass the time. But I didn't realise how venomous (another new word!) he had become. I should have told you sooner but maybe it wouldn't have made things better between you. I know how bitter you were about the way he treated you and we've both had lucky escapes.

BTW Claudio is turning out to have more than a flash forehand. He's serving up a real treat tonight by taking me out for dinner. I hope you're impressed that I can even joke in English.

Anyway, I wanted to say 'no hard feelings' and hope it all gets sorted in the end. I don't believe everything I read in the papers and no longer bother to look. Take care and hope to hear you're okay. Don't worry, all top secret and confidential. I'll not tell anyone what I know about your whereabouts or even that we are in contact.

Love,

Cosette x

* * *

Hi Cosette

Great to hear things are hotting up with Claudio. I find Italian men quite irresistible myself. They put English

men, with their pale skins and mealy-mouthed manners, well in the shade. It's their style and panache
(look it up! Ha ha) and they certainly know how to
treat a woman. It all stems from their mothers!
Don't worry about not telling on Scott's childish
stalking pranks. He thought he was being clever,
turning the tables. I need to apologise myself for the
bloodied badger. It was definitely not meant for you. It
was meant for someone else entirely (you can guess
who now!!) but they lived in a cul-de-sac and when I
went to drop it off, I spotted new CCTV cameras outside their front door. I avoid these spy devices like the
plague. So on the way home I decided to drop by
Scott's and leave it there. It was never meant for you
to open but I couldn't let it go to waste. I managed to
convince the police someone had left it on my
doorstep, Scott most likely, before I returned it to
where it had come. I'd love to have seen his face!
I won't let on where I'm living because I seem to be
on the police's most wanted list. I'm like Ted Bundy
who kept eluding capture or perhaps more Hannibal
Lecter, who phoned home from the tropics as he prepared to eat his next victim. No, but seriously, I'm
having lots of fun and I've got plenty to occupy my
time.
Good luck with Claudio

Bev x

I reread what I've typed. It's enough. It feels good to have told Cosette about the badger incident. All that blood must have curdled her young brain and the telling proves that I must have a semblance of a conscience. I don't say who the badger was meant for, just in case. I'll avoid putting too much on digital record.

Ms Evans might have started taking the stalking threats more seriously if she'd received the butchered animal, because she kept palming off my online and phone stalking campaign as the actions of another random 'pyscho' patient. In the end it didn't matter. I'd have gone for her anyway and she got her punishment.

As I click 'send' I wonder how Ms Evans' recovery is progressing. But as I glance at the clock, I realise now is not the time to worry about her. The minutes are ticking on towards the hour. One minute to go. I close down the laptop and turn back to look out over the top of my balcony.

It's two on the dot. Jeez, he's still that regular. Here they come. His left arm is round her ever ballooning waist and his right hand is cradling the bump. Danielle's ankles are even more swollen than first time round and I can't help but wonder if Scott is okay with the unsightliness. I'll make sure my slim ankles are pertly displayed when I suddenly make my appearance.

They amble up towards the piazza, past the church whose bells have started their lunchtime clanking peels of praise and thunder through the region. A pigeon shoots out from the roof, catapulted upwards by the blast, like a bullet from a smoking gun.

I'm not in any hurry. I've been watching them for days now. They're not likely to change their routine, not until the baby is born at least. Today I'm going to sit back, watch the show and relish the anticipation.

I pull on my sun hat, with its wide brim, replace the large Chanel sunglasses behind my ears and reel back in my painted wiggling toes. Scott is unlikely to spot them but just in case. I lift up my phone and start taking pictures for my scrapbook. Today's shots will be the 'before' snaps. I'm not sure the 'after' shots will be so relaxed or easily taken.

All I know for certain is that when I finally do walk down the stairs and join them in the square, it will all be just a matter of coincidence.

ACKNOWLEDGMENTS

Writing is frequently a solitary, lonely task, but it is the people along the way who keep you going with their unwavering encouragement and belief.

I would like to thank my friends, my family and all those who read my books and ask me every day how work is progressing. A special thanks to my enthusiastic reviewers who take time out to give honest opinions.

I am so grateful to the team at Boldwood Books for relaunching *Right Behind You* and giving it another chance to get back out into the world. Special thanks to Emily Yau, my amazing editor, for her enthusiasm and dedication, and for helping to bring my books to life.

Personal thanks, as always, must go to Linda, my big sis, who encourages me all the way with a tireless belief that I can succeed. To Lindsay, my gorgeous niece, who devours my books. Like me, a fan of dark psychological fiction, Lindsay tells me what works and what might be better left to the imagination. To Susan, my BFF, who reads everything I write and supports me all the way.

As an author who shies away from Beta readers before submission, I rely on self-belief, with one exception. Margaret Fitzpatrick is a special friend. A trusted colleague, whose opinion and suggestions I never question. She is my first and only reader, who trawls my early drafts and lets me know if I'm on the right track. Thank you, Margaret.

And once again, thanks to Neil and James. Neil for his constant support and James who is no closer to reading my books, but occasionally posts on Instagram a screenshot of his mother's Amazon chart ranking. What more could a writer wish for?

MORE FROM DIANA WILKINSON

We hope you enjoyed reading *Right Behind You.* If you did, please leave a review.

If you'd like to gift a copy, this book is also available as an ebook, hardback, large print, digital audio download and audiobook CD.

Sign up to Diana Wilkinson's mailing list for news, competitions and updates on future books.

https://bit.ly/DianaWilkinsonNews

One Down, another page-turning psychological thriller from Diana Wilkinson, is available now...

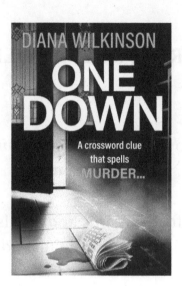

ABOUT THE AUTHOR

Diana Wilkinson (née Kennett) graduated from Durham University with a degree in geography. After a short spell in teaching, she spent most of her working life in the business of tennis development.

A former Irish international player, Diana finally stepped off the court to become a full-time writer. The inspiration for much of her work has come from the ladies she coached over the years and from confidences shared over coffee.

In 2022, Diana signed a three-book deal with Boldwood Books, and her debut, *One Down*, is the first of three psychological thrillers soon to be released.

Diana's novels are set in and around North London, in areas where Diana lived and worked for many years.

Born and bred in Belfast, Northern Ireland, during the height of the civil unrest, she now lives in

Hertfordshire, England, with her husband, Neil, and son, James.

Follow Diana on social media:

twitter.com/DiWilkinson2020

facebook.com/DiKennett

instagram.com/dianakennett37

THE *Murder* LIST

THE MURDER LIST IS A NEWSLETTER DEDICATED TO SPINE-CHILLING FICTION AND GRIPPING PAGE-TURNERS!

SIGN UP TO MAKE SURE YOU'RE ON OUR HIT LIST FOR EXCLUSIVE DEALS, AUTHOR CONTENT, AND COMPETITIONS.

SIGN UP TO OUR NEWSLETTER

BIT.LY/THEMURDERLISTNEWS

Boldwood

Boldwood Books is an award-winning fiction publishing company seeking out the best stories from around the world.

Find out more at www.boldwoodbooks.com

Join our reader community for brilliant books, competitions and offers!

Follow us
@BoldwoodBooks
@BookandTonic

Sign up to our weekly deals newsletter

https://bit.ly/BoldwoodBNewsletter